CLOTEL

William Wells Brown

ARNO PRESS and THE NEW YORK TIMES
NEW YORK 1969

AFRO-AMERICAN CULTURE SERIES

General Editor
ULYSSES LEE

WHEN THE FUGITIVE SLAVE BORN WILLIAM, called Sanford, and in freedom renamed for his protector, Wells Brown, published an anti-slavery novel in London in 1853, he became the father of American Negro fiction. The year before, *Uncle Tom's Cabin* had proved the novel a useful means of antislavery agitation, and William Wells Brown, a militant aboli-tionist, as earlier he had shaped his speeches, autobiographies, and travel writings, formed his book into a weapon against chattel slavery and racial discrimination in America. His novel, which like its author bore a series of names, was published four times.

The title of the first edition, *Clotel, or, the President's Daughter,* refers to the scandalous rumor that Thomas Jefferson had had a slave wife and children. This not only insured the book's notoriety, but more importantly, it also dramatized the American dilemma: the gulf between the democratic theories of the Dec-laration of Independence quoted on the novel's title page, and the racist practices which enslaved and degraded black people in a democratic land.

Brown, who believed his father to have been a white man, and who had shared antislavery platforms with the celebrated light-skinned fugitive, Ellen Craft, built his plots around three generations of whiteslaves. The book begins with the sale of the mulatto woman, Currer, long-discarded consort of Jefferson, and her fair aristocratic daughters. Separated from both her children, Currer is sold to a hypocritical minister and dies midway through the novel. A minor story line involves her master's daughter, who, expounding both abolitionism and Christianity, refutes her proslavery father and converts her antislavery lover; ultimately she and her new husband free the slaves and settle them in Ohio. A second minor plot follows Currer's lovely younger daughter, who is bought, educated, and married by a white New England physician. When, after his death, she is sold into slavery by her husband's creditors, she quickly perishes. The main narrative follows Currer's beautiful older daughter, Clotel, mistress to a Virginia gentleman. Although Clotel bears his child, her weak lover marries a white woman who sells her and enslaves her daughter. Determined to be reunited with the child, Clotel escapes and returns to Virginia, where she is seized as a fugitive and taken to the slave pens in Washington. When she again attempts escape, slave catchers trap her on the Long Bridge across the Potomac. Within sight of the Capitol, the president's daughter jumps to her death to avoid recapture. The final plot ends more happily. Unlike her grandmother, aunt, and mother, Clotel's daughter, Mary, loves a slave rebel, the heroic mulatto, George. Under sentence of death for participating in Nat Turner's insurrection, George is persuaded to let Mary take his place in prison. He escapes to Canada, and years later the lovers are reunited.

Amid this tangle of melodramatic whiteslave plots, William Wells Brown—who had been held in bondage on farms in Kentucky and Missouri, on steamboats plying the Mississippi River between St. Louis and New Orleans, and in the city of St. Louis; who had worked in the field and the house, in a doctor's office, in a tavern, in printing, tailoring, and barber shops, on ships and in stables; who had, when a child, been hunted by dogs as he hid in the woods, and had later made a disastrous attempt to reach Canada, before successfully escaping from slavery in 1834—includes sketches of the life he has known. The freshness of *Clotel* is in these realistic passages: in the scenes of slave life in coffles and gangs, in quarters, pens, and warehouses; glimpses of rebellious slaves; parodies of slave sermons; tales of ruses used by runaways; anecdotes depicting Jim Crow in the North. The description of a slave hunt and lynching strikes a note of horror, but not all of the interjections are grim. The scene of the slaves being prepared for market, like the dramatization of their religious training, and the toast offered by Jack, provide touches of rough, ironic humor which Brown uses as a weapon against both white mastery and black acceptance of doctrines of white supremacy.

The vitality of the book lies in these passages, but their tone grates harshly against its conventional plots and genteel characters. The sentimental novel was not an adequate vehicle to express black experience, and Brown did not republish his book in this form when, his freedom bought by British abolitionists, he returned to America in 1854 to continue his work as writer and reformer.

Revised and renamed *Miralda, or the Beautiful Quadroon: A Romance of American Slavery, Founded on Fact,* the novel appeared as a serial in the *Weekly Anglo-African* during the winter of 1860–61. The initial situation, the sale of a mulatto mother and her fair daughters, is retained, although now they are only incidentally linked to Jefferson. The secondary story line concerning the white lovers is omitted, and that dealing with the younger daughter is submerged. The plot concerning Clotel, here renamed Isabelle, which dramatizes the victimization of a whiteslave by her lover-master, is made secondary. The central narrative now follows her daughter, here called Miralda, whose adventures are expanded from three chapters to sixteen. Although the heroine remains essentially the same figure seen in *Clotel,* and the outlines of her adventures are not varied, the Mary-Miralda story has been radically changed because the man whom she loves is no longer the rebellious mulatto, George, but the black rebel, Jerome. In this version, George-Jerome is a heroic African who scorns to submit to a whipping, knocks down his tyrannical master, and escapes. Imprisoned and condemned, he defies his captors, saying, "If I had my life to live over again, I would use all the energies which God has given me to get up an insurrection." George-Jerome's flight North and his adventures in England are developed at length, and in the final passages, showing Miralda's reconciliation with her guilt-stricken planter father, American color prejudice is attacked.

Because some of the realistic scenes of slave life are omitted or diluted—for example, the lynching and the scene showing the religious instruction of the slaves do not reappear, and the description of the slave pens is abbreviated—the shifts in tone are less abrupt than in *Clotel.* But though individual passages are not as forceful, the realism which gave substance to the first edition is not completely lacking in *Miralda.* The book gains coherence as a result of the deletion of much of the distracting poetry and polemic, its simplification of plots, and its incorporation of some of the digressions into the fabric of the tale. In its portrayal of a militant black hero, *Miralda* presents a figure new in American fiction.

The third version is not so fortunate. In 1864 Brown again republished his book, this time as *Clotelle: A Tale of the Southern States.* The titles become confusing. Here the structure and characters are essentially those of *Miralda,* but the whiteslave heroine who takes her lover's place in prison has been renamed Clotelle. In this revision the realistic passages have been weakened still more. The tone is now smooth: the rough humor, stark brutality, and pointed debate which give *Clotel* immediacy are trimmed, toned down, almost obliterated. What remains is a conventional antislavery novel.

The 1864 edition was brought up to date and republished as *Clotelle; or, the Colored Heroine* in 1867. Brown, who is best known as a historian, was then writing a history of black troops in the Civil War, and he added four new chapters in which Mary-Miralda-Clotelle and George-Jerome return to America to aid in the struggle.

While the importance of *Clotel* as the first American Negro novel is undisputed, recently critics, distressed by Brown's preoccupation with aristocratic white-skinned heroines, have accused him of setting black fiction upon a false path. It is true that he drew sentimental mulatto heroines again and again, but it should be noted that as he reworked his materials, Brown shifted his focus from the "tragic mulatto" victimized by a white lover, to the white-slave who found happiness with a rebel; and that he envisioned a romantic hero who was both beautiful and black. More important, however, for the future of American Negro literature than these genteel figures, is the glimpse Brown gives of a vernacular black hero. Though early in the book Black Sam is ridiculed for rejecting his blackness—his buttered hair is lampooned in much the same way that in our time Malcolm derided conks—we later see another Black Sam. The scenes where he secretly celebrates a hated master's death, while outwardly expressing conventional sorrow, and later where he assumes responsibility for managing the estate and helping his fellow slaves prepare for freedom, hint at a figure with some of the force and complexity of the slave narrators. Although only fragmentary in *Clotel,* and absent in later editions, in these sketches of an ironic, tough black man, William Wells Brown suggests a character who would prove most fruitful for black fiction. *Clotel* was not a false beginning.

SELECTED WORKS BY WILLIAM WELLS BROWN

Narrative of William W. Brown, a Fugitive Slave, Written by Himself. Boston, 1847. Revised and retitled *Narrative of William W. Brown, an American Slave, Written by Himself.* Boston, 1847.

A Lecture Delivered Before the Female Anti-Slavery Society of Salem, at Lyceum Hall, November 14, 1847. Boston, 1847.

The Anti-Slavery Harp. Boston, 1848.

A Description of William Wells Brown's Original Panoramic Views of the Scenes in the Life of an American Slave. . . . London, n.d.

Three Years in Europe: or, Places I Have Seen and People I Have Met . . . with a memoir of the author, by *William Farmer, Esq.* London and Edinburgh, 1852.

Clotel; or, the President's Daughter: A Narrative of Slave Life in the United States. With a Sketch of the Author's Life. London, 1853. Revised and retitled *Miralda; or, the Beautiful Quadroon. A Romance of American Slavery. Founded on Fact. Weekly Anglo-African* (November 30, 1860–March 16, 1861). Revised and retitled *Clotelle: A Tale of the Southern States.* Boston, 1864. This edition was republished in facsimile with a biographical introduction by Maxwell Whiteman. Philadelphia, 1955. Revised and retitled *Clotelle; or, the Colored Heroine.* Boston, 1867.

St. Domingo: Its Revolutions and Its Patriots. . . . Boston, 1855.

The American Fugitive in Europe. Sketches of Places and People Abroad. With a Memoir of the Author. Boston, Cleveland, and New York, 1855. A revision of *Three Years*.

The Black Man, His Antecedents, His Genius, and His Achievements. New York and Boston, 1863.

The Negro in the American Rebellion: His Heroism and His Fidelity. Boston. 1867.

The Rising Son; or, the Antecedents and Advancement of the Colored Race. Boston, 1874. A revision of *The Black Man*.

My Southern Home; or, the South and its People. Boston, 1880.

SELECTED BIOGRAPHY AND CRITICISM

Bone, Robert. *The Negro Novel in America.* Rev. ed. New Haven and London, 1965.

Bontemps, Arna. "The Negro Contribution to American Letters," *The American Negro Reference Book,* edited by John P. Davis, Pp. 850–79. Englewood Cliffs, New Jersey. 1966.

Brawley, Benjamin (ed.). *Early American Negro Writers.* Chapel Hill, N.C., 1935.

[Brown, Josephine]. *Biography of an American Bondman: By His Daughter.* Boston, 1856.

Brown, Sterling A. *The Negro in American Fiction.* Bronze Booklet No. 6. Washington, D.C., 1937.

Farrison, W. Edward. "Brown's First Drama," *CLAJ,* II (December, 1958), 104–10.

————. "A Flight Across Ohio: The Escape of William Wells Brown From Slavery," *The Ohio State Archaeological and Historical Q.,* LXI (July, 1952), 272–82.

————. "The Origins of Brown's Clotel," *Phylon,* XV (1954), 347–54.

————. "William Wells Brown, America's First Negro Man of Letters," *Phylon,* IX (1948), 13–23.

————. "William Wells Brown in Buffalo," *J. Negro History,* XXXIX (October, 1954), 298–314.

————. "William Wells Brown, Social Reformer," *J. Negro Education,* XVII–XVIII (Winter, 1949), 29–39.

Gloster, Hugh M. *Negro Voices in American Fiction.* Chapel Hill, N.C., 1948.

Jackson, Blyden. "A Golden Mean for the Negro Novel," *CLAJ,* II (1959), 81–87.

————. "The Negro's Negro in Negro Literature," *Michigan Q. R.,* IV (1965), 290–95.

Loggins, Vernon. *The Negro Author: His Development in America to 1900.* Port Washington, N.Y., 1964. First published in 1931.

Redding, J. Saunders. *To Make a Poet Black*. Chapel Hill, N.C., 1939.

[Woodson, Carter G.]. "William Wells Brown," *Dictionary of American Biography*. Edited by Allen Johnson and Dumas Malone, II, 161. New York, 1929, 1958.

Jean Fagan Yellin

DEPARTMENT OF ENGLISH

PACE COLLEGE

CLOTEL

NEGRO DENTISTRY. *Page* 130.

CLOTEL;

OR,

THE PRESIDENT'S DAUGHTER:

A Narrative of Slave Life

IN

THE UNITED STATES.

BY

WILLIAM WELLS BROWN,

A FUGITIVE SLAVE, AUTHOR OF "THREE YEARS IN EUROPE."

With a Sketch of the Author's Life.

"WE hold these truths to be self-evident: that all men are created equal; that they
are endowed by their Creator with certain inalienable rights, and that among these are
LIFE, LIBERTY, and the PURSUIT OF HAPPINESS." — *Declaration of American Independence.*

LONDON:
PARTRIDGE & OAKEY, PATERNOSTER ROW;
AND 70, EDGWARE ROAD.
1853.

PARTRIDGE AND OAKEY, PRINTERS, PADDINGTON.

PREFACE.

MORE than two hundred years have elapsed since the first cargo of slaves was landed on the banks of the James River, in the colony of Virginia, from the West coast of Africa. From the introduction of slaves in 1620, down to the period of the separation of the Colonies from the British Crown, the number had increased to five hundred thousand; now there are nearly four million. In fifteen of the thirty-one States, Slavery is made lawful by the Constitution, which binds the several States into one confederacy.

On every foot of soil, over which *Stars* and *Stripes* wave, the negro is considered common property, on which any white man may lay his hand with perfect impunity. The entire white population of the United States, North and South, are bound by their oath to the constitution, and their adhesion to the Fugitive Slave Law, to hunt down the runaway slave and return him to his claimant, and to suppress any effort that may be made by the slaves to gain their freedom by physical force. Twenty-five millions of whites have banded themselves in solemn conclave to keep four millions of blacks in their chains. In all grades of society are to be found men who either hold, buy, or sell slaves, from the statesmen and doctors of divinity, who can own their hundreds, down to the person who can purchase but one.

Were it not for persons in high places owning slaves, and thereby giving the system a reputation, and especially professed Christians, Slavery would long since have been abolished. The influence of the great "honours the corruption, and chastisement doth therefore hide his head." The great aim of the true friends of the slave should be to lay bare the institution, so that the gaze of the world may be upon it, and cause the wise, the prudent, and the pious to withdraw their support from it, and leave it to its own fate. It does the cause of emancipation but little good to cry out in tones of execration against the traders, the kidnappers, the hireling overseers, and brutal drivers, so long as nothing is said to fasten the guilt on those who move in a higher circle.

The fact that slavery was introduced into the

American colonies, while they were under the control of the British Crown, is a sufficient reason why Englishmen should feel a lively interest in its abolition; and now that the genius of mechanical invention has brought the two countries so near together, and both having one language and one literature, the influence of British public opinion is very great on the people of the New World.

If the incidents set forth in the following pages should add anything new to the information already given to the Public through similar publications, and should thereby aid in bringing British influence to bear upon American slavery, the main object for which this work was written will have been accomplished.

W. WELLS BROWN.

22, *Cecil Street, Strand, London.*

CONTENTS.

CONTENTS.

NARRATIVE

OF THE

LIFE AND ESCAPE

OF

WILLIAM WELLS BROWN.

———◆———

" SHALL tongues be mute when deeds are wrought
  Which well might shame extremest Hell?
  Shall freemen lack th' indignant thought?
  Shall Mercy's bosom cease to swell?
  Shall Honour bleed?—shall Truth succumb?
  Shall pen, and press, and *soul* be dumb?"—*Whittier.*

WILLIAM WELLS BROWN, the subject of this narrative,
was born a slave in Lexington, Kentucky, not far
from the residence of the late Hon. Henry Clay.
His mother was the slave of Doctor John Young.
His father was a slaveholder, and, besides being a
near relation of his master, was connected with the
Wicklief family, one of the oldest, wealthiest, and
most aristocratic of the Kentucky planters.   Dr.
Young was the owner of forty or fifty slaves, whose
chief employment was in cultivating tobacco, hemp,
corn, and flax.   The Doctor removed from Lexington,

B

when William was five or six years old, to the state
of Missouri, and commenced farming in a beautiful
and fertile valley, within a mile of the Missouri
river.

Here the slaves were put to work under a harsh
and cruel overseer named Cook. A finer situation
for a farm could not have been selected in the state.
With climate favourable to agriculture, and soil
rich, the products came in abundance. At an early
age William was separated from his mother, she
being worked in the field, and he as a servant in his
master's medical department. When about ten
years of age, the young slave's feelings were much
hurt at hearing the cries of his mother, while being
flogged by the negro driver for being a few minutes
behind the other hands in reaching the field. He
heard her cry, " Oh, pray! oh, pray! oh, pray!"
These are the words which slaves generally utter
when imploring mercy at the hands of their oppressors. The son heard it, though he was some way
off. He heard the crack of the whip and the groans
of his poor mother. The cold chill ran over him,
and he wept aloud; but he was a slave like his
mother, and could render her no assistance. He
was taught by the most bitter experience, that
nothing could be more heart-rending than to see
a dear and beloved mother or sister tortured by
unfeeling men, and to hear her cries, and not be
able to render the least aid. When William was
twelve years of age, his master left his farm and
took up his residence near St. Louis. The Doctor

having more hands than he wanted for his own
use, William was let out to a Mr. Freeland, an
innkeeper. Here the young slave found himself
in the hands of a most cruel and heartless master.
Freeland was one of the real chivalry of the South;
besides being himself a slaveholder, he was a
horse-racer, cock-fighter, gambler, and, to crown
the whole, an inveterate drunkard. What else but
bad treatment could be expected from such a character? After enduring the tyrannical and inhuman
usage of this man for five or six months, William
resolved to stand it no longer, and therefore ran
away, like other slaves who leave their masters,
owing to severe treatment; and not knowing where
to flee, the young fugitive went into the forest, a
few miles from St. Louis. He had been in the
woods but a short time, when he heard the barking
and howling of dogs, and was soon satisfied that he
was pursued by the negro dogs; and, aware of their
ferocious nature, the fugitive climbed a tree, to save
himself from being torn to pieces. The hounds
were soon at the trunk of the tree, and remained
there, howling and barking, until those in whose
charge they were came up. The slave was
ordered down, tied, and taken home. Immediately
on his arrival there, he was, as he expected, tied up
in the smoke-house, and whipped till Freeland was
satisfied, and then smoked with tobacco stems. This
the slaveholder called "*Virginia play*." After being
well whipped and smoked, he was again set to work.
William remained with this monster a few months

longer, and was then let out to Elijah P. Lovejoy, who years after became the editor of an abolition newspaper, and was murdered at Alton, Illinois, by a mob of slaveholders from the adjoining state of Missouri. The system of letting out slaves is one among the worst of the evils of slavery. The man who hires a slave, looks upon him in the same light as does the man who hires a horse for a limited period; he feels no interest in him, only to get the worth of his money. Not so with the man who owns the slave; he regards him as so much property, of which care should be taken. After being let out to a steamer as an under-steward, William was hired by James Walker, a slave-trader. Here the subject of our memoir was made superintendent of the gangs of slaves that were taken to the New Orleans market. In this capacity, William had opportunities, far greater than most slaves, of acquiring knowledge of the different phases of the "*peculiar institution*." Walker was a negro speculator, who was amassing a fortune by trading in the bones, blood, and nerves, of God's children. The thoughts of such a traffic causes us to exclaim with the poet,

> "—— Is there not some chosen curse,
>   Some hidden thunder in the stores of heaven,
>   Red with uncommon wrath, to blast the man
>   Who gains his fortune from the blood of souls ?"

Between fifty and sixty slaves were chained together, put on board a steam-boat bound for New Orleans, and started on the voyage. New and strange scenes began to inspire the young slave with the hope of escaping to a land of freedom. There was in the boat a large room on the lower deck in which the slaves were kept, men and women promiscuously, all chained two and two together, not even leaving the poor slaves the privilege of choosing their partners. A strict watch was kept over them, so that they had no chance of escape. Cases had occurred in which slaves had got off their chains and made their escape at the landing-places, while the boat stopped to take in wood. But with all their care they lost one woman who had been taken from her husband and children, and having no desire to live without them, in the agony of her soul jumped overboard and drowned herself. Her sorrows were greater than she could bear; slavery and its cruel inflictions had broken her heart. She, like William, sighed for freedom, but not the freedom which even British soil confers and inspires, but freedom from torturing pangs, and overwhelming grief.

At the end of the week they arrived at New Orleans, the place of their destination. Here the slaves were placed in a negro pen, where those who wished to purchase could call and examine them. The negro pen is a small yard surrounded by buildings, from fifteen to twenty feet wide, with the exception of a large gate with iron bars. The slaves are kept in the buildings during the night, and turned into the pen during the day. After the best of the gang were sold off, the balance was taken to the Exchange coffee-house auction-rooms, and sold at public auction. After the sale of the last slave, William and Mr. Walker left New Orleans for St. Louis.

After they had been at St. Louis a few weeks another cargo of human flesh was made up. There were amongst the lot several old men and women, some of whom had grey locks. On their way down to New Orleans William had to prepare the old slaves for market. He was ordered to shave off the old men's whiskers, and to pluck out the grey hairs where they were not too numerous; where they were, he coloured them with a preparation of blacking with a blacking brush. After having gone through the blacking process, they looked ten or fifteen years younger. William, though not well skilled in the use of scissors and razor, performed the office of the barber tolerably. After the sale of this gang of negroes they returned to St. Louis, and a second cargo was made up. In this lot was a woman who had a child at the breast, yet was compelled to travel through the interior of the country on foot with the other slaves. In a published memoir of his life, William says, "The child cried during the most of the day, which displeased Mr. Walker, and he told the mother that if her child did not stop crying, he would stop its mouth. After a long and weary journey under a burning sun, we put up for the night at a country inn. The following morning, just as they were about to start, the child again commenced crying. Walker stepped up to her and told her to give the child to him. The mother tremblingly obeyed. He took the child by one arm, as any one would a cat by the leg, and walked into the house where they had been staying, and said to the lady, 'Madam, I will make you a present of this little nigger; it keeps making such a noise that I can't bear it.' 'Thank you, sir,' said the lady. The mother, as soon as she saw that her child was to be left, ran up to Mr. Walker, and falling on her knees, begged of him in an agony of despair, to let her have her child. She clung round his legs so closely, that for some time he could not kick her off; and she cried, 'O my child, my child. Master, do let me have my dear, dear child. Oh! do, do. I will stop its crying, and love you for ever if you will only let me have my child again.' But her prayers were not heeded, they passed on, and the mother was separated from her child for ever.

" After the woman's child had been given away, Mr. Walker rudely commanded her to retire into the ranks with the other slaves. Women who had children were not chained, but those who had none were. As soon as her child was taken she was chained to the gang."

Some time after this, Walker bought a woman who had a blind child; it being considered worthless, it was given to the trader by the former owner of the woman on the score of humanity, he saying that he wished to keep mother and child together. At first Walker declined taking the child, saying that it would be too much trouble, but the mother wishing to have her boy with her, begged him to take it, promising to carry it the whole distance in her arms. Consequently he took the child, and the gang started on their route to the nearest steamboat landing, which was above one hundred miles. As might have been expected, the woman was unable to carry the boy and keep up with the rest of the gang. They put up at night at a small town, and the next morning, when about to start, Walker took the little boy from its mother and sold it to the innkeeper for the small sum of *one dollar*. The poor woman was so frantic at the idea of being separated from her only child, that it seemed impossible to get her to leave it. Not until the chains were put upon her limbs, and she fastened to the other slaves, could they get her to leave the spot. By main force this slave mother was compelled to go on and leave her child behind. Some days after, a lady from one of the free states was travelling the same road and put up at the same inn : she saw the child the morning after her arrival, and heard its history from one of the slaves, which was confirmed by the innkeeper's wife. A few days after, the following poem appeared in one of the newspapers, from the pen of the lady who had seen the blind child :—

" Come back to me, mother ! why linger away
    From thy poor little blind boy, the long weary day !
    I mark every footstep, I list to each tone,
    And wonder my mother should leave me alone !
    There are voices of sorrow and voices of glee,
    But there's no one to joy or to sorrow with me ;
    For each hath of pleasure and trouble his share,
    And none for the poor little blind boy will care.

" My mother, come back to me ! close to thy breast
    Once more let thy poor little blind one be pressed ;
    Once more let me feel thy warm breath on my cheek,
    And hear thee in accents of tenderness speak !

O mother! I've no one to love me — no heart
Can bear like thy own in my sorrows a part;
No hand is so gentle, no voice is so kind!
Oh! none like a mother can cherish the blind!

" Poor blind one! no mother thy wailing can hear,
No mother can hasten to banish thy fear;
For the slave-owner drives her, o'er mountain and wild,
And for one paltry dollar hath sold thee, poor child!
Ah! who can in language of mortals reveal
The anguish that none but a mother can feel,
When man in his vile lust of mammon hath trod
On her child, who is stricken and smitten of God?

" Blind, helpless, forsaken, with strangers alone,
She hears in her anguish his piteous moan,
As he eagerly listens — but listens in vain,
To catch the loved tones of his mother again!
The curse of the broken in spirit shall fall
On the wretch who hath mingled this wormwood and gall,
And his gain like a mildew shall blight and destroy,
Who hath torn from his mother the little blind boy."

The thought that man can so debase himself as to
treat a fellow-creature as here represented, is enough
to cause one to blush at the idea that such men are
members of a civilised and Christian nation.

Nothing was more grievous to the sensitive
feelings of William, than seeing the separation of
families by the slave-trader: husbands taken from
their wives, and mothers from their children, without
the least appearance of feeling on the part of those
who separated them. While at New Orleans, on one
occasion, William saw a slave murdered. The

circumstances were as follows:—In the evening, between seven and eight o'clock, a slave came running down the levee, followed by several men and boys. The whites were crying out, "Stop that nigger! stop that nigger!" while the poor panting slave, in almost breathless accents, was repeating, "I did not steal the meat—I did not steal the meat." The poor man at last took refuge in the river. The whites who were in pursuit of him, ran on board of one of the boats to see if they could discover him. They finally espied him under the bow of the steamboat "Trenton." They got a pike-pole, and tried to drive him from his hiding-place. When they struck at him he would dive under the water. The water was so cold, that it soon became evident that he must come out or be drowned.

While they were trying to drive him from under the boat or drown him, he in broken and imploring accents said, "I did not steal the meat; I did not steal the meat. My master lives up the river. I want to see my master. I did not steal the meat. Do let me go home to master." After punching and striking him over the head for some time, he at last sunk in the water, to rise no more alive.

On the end of the pike-pole with which they had been striking him was a hook, which caught in his clothing, and they hauled him up on the bow of the boat. Some said he was dead; others said he was "playing 'possum;'" while others kicked him to make him get up; but it was of no use—he was dead.

As soon as they became satisfied of this they commenced leaving one after another. One of the hands on the boat informed the captain that they had killed the man, and that the dead body was lying on the deck. The captain, whose name was Hart, came on deck, and said to those who were remaining, "You have killed this nigger; now take him off my boat." The dead body was dragged on shore and left there. William went on board of the boat where the gang of slaves were, and during the whole night his mind was occupied with what he had seen. Early in the morning he went on shore to see if the dead body remained there. He found it in the same position that it was left the night before. He watched to see what they would do with it. It was left there until between eight and nine o'clock, when a cart, which took up the trash from the streets, came along, and the body was thrown in, and in a few minutes more was covered over with dirt, which they were removing from the streets.

At the expiration of the period of his hiring with Walker, William returned to his master, rejoiced to have escaped an employment as much against his own feelings as it was repugnant to human nature. But this joy was of short duration. The Doctor wanted money, and resolved to sell William's sister and two brothers. The mother had been previously sold to a gentleman residing in the city of St. Louis. William's master now informed him that he intended to sell him, and, as he was his own nephew, he gave him the privilege of finding some one to purchase him, who would treat him better than if he was sold on the auction block. William tried to make some arrangement by which he could purchase his own freedom, but the old Doctor would hear nothing of the kind. If there is one thing more revolting in the trade of human flesh than another, it is the selling of one's own blood relations.

He accordingly set out for the city in search of a new master. When he arrived there, he proceeded to the gaol with the hope of seeing his sister, but was again disappointed. On the following morning he made another attempt, and was allowed to see her once, for the last time. When he entered the room where she was seated in one corner, alone and disconsolate, there were four other women in the room, belonging to the same man, who were bought, the gaoler said, for the master's own use.

William's sister was seated with her face towards the door when he entered, but her gaze was transfixed on nothingness, and she did not look up when he walked up to her; but as soon as she observed him she sprang up, threw her arms around his neck, leaned her head upon his breast, and without uttering a word, in silent, indescribable sorrow, burst into tears. She remained so for some minutes, but when she recovered herself sufficiently to speak, she urged him to take his mother immediately, and try to get to the land of freedom. She said there was no hope for herself, she must live and die a slave. After giving her some advice, and taking a ring from his finger, he bade her farewell for ever.

Reader, did ever a fair sister of thine go down to the grave prematurely, if so, perchance, thou hast drank deeply from the cup of sorrow? But how infinitely better is it for a sister to "go into the silent land" with her honour untarnished, but with bright hopes, than for her to be sold to sensual slave-holders.

William had been in the city now two days, and as he was to be absent for only a week, it was well that he should make the best use of his time if he intended to escape. In conversing with his mother, he found her unwilling to make the attempt to reach the land of liberty, but she advised him by all means to get there himself if he possibly could. She said, as all her children were in slavery, she did not wish to leave them; but he loved his mother so intensely, that he could not think of leaving without her. He consequently used all his simple eloquence to induce her to fly with him, and at last he prevailed. They consequently fixed upon the next night as the time for their departure. The time at length arrived, and they left the city just as the clock struck nine. Having found a boat, they crossed the river in it. Whose boat it was he did not know; neither did he care: when it had served his purpose, he turned it adrift, and when he saw it last, it was going at a good speed down the river. After walking in the main road as fast as they could all night, when the morning came they made for the woods, and remained there during the day, but when night came again, they proceeded on their journey with nothing but the North Star to guide them. They continued to travel by night, and to bury themselves in the silent solitudes of the forest by day. Hunger and fatigue could not stop them, for the prospect of freedom at the end of the journey nerved them up. The very thought of leaving slavery, with its democratic whips, republican chains, and bloodhounds, caused the hearts of the weary fugitives to leap with joy. After travelling ten nights and hiding in the woods during the day for fear of being arrested and taken back, they thought they might with safety go the rest of their way by daylight. In nearly all the free states there are men who make a business of catching runaway slaves and returning them to their owners for the reward that may be offered; some of these were on the alert for William and his mother, for they had already seen the runaways advertised in the St. Louis newspapers.

All at once they heard the click of a horse's hoof, and looking back saw three men on horseback galloping towards them. They soon came up, and demanded them to stop. The three men dismounted, arrested them on a warrant, and showed them a handbill, offering two hundred dollars for their apprehension and delivery to Dr. Young and Isaac Mansfield in St. Louis.

While they were reading the handbill, William's mother looked him in the face, and burst into tears. "A cold chill ran over me," says he, "and such a sensation I never experienced before, and I trust I never shall again." They took out a rope and tied him, and they were taken back to the house of the individual who appeared to be the leader. They then had something given them to eat, and were separated. Each of them was watched over by two men during the night. The religious characteristic of the American slaveholder soon manifested itself, as before the family retired to rest they were all called together to attend prayers; and the very man who, but a few hours before, had arrested poor panting, fugitive slaves, now read a chapter from the Bible and offered a prayer to God; as if that benignant and omnipotent One consecrated the infernal act he had just committed.

The next morning they were chained and handcuffed, and started back to St. Louis. A journey of three days brought the fugitives again to the place they had left twelve days previously with the hope that they would never return. They were put in prison to await the orders of their owners. When a slave attempts to escape and fails, he feels sure of either being severely punished, or sold to the negro traders and taken to the far south, there to be worked up on a cotton, sugar, or rice plantation. This William and his mother dreaded. While they were in suspense as to what would be their fate, news came to them that the mother had been sold to a slave speculator. William was soon sold to a merchant residing in the city, and removed to his new owner's dwelling. In a few days the gang of slaves, of which William's mother was one, were taken on board a steamer to be carried to the New Orleans market. The young slave obtained permission from his new owner to go and take a last farewell of his mother. He went to the boat, and found her there, chained to another woman, and the whole number of slaves, amounting to some fifty or sixty, chained in the same manner. As the son approached his mother she moved not, neither did she weep; her emotions were too deep for tears. William approached her, threw his arms around her neck, kissed her, fell upon his knees begging her forgiveness, for he thought he was to blame for her sad condition, and if he had not persuaded her to accompany him she might not have been in chains then.

She remained for some time apparently unimpressionable, tearless, sightless, but in the innermost depths of her heart moved mighty passions. William says, "She finally raised her head, looked me in the face, and such a look none but an angel can give, and said, 'My dear son, you are not to blame for my being here. You have done nothing more nor less than your duty. Do not, I pray you, weep for me; I cannot last long upon a cotton plantation. I feel that my heavenly Master will soon call me home, and then I shall be out of the hands of the slaveholders.' I could hear no more—my heart struggled to free itself from the human form. In a moment she saw Mr. Mansfield, her master, coming toward that part of the boat, and she whispered in my ear, 'My child, we must soon part to meet no more on this side of the grave. You have ever said that you would not die a slave; that you would be a freeman. Now try to get your liberty! You will soon have no one to look after but yourself!' and just as she whispered the last sentence into my ear, Mansfield came up to me, and with an oath said, 'Leave here this instant; you have been the means of my losing one hundred dollars to get this wench back '—at the same time kicking me with a heavy pair of boots. As I left her she gave one shriek, saying, 'God be with you!' It was the last time that I saw her, and the last word I heard her utter.

"I walked on shore. The bell was tolling. The boat was about to start. I stood with a heavy heart, waiting to see her leave the wharf. As I thought of my mother, I could but feel that I had lost

> 'The glory of my life,
> My blessing and my pride!
> I half forgot the name of slave,
> When she was by my side.'

"The love of liberty that had been burning in my bosom had well-nigh gone out. I felt as though I was ready to die. The boat moved gently from the wharf, and while she glided down the river, I realised that my mother was indeed

> 'Gone—gone—sold and gone,
> To the rice swamp, dark and lone!'

"After the boat was out of sight I returned home; but my thoughts were so absorbed in what I had witnessed, that I knew not what I was about. Night came, but it brought no sleep to my eyes." When once the love of freedom is born in the slave's mind, it always increases and brightens, and William having heard so much about Canada, where a number of his acquaintances had found a refuge and a home, he heartily desired to join them. Building castles in the air in the daytime ; incessantly thinking of freedom, he would dream of the land of liberty, but on waking in the morning would weep to find it but a dream.

> " He would dream of Victoria's domain,
> And in a moment he seemed to be there ;
> But the fear of being taken again,
> Soon hurried him back to despair."

Having been for some time employed as a servant in an hotel, and being of a very active turn, William's new owner resolved to let him out on board a steamboat. Consequently the young slave was hired out to the steamer St. Louis, and soon after sold to Captain Enoch Price, the owner of that boat. Here he was destined to remain but a short period, as Mrs. Price wanted a carriage-driver, and had set her heart upon William for that purpose.

Scarcely three months had elapsed from the time that William became the property of Captain Price, ere that gentleman's family took a pleasure trip to New Orleans, and William accompanied them. From New Orleans the family proceeded to Louisville. The hope of escape again dawned upon the slave's mind, and the trials of the past were lost in hopes for the future. The love of liberty, which had been burning in his bosom for years, and which at times

had been well nigh extinguished, was now resus-
citated. Hopes nurtured in childhood, and strength-
ened as manhood dawned, now spread their sails to
the gales of his imagination. At night, when all
around was peaceful, and in the mystic presence of
the everlasting starlight, he would walk the steamer's
decks, meditating on his happy prospects, and sum-
moning up gloomy reminiscences of the dear hearts
he was leaving behind him. When not thinking
of the future his mind would dwell on the past.
The love of a dear mother, a dear and affectionate
sister, and three brothers yet living, caused him to
shed many tears. If he could only be assured of
their being dead, he would have been comparatively
happy; but he saw in imagination his mother in the
cotton-field, followed by a monster task-master, and
no one to speak a consoling word to her. He beheld
his sister in the hands of the slave-driver, compelled
to submit to his cruelty, or, what was unutterably
worse, his lust; but still he was far away from them,
and could not do anything for them if he remained
in slavery; consequently he resolved, and consecrated
the resolve with a prayer, that he would start on the
first opportunity.

That opportunity soon presented itself. When
the boat got to the wharf where it had to stay for
some time, at the first convenient moment Brown
made towards the woods, where he remained until
night-time. He dared not walk during the day,
even in the state of Ohio; he had seen so much of

c 2

the perfidy of white men, and resolved, if possible, not to get into their hands. After darkness covered the world, he emerged from his hiding-place; but he did not know east from west, or north from south; clouds hid the North Star from his view. In this desolate condition he remained for some hours, when the clouds rolled away, and his friend, with its shining face—the North Star—welcomed his sight. True as the needle to the pole he obeyed its attractive beauty, and walked on till daylight dawned.

It was winter-time; the day on which he started was the 1st of January, and, as it might be expected, it was intensely cold; he had no overcoat, no food, no friend, save the North Star, and the God which made it. How ardently must the love of freedom burn in the poor slave's bosom, when he will pass through so many difficulties, and even look death in the face, in winning his birth-right, freedom. But what crushed the poor slave's heart in his flight most was, not the want of food or clothing, but the thought that every white man was his deadly enemy. Even in the free states the prejudice against colour is so strong, that there appears to exist a deadly antagonism between the white and coloured races.

William in his flight carried a tinder-box with him, and when he got very cold he would gather together dry leaves and stubble and make a fire, or certainly he would have perished. He was determined to enter into no house, fearing that he might meet a betrayer.

It must have been a picture which would have inspired an artist, to see the fugitive roasting the ears of corn that he found or took from barns during the night, at solitary fires in the deep solitudes of woods.

The suffering of the fugitive was greatly increased by the cold, from the fact of his having just come from the warm climate of New Orleans. Slaves seldom have more than one name, and William was not an exception to this, and the fugitive began to think of an additional name. A heavy rain of three days, in which it froze as fast as it fell, and by which the poor fugitive was completely drenched, and still more chilled, added to the depression of his spirits already created by his weary journey. Nothing but the fire of hope burning within his breast could have sustained him under such overwhelming trials,

> " Behind he left the whip and chains,
> Before him were sweet Freedom's plains."

Through cold and hunger, William was now ill, and he could go no further. The poor fugitive resolved to seek protection, and accordingly hid himself in the woods near the road, until some one should pass. Soon a traveller came along, but the slave dared not speak. A few moments more and a second passed, the fugitive attempted to speak, but fear deprived him of voice. A third made his appearance. He wore a broad-brimmed hat and a long coat, and was evidently walking only for exercise. William scanned him well, and though not much skilled in physiognomy, he concluded he was the man. William approached him, and asked him if he knew any one who would help him, as he was sick? The gentleman asked whether he was not a slave. The poor slave hesitated; but, on being told that he had nothing to fear, he answered, " Yes." The gentleman told him he was in a pro-slaving neighbourhood, but, if he would wait a little, he would go and get a covered waggon, and convey him to his house. After he had gone, the fugitive meditated whether he should stay or not, being apprehensive that the broad-brimmed gentleman had gone for some one to assist him: he however concluded to remain.

After waiting about an hour—an hour big with fate to him—he saw the covered waggon making its appearance, and no one on it but the person he before accosted. Trembling with hope and fear, he entered the waggon, and was carried to the person's house. When he got there, he still halted between two opinions, whether he should enter or take to his heels; but he soon decided after seeing the glowing face of the wife. He saw something in her that bid him welcome, something that told him he would not be betrayed.

He soon found that he was under the shed of a Quaker, and a Quaker of the George Fox stamp. He had heard of Quakers and their kindness; but was not prepared to meet with such hospitality as now greeted him. He saw nothing but kind looks, and heard nothing but tender words. He began to feel the pulsations of a new existence. White men always scorned him, but now a white benevolent woman felt glad to wait on him; it was a revolution in his experience. The table was loaded with good things, but he could not eat. If he were allowed the privilege of sitting in the kitchen, he thought he could do justice to the viands. The surprise being over his appetite soon returned.

"I have frequently been asked," says William, "how I felt upon finding myself regarded as a man by a white family; especially having just run away from one. I cannot say that I have ever answered the question yet. The fact that I was, in all probability, a freeman, sounded in my ears like a charm. I am satisfied that none but a slave could place such an appreciation upon liberty as I did at that time. I wanted to see my mother and sister, that I might tell them that "I was free!" I wanted to see my fellow-slaves in St. Louis, and let them know that the chains were no longer upon my limbs. I wanted to see Captain Price, and let him learn from my own lips that I was no more a chattel, but a MAN. I was anxious, too, thus to inform Mrs. Price that she must get another coachman, and I wanted to see Eliza more than I did Mr. Price or Mrs. Price. The fact that I was a freeman—could walk, talk, eat, and sleep as a man, and no one to stand over me with the blood-clotted cow-hide—all this made me feel that I was not myself."

The kind Quaker, who so hospitably entertained William, was called Wells Brown. He remained with him about a fortnight, during which time he was well fed and clothed. Before leaving, the Quaker asked him what was his name besides William? The fugitive told him he had no other. "Well," said he, "thee must have another name. Since thee has got out of slavery, thee has become a man, and men always have two names."

William told him that as he was the first man to extend the hand of friendship to him, he would give him the privilege of naming him.

"If I name thee," said he, "I shall call thee Wells Brown, like myself.

"But," said he, "I am not willing to lose my name of William. It was taken from me once against my will, and I am not willing to part with it on any terms."

"Then," said the benevolent man, "I will call thee William Wells Brown."

"So be it," said William Wells Brown, and he has been known by this name ever since.

After giving the newly-christened freeman "a name," the Quaker gave him something to aid him to get "a local habitation." So, after giving him some money, Brown again started for Canada. In four days he reached a public-house, and went in to warm himself. He soon found that he was not out of the reach of his enemies. While warming himself, he heard some men in an adjoining bar-room talking about some runaway slaves. He thought it was time to be off, and, suiting the action to the thought, he was soon in the woods out of sight. When night came, he returned to the road and walked on; and so, for two days and two nights, till he was faint and ready to perish of hunger.

In this condition he arrived in the town of Cleveland, Ohio, on the banks of Lake Erie, where he determined to remain until the spring of the year, and then to try and reach Canada. Here he was compelled to work merely for his food. "Having lived in that way," said he in a speech at a public meeting in Exeter Hall, "for some weeks, I obtained a job, for which I received a shilling. This was not only the only shilling I had, but it was the first I had received after obtaining my freedom, and that shilling made me feel, indeed, as if I had a considerable stock in hand. What to do with my shilling I did not know. I would not put it into the bankers' hands, because, if they would have received it, I would not trust them. I would not lend it out, because I was afraid I should not get it back again. I carried the shilling in my pocket for some time, and finally resolved to lay it out; and after considerable thinking upon the subject, I laid out 6d. for a spelling-book, and the other 6d. for sugar candy or barley sugar. Well, now, you will all say that the one 6d. for the spelling-book was well laid out; and I am of opinion that the other was well laid out too; for the family in which I worked for my bread had two little boys, who attended the school every day, and I wanted to convert them into teachers; so I thought that nothing would act like a charm so much as a little barley sugar. The first day I got my book and stock in trade, I put the book into my bosom, and went to saw wood in the wood-house on a very cold day. One of the boys, a little after four o'clock, passed through the wood-house with a bag of books. I called to him, and I said to him, 'Johnny, do you see this?' taking a stick of barley sugar from my pocket and showing it to him. Says he, 'Yes; give me a taste of it.' Said I, 'I have got a spelling-book too,' and I showed that to him. 'Now,' said I, 'if you come to me in my room, and teach me my A, B, C, I will give you a whole stick.' 'Very well,' said he, 'I will; but let me taste it.' 'No; I can't.' 'Let me have it now.' Well, I thought I had better give him a little taste, until the right time came; and I marked the barley sugar about a quarter of an inch down, and told him to bite that far and no farther. He made a grab, and bit half the stick, and ran off laughing. I put the other piece in my pocket, and after a little while the other boy, little David, came through the wood-house with his books. I said nothing about the barley sugar, or my wish to get education. I knew the other lad would communicate the news to him. In a little while he returned, and said, 'Bill, John says you have got some barley sugar.' Well,' I said, 'what of that?' 'He said you gave him some; give

me a little taste.' 'Well, if you come to-night
and help me to learn my letters, I will give you
a whole stick.' 'Yes; but let me taste it.' 'Ah!
but you want to bite it.' 'No, I don't, but
just let me taste it.' Well, I thought I had better
show it to him. 'Now,' said he, 'let me touch my
tongue against it.' I thought then that I had better
give him a taste, but I would not trust him so far
as I trusted John; so I called him to me, and got
his head under my arm, and took him by the chin,
and told him to hold out his tongue; and as he did
so, I drew the barley sugar over very lightly. He said,
'That's very nice; just draw it over again.' 'I could
stand here and let you draw it across my tongue
all day.' The night came on; the two boys came
out of their room up into the attic where I was
lodging, and there they commenced teaching me the
letters of the alphabet. We all laid down upon the
floor, covered with the same blanket; and first one
would teach me a letter, and then the other, and I
would pass the barley sugar from one side to the
other. I kept those two boys on my sixpenny worth
of barley sugar·for about three weeks. Of course I
did not let them know how much I had. I first
dealt it out to them a quarter of a stick at a time.
I worked along in that way, and before I left that
place where I was working for my bread, I got so
that I could spell. I had a book that had the word
baker in it, and the boys used to think that when
they got so far as that, they were getting on pretty

well. I had often passed by the school-house, and
stood and listened at the window to hear them spell,
and I knew that when they could spell *baker* they
thought something of themselves; and I was glad
when I got that far. Before I left that place I
could read. Finally, from that I went on until I
could write. How do you suppose I first commenced
writing? for you will understand that up to the
present time I never spent a day in school in my
life, for I had no money to pay for schooling, so that
I had to get my learning first from one and then from
another. I carried a piece of chalk in my pocket,
and whenever I met a boy I would stop him and
take out my chalk and get at a board fence and then
commence. First I made some flourishes with no
meaning, and called a boy up, and said, 'Do you see
that? Can you beat that writing?' Said he, 'That's
not writing.' Well, I wanted to get so as to write
my own name. I had got out of slavery with only
one name. While escaping, I received the hospitality
of a very good man, who had spared part of his name
to me, and finally my name got pretty long, and I
wanted to be able to write it. 'Now, what do you
call that?' said the boy, looking at my flourishes. I
said, 'Is not that *William Wells Brown?*' 'Give
me the chalk,' says he, and he wrote out in large
letters ' *William Wells Brown,*' and I marked up the
fence for nearly a quarter of a mile, trying to copy,
till I got so that I could write my name. Then I
went on with my chalking, and, in fact, all board

fences within half a mile of where I lived were marked over with some kind of figures I had made, in trying to learn how to write. I next obtained an arithmetic, and then a grammar, and I stand here to-night, without having had a day's schooling in my life." Such were some of the efforts made by a fugitive slave to obtain for himself an education. Soon after his escape, Brown was married to a free coloured woman, by whom he has had three daughters, one of whom died in infancy. Having tasted the sweets of freedom himself, his great desire was to extend its blessing to his race, and in the language of the poet he would ask himself,

> " Is true freedom but to break
> Fetters for our own dear sake
> And with leathern hearts forget
> That we owe mankind a debt?

> " No! true freedom is to share
> All the chains our brothers wear,
> And with heart and hand to be
> Earnest to make others free."

While acting as a servant to one of the steamers on Lake Erie, Brown often took fugitives from Cleveland and other ports to Buffalo, or Detroit, from either of which places they could cross to Canada in an hour. During the season of 1842, this fugitive slave conveyed no less than *sixty-nine* runaway slaves across Lake Erie, and placed them safe on the soil of Canada. The following interesting account of Brown's first going into business for himself, which we transcribe from his "Three Years in Europe," will show the energy of the man. He says, "In the autumn of 1835, having been cheated out of the previous summer's earnings by the captain of the steamer in which I had been employed running away with the money, I was, like the rest of the men, left without any means of support during the winter, and therefore had to seek employment in the neighbouring towns. I went to the town of Monroe in the state of Michigan, and while going through the principal streets looking for work, I passed the door of the only barber in the town, whose shop appeared to be filled with persons waiting to be shaved. As there was but one man at work, and as I had, while employed in the steamer, occasionally shaved a gentleman who could not perform that office himself, it occurred to me that I might get employment here as a journeyman barber. I therefore made immediate application for work, but the barber told me he did not need a hand. But I was not to be put off so easily, and after making several offers to work cheap, I frankly told him, that if he would not employ me, I would get a room near him, and set up an opposition establishment. This threat, however, made no impression on the barber; and as I was leaving, one of the men, who were waiting to be shaved, said, ' If you want a room in which to commence business, I have one on the opposite side of the street.' This man followed me out ; we went over, and I looked at the room.

He strongly urged me to set up, at the same time promising to give me his influence. I took the room, purchased an old table, two chairs, got a pole with a red stripe painted around it, and the next day opened, with a sign over the door, 'Fashionable Hair-dresser from New York, Emperor of the West.' I need not add that my enterprise was very annoying to the 'shop over the way,' especially my sign, which happened to be the most extensive part of the concern. Of course I had to tell all who came in, that my neighbour on the opposite side did not keep clean towels, that his razors were dull, and, above all, he never had been to New York to see the fashions. Neither had I. In a few weeks I had the entire business of the town, to the great discomfiture of the other barber. At this time, money matters in the Western States were in a sad condition. Any person who could raise a small amount of money was permitted to establish a bank, and allowed to issue notes for four times the sum raised. This being the case, many persons borrowed money merely long enough to exhibit to the bank inspectors, and the borrowed money was returned, and the bank left without a dollar in its vaults, if, indeed, it had a vault about its premises. The result was, that banks were started all over the Western States, and the country flooded with worthless paper. These were known as the 'Wild Cat Banks.' Silver coin being very scarce, and the banks not being allowed to issue notes for a smaller amount than one dollar, several persons put out notes of from 6 to 75 cents in value; these were called 'Shinplasters.' The Shinplaster was in the shape of a promissory note, made payable on demand. I have often seen persons with large rolls of these bills, the whole not amounting to more than five dollars. Some weeks after I had commenced business on my 'own hook,' I was one evening very much crowded with customers; and while they were talking over the events of the day, one of them said to me, 'Emperor, you seem to be doing a thriving business. You should do as other business men, issue your Shinplasters.' This of course, as it was intended, created a laugh; but with me it was no laughing matter, for from that moment I began to think seriously of becoming a banker. I accordingly went a few days after to a printer, and he, wishing to get the job of printing, urged me to put out my notes, and showed me some specimens of engravings that he had just received from Detroit. My head being already filled with the idea of the bank, I needed but little persuasion to set the thing finally afloat. Before I left the printer the notes were partly in type, and I studying how I should keep the public from counterfeiting them. The next day, my Shinplasters were handed to me, the whole amount being twenty dollars; and, after being duly signed, were ready for circulation. The first night I had my money, my head was so turned and dizzy, that I could not sleep. In fact, I slept but little for weeks after the issuing of my bills.

This fact satisfied me, that people of wealth pass many sleepless hours. At first my notes did not take well; they were too new, and viewed with a suspicious eye. But through the assistance of my customers, and a good deal of exertion on my part, my bills were soon in circulation; and nearly all the money received in return for my notes was spent in fitting up and decorating my shop. Few bankers get through this world without their difficulties, and I was not to be an exception. A short time after my money had been out, a party of young men, either wishing to pull down my vanity, or to try the soundness of my bank, determined to give it 'a run.' After collecting together a number of my bills, they came one at a time to demand other money for them; and I, not being aware of what was going on, was taken by surprise. One day as I was sitting at my table, stropping some new razors I had just purchased with the avails of my Shinplasters, one of the men entered and said, 'Emperor, you will oblige me if you will give me some other money for these notes of yours.' I immediately cashed the notes with the most worthless of the Wild Cat money that I had on hand, but which was a lawful tender. The young man had scarcely left, when a second appeared with a similar amount, and demanded payment. These were cashed, and soon a third came with his roll of notes. I paid these with an air of triumph, although I had but half a dollar left. I began now to think seriously what I should do, or how to act,

D

provided another demand should be made. While I was thus engaged in thought, I saw the fourth man crossing the street, with a handful of notes, evidently my Shinplasters. I instantaneously shut the door, and looking out of the window said, 'I have closed business for to-day : come to-morrow and I will see you.' In looking across the street, I saw my rival standing at his shopdoor, grinning and clapping his hands at my apparent downfal. I was completely 'done *Brown*' for the day. However, I was not to be 'used up' in this way; so I escaped by the back door, and went in search of my friend, who had first suggested to me the idea of issuing my notes. I found him, told him of the difficulty I was in, and wished him to point out a way by which I might extricate myself. He laughed heartily at my sad position, and then said, 'You must act as all bankers do in this part of the country.' I inquired how they did; and he said, 'when your notes are brought to you, you must redeem them, and then send them out and get other money for them; and, with the latter, you can keep cashing your own Shinplasters.' This was, indeed, a new idea for me. I immediately commenced putting in circulation the notes which I had just redeemed, and my efforts were crowned with such success, that, together with the aid of my friend, who, like a philanthropist and Western Christian as he was, before I slept that night, my Shinplasters were again in circulation, and my bank once more on a sound basis."

In proportion as his mind expanded under the more favourable circumstances in which Brown was placed, he became anxious, not merely for the redemption of his race from personal slavery, but for the moral and religious elevation of those who were free. Finding that habits of intoxication were too prevalent among his coloured brethren, he, in conjunction with others, commenced a temperance reformation in their body. Such was the success of their efforts that, in three years, in the city of Buffalo alone, a society of upwards of 500 members was raised out of a coloured population of less than 700. Of that society Mr. Brown was thrice elected president. The intellectual powers of our author, coupled with his intimate acquaintance with the workings of the slave system, early recommended him to the Abolitionists, as a man eminently qualified to arouse the attention of the people of the Northern States to the great national sin of America. In 1843, he was engaged by the Western New York Anti-Slavery Society as a lecturing agent. From 1844 to 1847, he laboured in the Anti-Slavery cause in connection with the American Anti-Slavery Society; and from that period up to the time of his departure for Europe, in 1849, he was an agent of the Massachusetts Anti-Slavery Society. The records of these societies furnish abundant evidence of the success of his labours. From the Massachusetts Anti-Slavery Society he early received the following testimonial. "Since Mr. Brown became an agent of this society, he has lectured in very many of the towns of this commonwealth, and gained for himself, the respect and esteem of all whom he met. Himself a fugitive slave, he can experimentally describe the situation of those in bonds as bound with them; and he powerfully illustrates the diabolism of that system which keeps in chains and darkness a host of minds, which, if free and enlightened, would shine among men like stars in the firmament." Another member of that society speaks thus of him :—"I need not attempt any description of the ability and efficiency which characterised the speeches of William Wells Brown throughout the meeting. To you who know him so well, it is enough to say that his lectures were worthy of himself. He has left an impression on the minds of the people, that few could have done. Cold indeed must be the hearts that could resist the appeals of so noble a specimen of humanity, in behalf of a crushed and despised race."

In 1847, Mr. Brown wrote a narrative of his life and escape from slavery, which rapidly ran through several editions. A copy of this he forwarded to his old master, from whom he had escaped, and soon after a friend of Mr. Brown's received the following letter :

" St. Louis, Jan. 10*th*, 1848.

" Sir,—I received a pamphlet, or a narrative, so called on the title-page, of the Life of William W. Brown, a fugitive slave, purporting to have been written by himself; and in his book I see a letter from you to the said William W. Brown. This said Brown is named William; he is a slave belonging to me, and ran away from me the first day of January, 1834.

"I purchased him of Mr. S. Willi, the last of September, 1833. I paid six hundred and fifty dollars for him. If I had wanted to speculate on him, I could have sold him for three times as much as I paid for him. I was offered two thousand dollars for him in New Orleans at one time, and fifteen hundred dollars for him at another time, in Louisville, Kentucky. But I would not sell him. I was told that he was going to run away, but I did not believe the man, for I had so much confidence in William. I want you to see him, and see if what I say is not the truth. I do not want him as a slave, but I think that his friends, who sustain him and give him the right hand of fellowship, or he himself, could afford to pay my agent in Boston three hundred and twenty five dollars, and I will give him free papers, so that he may go wherever he wishes to. Then he can visit St. Louis, or any other place he may wish.

"This amount is just half what I paid for him. Now, if this offer suits Mr. Brown, and the Anti-Slavery Society of Boston, or Massachusetts, let me know, and I will give you the name of my agent in Boston, and forward the papers, to be given to William W. Brown as soon as the money is paid.

" Yours respectfully,
" ENOCH PRICE."

" To Emund Quincy, Esq."

While Mr. Brown would most gladly have accepted manumission papers, relieving him from all future claim of the slaveholder, and thereby making his freedom more secure, he yet felt that he could not conscientiously purchase his liberty, because, by so doing, he would be putting money into the pockets of the manstealer which did not justly belong to him. He therefore refused the offer of Mr. Price. Notwithstanding the celebrity he had acquired in the North, as a man of genius and talent, and the general respect his high character had gained him, the slave spirit of America denied him the rights of a citizen. By the constitution of the United States he was every moment liable to be arrested, and returned to the slavery from which he had fled. His only protection from such a fate was the anomaly of the ascendancy of the public opinion over the law of the country.

It has been for years thought desirable and advantageous to the cause of Negro emancipation in America, to have some talented man of colour always in Great Britain, who should be a living refutation of the doctrine of the inferiority of the African race; and it was moreover felt that none could so powerfully advocate the cause of " those in bonds" as one who had actually been " bound with them." Mr. Brown having received repeated invitations from distinguished English Abolitionists to visit Great Britain, and being chosen a delegate to the Paris Peace Congress of 1849 by the American Peace Society, and also by a convention of the coloured people of Boston, he resolved to acquiesce in the wishes of his numerous friends, and accordingly sailed from the United States on the 18th of July, 1849.

On leaving America he bore with him the following testimony from the Board of Managers of the Massachusetts Anti-Slavery Society:—

"In consequence of the departure for England of their esteemed friend and faithful co-labourer in the cause of the American slave, William W. Brown, the Board of Management of the Massachusetts Anti-Slavery Society would commend him to the confidence, respect, esteem, and hospitality of the friends of emancipation wherever he may travel:—

"1. Because he is a fugitive slave from the American house of bondage, and on the soil which gave him birth can find no spot on which he can stand in safety from his pursuers, protected by law.

"2. Because he is a man, and not a chattel; and while as the latter, he may at any time be sold at public vendue under the American star-spangled banner, we rejoice to know that he will be recognised and protected as the former under the flag of England.

"3. Because, for several years past, he has nobly consecrated his time and talents, at great personal hazard, and under the most adverse circumstances, to the uncompromising advocacy of the cause of his enslaved countrymen.

"4. Because he visits England for the purpose of

increasing, consolidating, and directing British humanity and piety against that horrible system of slavery in America, by which three millions of human beings, by creation the children of God, are ranked with four-footed beasts, and treated as marketable commodities.

"5. Because he has long been in their employment as a lecturing agent in Massachusetts, and has laboured with great acceptance and success; and from the acquaintance thus formed, they are enabled to certify that he has invariably conducted himself with great circumspection, and won for himself the sympathy, respect, and friendship of a very large circle of acquaintance."

The Coloured convention unanimously passed the following resolution :

"*Resolved*, — That we bid our brother, William Wells Brown, God speed in his mission to Europe, and commend him to the hospitality and encouragement of all true friends of humanity."

In a letter to an American journal, announcing his arrival at Liverpool, he speaks as follows : —

"No person of my complexion can visit this country without being struck with the marked difference between the English and the Americans. The prejudice which I have experienced on all and every occasion in the United States, and to some degree on board the *Canada*, vanished as soon as I set foot on the soil of Britain. In America I had been bought and sold as a slave, in the Southern States. In the so-called Free States I had been treated as one born to occupy an inferior position; in steamers, compelled to take my fare on the deck; in hotels, to take my meals in the kitchen; in coaches, to ride on the outside; in railways, to ride in the 'Negro car;' and in churches, to sit in the 'Negro pew.' But no sooner was I on British soil than I was recognised as a man and an equal. The very dogs in the streets appeared conscious of my manhood. Such is the difference, and such is the change that is brought about by a trip of nine days in an Atlantic steamer. * * * For the first time in my life, I can say 'I am truly free.' My old master may make his appearance here, with the constitution of the United States in his pocket, the fugitive slave law in one hand and the chains in the other, and claim me as his property; but all will avail him nothing. I can here stand and look the tyrant in the face, and tell him that I am his equal! England is, indeed, the 'land of the free, and the home of the brave.'"

The reception of Mr. Brown at the Peace Congress in Paris was most flattering. He admirably maintained his reputation as a public speaker. His brief address upon that "war spirit of America which holds in bondage nearly four millions of his brethren," produced a profound sensation. At its conclusion the speaker was warmly greeted by Victor Hugo, the Abbé Duguerry, Emile de Girardin, Richard Cobden, and every man of note in the assembly. At the soirée given by M. de Tocquerelle, the Minister for Foreign Affairs, and the other fêtes given to the members of the Congress, Mr. Brown was received with marked attention.

Having finished his Peace Mission in France, he returned to England, where he was received with a hearty welcome by some of the most influential abolitionists of this country. Most of the fugitive slaves, and in fact nearly all of the coloured men who have visited Great Britain from the United States, have come upon begging missions, either for some society or for themselves. Mr. Brown has been almost the only exception. With that independence of feeling, which those who are acquainted with him know to be one of his chief characteristics, he determined to maintain himself and family by his own exertions—by his literary labours, and the honourable profession of a public lecturer. From nearly all the cities and large provincial towns he received invitations to lecture or address public meetings. The mayors, or other citizens of note, presided over many of these meetings. At Newcastle-upon-Tyne a soirée was given him, and an address presented by the citizens. A large and influential meeting was held at Bolton, Lancashire, which was addressed by Mr. Brown, and at its close the ladies presented to him the following address :—

"An address, presented to Mr. William Wells Brown, the fugitive slave from America, by the ladies of Bolton, March 22nd, 1850 :—

"Dear friend and brother,—We cannot permit you to depart from among us without giving expression to the feelings which we entertain towards yourself personally, and to the sympathy which you have awakened in our breasts for the three millions of our sisters and brothers who still suffer and groan in the prison-house of American bondage. You came among us an entire stranger; we received you for the sake of your mission; and having heard the story of your personal wrongs, and gazed with horror on the atrocities of slavery as seen through the medium of your touching descriptions, we are resolved, henceforward, in reliance on divine assistance, to render what aid we can to the cause which you have so eloquently pleaded in our presence.

"We have no words to express our detestation of the crimes which, in the name of liberty, are committed in the country which gave you birth. Language fails to tell our deep abhorrence of the impiety of those who, in the still more sacred name of religion, rob immortal beings not only of an earthly citizenship, but do much to prevent them from obtaining a heavenly one; and, as mothers and daughters, we embrace this opportunity of giving utterance to our utmost indignation at the cruelties perpetrated upon our sex, by a people professedly acknowledging the equality of all mankind. Carry with you, on your return to the land of your nativity, this our solemn protest against the wicked institution which, like a dark and baleful cloud, hangs over it; and

ask the unfeeling enslavers, as best you can, to open
the prison doors to them that are bound, and let the
oppressed go free.

"Allow us to assure you that your brief sojourn
in our town has been to ourselves, and to vast mul-
titudes, of a character long to be remembered; and
when you are far removed from us, and toiling, as
we hope you may be long spared to do, in this
righteous enterprise, it may be some solace to your
mind to know that your name is cherished with
affectionate regard, and that the blessing of the Most
High is earnestly supplicated in behalf of yourself,
your family, and the cause to which you have consecrated your distinguished talents."

A most respectable and enthusiastic public meeting
was held at Sheffield, to welcome Mr. Brown, and
the next day he was invited to inspect several of the
large establishments there. While going through the
manufactory of Messrs. Broadhead and Atkin, silver
and electroplaters, &c., in Love-street, and whilst he
was being shown through the works, a subscription
was hastily set on foot on his behalf, by the workmen
and women of the establishment, which was presented to Mr. Brown in the counting-house by a
deputation of the subscribers. The spokesman (the
designer to Messrs. Broadhead and Atkin) addressing
Mr. Brown on behalf of the workpeople, begged his
acceptance of the present as a token of esteem, as
well as an expression of their sympathy in the cause

he advocates, viz. that of the American slave. Mr. Brown briefly thanked the parties for their spontaneous free will offering, accompanied as it was by a generous expression of sympathy for his afflicted brethren and sisters in bondage.

Mr. Brown has been in England nearly four years, and since his arrival he has travelled above twenty thousand miles through Great Britain, addressed one hundred and thirty public meetings, lectured in twenty-three mechanics and literary institutions, and given his services to many of the benevolent and religious societies on the occasion of their anniversary meetings. After a lecture, which he delivered before the Whittington Club, he received from the managers of that institution the following testimonial:

> "*Whittington Club and Metropolitan Athenæum,*
> "189, *Strand, June* 21, 1850.

"My dear sir,

I have much pleasure in conveying to you the best thanks of the Managing Committee of this institution for the excellent lecture you gave here last evening, and also in presenting you in their names with an honorary membership of the club. It is hoped that you will often avail yourself of its privileges by coming amongst us. You will then see, by the cordial welcome of the members, that they protest against the odious distinctions made between man and man, and the abominable traffic of which you have been the victim.

"For my own part, I shall be happy to be serviceable to you in any way, and at all times be glad to place the advantages of the institution at your disposal.

        "I am, my dear sir,

                "Yours truly,

                        "WILLIAM STRUDWICKE,

"Mr. W. Wells Brown."   "Secretary."

On the 1st of August, 1851, a meeting of the most novel character was held at the Hall of Commerce, London, the chief actors being American fugitive slaves. That meeting was most ably presided over by Mr. Brown, and the speeches made on the occasion by fugitive slaves were of the most interesting and creditable description. Although a residence in Canada is infinitely preferable to slavery in America, yet the climate of that country is uncongenial to the constitutions of the Negroes, and their lack of education is an almost insuperable barrier to their social progress. The latter evil Mr. Brown attempted to remedy by the establishment of Manual Labour Schools in Canada for fugitive slaves. A public meeting, attended by between 3,000 and 4,000 persons, was held on the 6th of January 1851, in the City Hall, Glasgow, which was presided over by Alexander Hastie, Esq., M.P., at which resolutions were unanimously passed, approving of Mr. Brown's scheme; which scheme, however, never received that amount of support which would have enabled him to bring it into practice ; and the plan at present only re-

remains as an evidence of its author's ingenuity and desire for the elevation of his oppressed and injured race. Mr. Brown subsequently made, through the columns of the *Times*, a proposition for the emigration of American fugitive slaves, under fair and honourable terms, from Canada to the West Indies, where there is a great lack of that labour which they are so capable of undertaking. These efforts all show the willingness of this fugitive slave to aid those of his race. Last year Mr. Brown published his "Three Years in Europe; or, Places I have seen and People I have met." And his literary abilities may be partly judged of from the following commendations of that ably written work :—

"The extraordinary excitement produced by 'Uncle Tom's Cabin' will, we hope, prepare the public of Great Britain and America for this lively book of travels by a real fugitive slave. Though he never had a day's schooling in his life, he has produced a literary work not unworthy of a highly educated gentleman. Our readers will find in these letters much instruction, not a little entertainment, and the beatings of a manly heart, on behalf of a down-trodden race, with which they will not fail to sympathise."—*The Eclectic.*

"When he writes on the wrongs of his race, or the events of his own career, he is always interesting or amusing."—*The Athenæum.*

"The appearance of this book is too remarkable a literary event to pass without a notice. At the moment when attention in this country is directed to the state of the coloured people in America, the book appears with additional advantage; if nothing else were attained by its publication, it is well to have another proof of the capability of the Negro intellect. Altogether Mr. Brown has written a pleasing and amusing volume. Contrasted with the caricature and bombast of his white countrymen, Mr. Willis's description of 'People he has met,' a comparison suggested by the similarity of the title, it is both in intellect and in style a superior performance, and we are glad to bear this testimony to the literary merit of a work by a Negro author."—*The Literary Gazette.*

" That a man who was a slave for the first twenty years of his life, and who has never had a day's schooling, should produce such a book as this, cannot but astonish those who speak disparagingly of the African race."—*The Weekly News and Chronicle.*

" This remarkable book of a remarkable man cannot fail to add to the practical protests already entered in Britain against the absolute bondage of 3,000,000 of our fellow creatures. The impression of a self-educated son of slavery here set forth, must hasten the period when the senseless and impious denial of common claims to a common humanity, on the score of colour, shall be scouted with scorn in every civilised and Christian country. And when this shall be attained, among the means of destruction of the hideous abomination, his compatriots will remember with respect and gratitude the doings and sayings of William Wells Brown. The volume consists of a sufficient variety of scenes, persons, arguments, inferences, speculations, and opinions, to satisfy and amuse the most *exigeant* of those who read *pour se desennuyer;* while those who look deeper into things, and view with anxious hope the progress of nations and of mankind, will feel that the good cause of humanity and freedom, of Christianity, enlightenment, and brotherhood, cannot fail to be served by such a book as this."—*Morning Advertiser.*

"He writes with ease and ability, and his intelligent observations upon the great question to which he has devoted, and is devoting his life, will be read with interest, and will command influence and respect."—*Daily News.*

Mr. Brown is most assiduous in his studies even at the present time. The following extract from his writings will show how he spends most of his leisure hours:—

"It was eight o'clock before I reached my lodgings. Although fatigued by the day's exertions, I again resumed the reading of Roscoe's 'Leo X.,' and had nearly finished seventy-three pages, when the clock on St. Martin's Church apprised me that it was two. He who escapes from slavery at the age of twenty years without any education, as did the writer of this letter, must read when others are asleep, if he would catch up with the rest of the world. 'To be wise,' says Pope, 'is but to know how little can be known.' The true searcher after

E

truth and knowledge is always like a child; although gaining strength from year to year, he still 'learns to labour and to wait.' The field of labour is ever expanding before him, reminding him that he has yet more to learn ; teaching him that he is nothing more than a child in knowledge, and inviting him onward with a thousand varied charms. The son may take possession of the father's goods at his death, but he cannot inherit with the property the father's cultivated mind. He may put on the father's old coat, but that is all ; the immortal mind of the first wearer has gone to the tomb. Property may be bequeathed but knowledge cannot. Then let him who would be useful in his generation be up and doing. Like the Chinese student who learned perseverance from the woman whom he saw trying to rub a crowbar into a needle, so should we take the experience of the past to lighten our feet through the paths of the future."

The following testimonial to Mr. Brown's abilities, from an American journal of which Frederick Douglas is editor, shows that his talents are highly appreciated in that country:—

"We have the pleasure to lay before our readers another interesting letter from W. Wells Brown. We rejoice to find our friend still persevering in the pursuit of knowledge, and still more do we rejoice to find such marked evidence of his rapid progress as his several letters afford. But a few years ago he was a despised, degraded, whip-scarred slave, knowing nothing of letters; and now we find him writing accounts of his travels in a distant land, of which a man reared under the most favourable educational advantages might be proud."

We should have said that it was Mr. Brown's intention to have returned to the United States to his family ere this. But the passage of the infamous "Fugitive Slave Law" prevented his returning.

Mr. Brown's wife died in Buffalo N. Y. in Jan. 1851. He has two daughters who are now in this country, being trained for teachers. Of course we need not add that for their education they are entirely dependent on their father's exertions. During last year, the Rev. Edward Hore, of Ramsgate, through a willingness to assist Mr. Brown in returning to the United States, wrote to his former owner, and offered him £50, if he would relinquish all claim to him, and furnish the fugitive with papers of emancipation, but the following note from the slaveowner speaks for itself : —

" *St. Louis, Feb.* 16*th,* 1852.

"Rev. sir,—I received your note, dated Jan. 6th, concerning a runaway slave of mine now known by the name of William Wells Brown. You state that I offered to take three hundred and twenty five dollars for him, and give him free papers, in 1848. I did so then, but since that time the laws of the United States are materially changed. The Fugitive Slave

Bill has passed since then. I can now take him any-
where in the United States, and I have everything
arranged for his arrest if he lands at any port in the
United States. But I will give him papers of
emancipation, properly authenticated by our statutes,
for the sum of five hundred dollars (or £100) that
will make him as free as any white person. If this
suits your views, you can let me know, and I will
have the papers made out and forwarded to Boston,
to Joseph Gruley, of the firm of Charles Wilkins and
Co., 33, Long Wharf. The money must be paid before
the papers are handed over to your agent.

      "Respectfully your obedient servant,

"To the Rev. Edward Hore."   "ENOCH PRICE."

CLOTEL;

OR,

THE PRESIDENT'S DAUGHTER.

CHAPTER I.

THE NEGRO SALE.

"WHY stands she near the auction stand,
  That girl so young and fair?
What brings her to this dismal place,
  Why stands she weeping there?"

WITH the growing population of slaves in the Southern States of America, there is a fearful increase of half whites, most of whose fathers are slaveowners, and their mothers slaves. Society does not frown upon the man who sits with his mulatto child upon his knee, whilst its mother stands a slave behind his chair. The late Henry Clay, some years since, predicted that the abolition of negro slavery would be brought about by the amalgamation of the races. John Randolph, a distinguished slaveholder of Virginia, and a prominent statesman, said in a speech in the legislature of his native state, that "the blood of the first American statesmen coursed through the veins of the slave of the South." In all the cities and towns of the slave states, the real negro, or clear black, does not amount to more than one in every four of the slave population. This fact is, of itself, the best evidence of the degraded and immoral condition of the relation of master and slave in the United States of America.

In all the slave states, the law says : —" Slaves shall be deemed, sold, taken, reputed, and adjudged in law to be chattels personal in the hands of their owners and possessors, and their executors, administrators and assigns, to all intents, constructions, and purposes whatsoever." A slave is one who is in the power of a master to whom he belongs. The master may sell him, dispose of his person, his industry, and his labour. He can do nothing, possess nothing, nor acquire anything, but what must belong to his master. The slave is entirely subject to the will of his master, who may correct and chastise him, though not with unusual rigour, or so as to maim and mutilate him, or expose him to the danger of loss of life, or to cause his death. The slave, to remain a slave, must be sensible that there is no appeal from his master." Where the slave is placed by law entirely under the control of the man who claims him, body and soul, as property, what else could be expected than the most depraved social condition? The marriage relation, the oldest and most sacred institution given to man by his Creator, is unknown and unrecognised in the slave laws of the United States. Would that we could say, that the moral and religious teaching in the slave states were better than the laws; but, alas! we cannot. A few years since, some slave-holders became a little uneasy in their minds about the rightfulness of permitting slaves to take to themselves husbands and wives, while they still had others living, and applied to their religious teachers for advice; and the following will show how this grave and important subject was treated : —

"Is a servant, whose husband or wife has been sold by his or her master into a distant country, to be permitted to marry again?"

The query was referred to a committee, who made the following report; which, after discussion, was adopted : —

"That, in view of the circumstances in which servants in this country are placed, the committee are unanimous in the opinion, that it is better to permit servants thus circumstanced to take another husband or wife."

Such was the answer from a committee of the "Shiloh Baptist Association;" and instead of receiving light, those who asked the question were plunged into deeper darkness!

A similar question was put to the "Savannah River Association," and the answer, as the following will show, did not materially differ from the one we have already given : —

"Whether, in a case of involuntary separation, of such a character as to preclude all prospect of future intercourse, the parties ought to be allowed to marry again."

Answer —

"That such separation among persons situated as our slaves are, is civilly a separation by death; and they believe that, in the sight of God, it would be so viewed. To forbid second marriages in such cases would be to expose the parties, not only to stronger hardships and strong temptation, but to church-censure for acting in obedience to their masters, who cannot be expected to acquiesce in a regulation at variance with justice to the slaves, and to the spirit of that command which regulates marriage among Christians. The slaves are not free agents; and a dissolution by death is not more entirely without their consent, and beyond their control, than by such separation."

Although marriage, as the above indicates, is a matter which the slaveholders do not think is of any importance, or of any binding force with their slaves; yet it would be doing that degraded class an injustice, not to acknowledge that many of them do regard it as a sacred obligation, and show a willingness to obey the commands of God on this subject. Marriage is, indeed, the first and most important institution of human existence — the foundation of all civilisation and culture—the root of church and state. It is the most intimate covenant of heart formed among mankind; and for many persons the only relation in which they feel the true sentiments of humanity. It gives scope for every human virtue, since each of these is developed from the love and

confidence which here predominate. It unites all
which ennobles and beautifies life,— sympathy, kindness of will and deed, gratitude, devotion, and
every delicate, intimate feeling. As the only asylum
for true education, it is the first and last sanctuary of
human culture. As husband and wife through each
other become conscious of complete humanity, and
every human feeling, and every human virtue; so
children, at their first awakening in the fond covenant of love between parents, both of whom are
tenderly concerned for the same object, find an image
of complete humanity leagued in free love. The
spirit of love which prevails between them acts with
creative power upon the young mind, and awakens
every germ of goodness within it. This invisible
and incalculable influence of parental life acts more
upon the child than all the efforts of education, whether by means of instruction, precept, or exhortation.
If this be a true picture of the vast influence for good
of the institution of marriage, what must be the
moral degradation of that people to whom marriage is
denied? Not content with depriving them of all the
higher and holier enjoyments of this relation, by degrading and darkening their souls, the slaveholder
denies to his victim even that slight alleviation of his
misery, which would result from the marriage relation
being protected by law and public opinion. Such is
the influence of slavery in the United States, that the
ministers of religion, even in the so-called free states,
are the mere echoes, instead of the correctors, of
public sentiment.

We have thought it advisable to show that the
present system of chattel slavery in America under-
mines the entire social condition of man, so as to
prepare the reader for the following narrative of
slave life, in that otherwise happy and prosperous
country.

In all the large towns in the Southern States, there is a class of slaves who are permitted to hire their time of their owners, and for which they pay a high price. These are mulatto women, or quadroons, as they are familiarly known, and are distinguished for their fascinating beauty. The handsomest usually pays the highest price for her time. Many of these women are the favourites of persons who furnish them with the means of paying their owners, and not a few are dressed in the most extravagant manner. Reader, when you take into consideration the fact, that amongst the slave population no safeguard is thrown around virtue, and no inducement held out to slave women to be chaste, you will not be surprised when we tell you that immorality and vice pervade the cities of the Southern States in a manner unknown in the cities and towns of the Northern States. Indeed most of the slave women have no higher aspiration than that of becoming the finely-dressed mistress of some white man. And at negro balls and parties, this class of women usually cut the greatest figure.

At the close of the year —— the following advertisement appeared in a newspaper published in Richmond, the capital of the state of Virginia:— "Notice: Thirty-eight negroes will be offered for sale on Monday, November 10th, at twelve o'clock, being the entire stock of the late John Graves, Esq. The negroes are in good condition, some of them very prime; among them are several mechanics, able-bodied field hands, plough-boys, and women with children at the breast, and some of them very prolific in their generating qualities, affording a rare opportunity to any one who wishes to raise a strong and healthy lot of servants for their own use. Also several mulatto girls of rare personal qualities: two of them very superior. Any gentleman or lady

wishing to purchase, can take any of the above
slaves on trial for a week, for which no charge will
be made." Amongst the above slaves to be sold
were Currer and her two daughters, Clotel and Althesa; the latter were the girls spoken of in the
advertisement as "very superior." Currer was a
bright mulatto, and of prepossessing appearance,
though then nearly forty years of age. She had
hired her time for more than twenty years, during
which time she had lived in Richmond. In her
younger days Currer had been the housekeeper of a
young slaveholder; but of later years had been a
laundress or washerwoman, and was considered to
be a woman of great taste in getting up linen. The
gentleman for whom she had kept house was Thomas
Jefferson, by whom she had two daughters. Jefferson being called to Washington to fill a government
appointment, Currer was left behind, and thus she
took herself to the business of washing, by which
means she paid her master, Mr. Graves, and supported herself and two children. At the time of
the decease of her master, Currer's daughters, Clotel
and Althesa, were aged respectively sixteen and
fourteen years, and both, like most of their own sex
in America, were well grown. Currer early resolved
to bring her daughters up as ladies, as she termed it,
and therefore imposed little or no work upon them.
As her daughters grew older, Currer had to pay a
stipulated price for them; yet her notoriety as a
laundress of the first class enabled her to put an
extra price upon her charges, and thus she and her
daughters lived in comparative luxury. To bring
up Clotel and Althesa to attract attention, and especially at balls and parties, was the great aim of
Currer. Although the term "negro ball" is applied
to most of these gatherings, yet a majority of the
attendants are often whites. Nearly all the negro

parties in the cities and towns of the Southern States are made up of quadroon and mulatto girls, and white men. These are democratic gatherings, where gentlemen, shopkeepers, and their clerks, all appear upon terms of perfect equality. And there is a degree of gentility and decorum in these companies that is not surpassed by similar gatherings of white people in the Slave States. It was at one of these parties that Horatio Green, the son of a wealthy gentleman of Richmond, was first introduced to Clotel. The young man had just returned from college, and was in his twenty-second year. Clotel was sixteen, and was admitted by all to be the most beautiful girl, coloured or white, in the city. So attentive was the young man to the quadroon during the evening that it was noticed by all, and became a matter of general conversation; while Currer appeared delighted beyond measure at her daughter's conquest. From that evening, young Green became 'the favourite visitor at Currer's house. He soon promised to purchase Clotel, as speedily as it could be effected, and make her mistress of her own dwelling; and Currer looked forward with pride to the time when she should see her daughter emancipated and free. It was a beautiful moonlight night in August, when all who reside in tropical climes are eagerly gasping for a breath of fresh air, that Horatio Green was seated in the small garden behind Currer's cottage, with the object of his affections by his side. And it was here that Horatio drew from his pocket the newspaper, wet from the press, and read the advertisement for the sale of the slaves to which we have alluded; Currer and her two daughters being of the number. At the close of the evening's visit, and as the young man was leaving, he said to the girl, " You shall soon be free and your own mistress."

As might have been expected, the day of sale

brought an unusual large number together to compete
for the property to be sold. Farmers who make a
business of raising slaves for the market were there;
slave-traders and speculators were also numerously
represented; and in the midst of this throng was
one who felt a deeper interest in the result of the
sale than any other of the bystanders; this was
young Green. True to his promise, he was there
with a blank bank check in his pocket, awaiting
with impatience to enter the list as a bidder for the
beautiful slave. The less valuable slaves were first
placed upon the auction block, one after another, and
sold to the highest bidder. Husbands and wives
were separated with a degree of indifference that is
unknown in any other relation of life, except that of
slavery. Brothers and sisters were torn from each
other; and mothers saw their children leave them
for the last time on this earth.

It was late in the day, when the greatest number
of persons were thought to be present, that Currer
and her daughters were brought forward to the place
of sale. Currer was first ordered to ascend the
auction stand, which she did with a trembling step.
The slave mother was sold to a trader. Althesa,
the youngest, and who was scarcely less beautiful
than her sister, was sold to the same trader for one
thousand dollars. Clotel was the last, and, as was
expected, commanded a higher price than any that
had been offered for sale that day. The appearance
of Clotel on the auction block created a deep sensation amongst the crowd. There she stood, with a
complexion as white as most of those who were
waiting with a wish to become her purchasers; her
features as finely defined as any of her sex of pure
Anglo-Saxon; her long black wavy hair done up in
the neatest manner; her form tall and graceful, and
her whole appearance indicating one superior to her

position. The auctioneer commenced by saying, that
" Miss Clotel had been reserved for the last, because
she was the most valuable. How much gentlemen?
Real Albino, fit for a fancy girl for any one. She
enjoys good health, and has a sweet temper. How
much do you say?" "Five hundred dollars."
"Only five hundred for such a girl as this? Gentlemen, she is worth a deal more than that sum; you
certainly don't know the value of the article you are
bidding upon. Here, gentlemen, I hold in my hand
a paper certifying that she has a good moral character." "Seven hundred." "Ah, gentlemen, that
is something like. This paper also states that she is
very intelligent." "Eight hundred." "She is a
devoted Christian, and perfectly trustworthy." "Nine
hundred." "Nine fifty." "Ten." "Eleven."
"Twelve hundred." Here the sale came to a dead
stand. The auctioneer stopped, looked around, and
began in a rough manner to relate some anecdotes
relative to the sale of slaves, which, he said, had
come under his own observation. At this juncture
the scene was indeed strange. Laughing, joking,
swearing, smoking, spitting, and talking kept up a
continual hum and noise amongst the crowd; while
the slave-girl stood with tears in her eyes, at one
time looking towards her mother and sister, and at
another towards the young man whom she hoped
would become her purchaser. " The chastity of this
girl is pure; she has never been from under her
mother's care; she is a virtuous creature." " Thirteen." "Fourteen." "Fifteen." "Fifteen hundred
dollars," cried the auctioneer, and the maiden was
struck for that sum. This was a Southern auction,
at which the bones, muscles, sinews, blood, and
nerves of a young lady of sixteen were sold for five
hundred dollars; her moral character for two hundred; her improved intellect for one hundred; her

Christianity for three hundred; and her chastity and virtue for four hundred dollars more. And this, too, in a city thronged with churches, whose tall spires look like so many signals pointing to heaven, and whose ministers preach that slavery is a God-ordained institution!

What words can tell the inhumanity, the atrocity, and the immorality of that doctrine which, from exalted office, commends such a crime to the favour of enlightened and Christian people? What indignation from all the world is not due to the government and people who put forth all their strength and power to keep in existence such an institution? Nature abhors it; the age repels it; and Christianity needs all her meekness to forgive it.

Clotel was sold for fifteen hundred dollars, but her purchaser was Horatio Green. Thus closed a negro sale, at which two daughters of Thomas Jefferson, the writer of the Declaration of American Independence, and one of the presidents of the great republic, were disposed of to the highest bidder!

> "O God! my every heart-string cries,
>   Dost thou these scenes behold
> In this our boasted Christian land,
>   And must the truth be told?
>
> "Blush, Christian, blush! for e'en the dark,
>   Untutored heathen see
> Thy inconsistency; and, lo!
>   They scorn thy God, and thee!"

CHAPTER II.

"My country, shall thy honoured name,
　　Be as a bye-word through the world?
Rouse! for, as if to blast thy fame,
　　This keen reproach is at thee hurled;
The banner that above thee waves,
　　Is floating o'er three million slaves."

DICK WALKER, the slave speculator, who had pur-
chasd Currer and Althesa, put them in prison until
his gang was made up, and then, with his forty slaves,
started for the New Orleans market. As many of
the slaves had been brought up in Richmond, and
had relations residing there, the slave trader determined to leave the city early in the morning, so
as not to witness any of those scenes so common
where slaves are separated from their relatives and
friends, when about departing for the Southern market.
This plan was successful; for not even Clotel, who
had been every day at the prison to see her mother
and sister, knew of their departure. A march of
eight days through the interior of the state, and they
arrived on the banks of the Ohio river, where they
were all put on board a steamer, and then speedily
sailed for the place of their destination.

Walker had already advertised in the New Orleans
papers, that he would be there at a stated time with
"a prime lot of able-bodied slaves ready for field
service; together with a few extra ones, between the
ages of fifteen and twenty-five." But, like most
who make a business of buying and selling slaves

F

for gain, he often bought some who were far advanced in years, and would always try to sell them for five or ten years younger than they actually were. Few persons can arrive at anything like the age of a negro, by mere observation, unless they are well acquainted with the race. Therefore the slave-trader very frequently carried out this deception with perfect impunity. After the steamer had left the wharf, and was fairly on the bosom of the Father of Waters, Walker called his servant Pompey to him, and instructed him as to "getting the negroes ready for market." Amongst the forty negroes were several whose appearance indicated that they had seen some years, and had gone through some services. Their grey hair and whiskers at once pronounced them to be above the ages set down in the trader's advertisement. Pompey had long been with the trader, and knew his business; and if he did not take delight in discharging his duty, he did it with a degree of alacrity, so that he might receive the approbation of his master. "Pomp," as Walker usually called him, was of real negro blood, and would often say, when alluding to himself, "Dis nigger is no counterfit; he is de genewine artekil." Pompey was of low stature, round face, and, like most of his race, had a set of teeth, which for whiteness and beauty could not be surpassed; his eyes large, lips thick, and hair short and woolly. Pompey had been with Walker so long, and had seen so much of the buying and selling of slaves, that he appeared perfectly indifferent to the heartrending scenes which daily occurred in his presence. It was on the second day of the steamer's voyage that Pompey selected five of the old slaves, took them into a room by themselves, and commenced preparing them for the market. "Well," said Pompey, addressing himself to the company, "I is de gentman dat is to get you ready, so dat you will bring marser a good price in de Orleans market. How old is you?" addressing himself to a man who, from appearance, was not less than forty. "If I live to see next corn-planting time I will either be forty-five or fifty-five, I don't know which." "Dat may be," replied Pompey; "But now you is only thirty years old; dat is what marser says you is to be." "I know I is more den dat," responded the man. "I knows nothing about dat," said Pompey; "but when you get in de market, an anybody axe you how old you is, an you tell 'em forty-five, marser will tie you up an gib you de whip like smoke. But if you tell 'em dat you is only thirty, den he wont." "Well den, I guess I will only be thirty when dey axe me," replied the chattel.

"What your name?" inquired Pompey. "Geemes," answered the man. "Oh, Uncle Jim, is it?" "Yes." "Den you must have off dem dare whiskers of yours, an when you get to Orleans you must grease dat face an make it look shiney." This was all said by Pompey in a manner which clearly showed that he knew what he was about. "How old is you?" asked Pompey of a tall, strong-looking man. "I was twenty-nine last potato-digging time," said the man. "What's your name?" "My name is Tobias, but dey call me 'Toby.'" "Well, Toby, or Mr. Tobias, if dat will suit you better, you is now twenty-three years old, an no more. Dus you hear dat?" "Yes," responded Toby. Pompey gave each to understand how old he was to be when asked by persons who wished to purchase, and then reported to his master that the "old boys" were all right. At eight o'clock on the evening of the third day, the lights of another steamer were seen in the distance, and apparently coming up very fast. This was a signal for a general commotion on the Patriot, and

F 2

everything indicated that a steamboat race was at hand. Nothing can exceed the excitement attendant upon a steamboat on the Mississippi river. By the time the boats had reached Memphis, they were side by side, and each exerting itself to keep the ascendancy in point of speed. The night was clear, the moon shining brightly, and the boats so near to each other that the passengers were calling out from one boat to the other. On board the Patriot, the firemen were using oil, lard, butter, and even bacon, with the wood, for the purpose of raising the steam to its highest pitch. The blaze, mingled with the black smoke, showed plainly that the other boat was burning more than wood. The two boats soon locked, so that the hands of the boats were passing from vessel to vessel, and the wildest excitement prevailed throughout amongst both passengers and crew. At this moment the engineer of the Patriot was seen to fasten down the safety-valve, so that no steam should escape. This was, indeed, a dangerous resort. A few of the boat hands who saw what had taken place, left that end of the boat for more secure quarters.

The Patriot stopped to take in passengers, and still no steam was permitted to escape. At the starting of the boat cold water was forced into the boilers by the machinery, and, as might have been expected, one of the boilers immediately exploded. One dense fog of steam filled every part of the vessel, while shrieks, groans, and cries were heard on every hand. The saloons and cabins soon had the appearance of a hospital. By this time the boat had landed, and the Columbia, the other boat, had come alongside to render assistance to the disabled steamer. The killed and scalded (nineteen in number) were put on shore, and the Patriot, taken in tow by the Columbia, was soon again on its way.

"BETTING" A NEGRO IN THE SOUTHERN STATES. *Page* 69.

J. JOHNSTON.

It was now twelve o'clock at night, and instead of the passengers being asleep the majority were gambling in the saloons. Thousands of dollars change hands during a passage from Louisville or St. Louis to New Orleans on a Mississippi steamer, and many men, and even ladies, are comple ely ruined. "Go call my boy, steward," said Mr. Smith, as he took his cards one by one from the table. In a few moments a fine looking, bright-eyed mulatto boy, apparently about fifteen years of age, was standing by his master's side at the table. "I will see you, and five hundred dollars better," said Smith, as his servant Jerry approached the table. "What price do you set on that boy?" asked Johnson, as he took a roll of bills from his pocket. "He will bring a thousand dollars, any day, in the New Orleans market," replied Smith. "Then you bet the whole of the boy, do you?" "Yes." "I call you, then," said Johnson, at the same time spreading his cards out upon the table. "You have beat me," said Smith, as soon as he saw the cards. Jerry, who was standing on top of the table, with the bank notes and silver dollars round his feet, was now ordered to descend from the table. "You will not forget that you belong to me," said Johnson, as the young slave was stepping from the table to a chair. "No, sir," replied the chattel. "Now go back to your bed, and be up in time to-morrow morning to brush my clothes and clean my boots, do you hear?" "Yes, sir," responded Jerry, as he wiped the tears from his eyes.

Smith took from his pocket the bill of sale and handed it to Johnson; at the same time saying, "I claim the right of redeeming that boy, Mr. Johnson. My father gave him to me when I came of age, and I promised not to part with him." "Most certainly, sir, the boy shall be yours, whenever you hand me

over a cool thousand," replied Johnson. The next
morning, as the passengers were assembling in the
breakfast saloons and upon the guards of the vessel,
and the servants were seen running about waiting
upon or looking for their masters, poor Jerry was
entering his new master's state-room with his boots.
"Who do you belong to?" said a gentleman to an old
black man, who came along leading a fine dog that he
had been feeding. "When I went to sleep last
night, I belonged to Governor Lucas; but I understand dat he is bin gambling all night, so I don't
know who owns me dis morning." Such is the un-
certainty of a slave's position. He goes to bed at
night the property of the man with whom he has
lived for years, and gets up in the morning the slave
of some one whom he has never seen before! To
behold five or six tables in a steamboat's cabin, with
half-a-dozen men playing at cards, and money, pis-
tols, bowie-knives, &c. all in confusion on the tables,
is what may be seen at almost any time on the Mississippi river.

On the fourth day, while at Natchez, taking in
freight and passengers, Walker, who had been on
shore to see some of his old customers, returned, accompanied by a tall, thin-faced man, dressed in black,
with a white neckcloth, which immediately proclaimed him to be a clergyman. "I want a good,
trusty woman for house service," said the stranger,
as they entered the cabin where Walker's slaves
were kept. "Here she is, and no mistake," replied
the trader. "Stand up, Currer, my gal; here's a
gentleman who wishes to see if you will suit him."
Althesa clung to her mother's side, as the latter rose
from her seat. "She is a rare cook, a good washer,
and will suit you to a T, I am sure." "If you buy
me, I hope you will buy my daughter too," said the
woman, in rather an excited manner. "I only want

one for my own use, and would not need another," said the man in black, as he and the trader left the room. Walker and the parson went into the saloon, talked over the matter, the bill of sale was made out, the money paid over, and the clergyman left, with the understanding that the woman should be delivered to him at his house. It seemed as if poor Althesa would have wept herself to death, for the first two days after her mother had been torn from her side by the hand of the ruthless trafficker in human flesh. On the arrival of the boat at Baton Rouge, an additional number of passengers were taken on board; and, amongst them, several persons who had been attending the races. Gambling and drinking were now the order of the day. Just as the ladies and gentlemen were assembling at the supper-table, the report of a pistol was heard in the direction of the Social Hall, which caused great uneasiness to the ladies, and took the gentlemen to that part of the cabin. However, nothing serious had occurred. A man at one of the tables where they were gambling had been seen attempting to conceal a card in his sleeve, and one of the party seized his pistol and fired; but fortunately the barrel of the pistol was knocked up, just as it was about to be discharged, and the ball passed through the upper deck, instead of the man's head, as intended. Order was soon restored; all went on well the remainder of the night, and the next day, at ten o'clock, the boat arrived at New Orleans, and the passengers went to the hotels and the slaves to the market!

> " Our eyes are yet on Afric's shores,
>   Her thousand wrongs we still deplore;
>   We see the grim slave trader there;
>   We hear his fettered victim's prayer;
>   And hasten to the sufferer's aid,
>   Forgetful of *our own ' slave trade.'*

" The Ocean ' Pirate's ' fiend-like form
  Shall sink beneath the vengeance-storm ;
  His heart of steel shall quake before
  The battle-din and havoc roar :
  The knave shall die, the Law hath said,
  While it protects our own ' *slave trade.*'

" What earthly eye presumes to scan
  The wily Proteus-heart of man ? —
  What potent hand will e'er unroll
  The mantled treachery of his soul ! —
  O where is he who hath surveyed
  The horrors of *our own ' slave trade ?*'

" There is an eye that wakes in light,
  There is a hand of peerless might ;
  Which, soon or late, shall yet assail
  And rend dissimulation's veil :
  Which *will* unfold the masquerade
  Which justifies *our own ' slave trade.*' "

CHAPTER III.

THE NEGRO CHASE.

WE shall now return to Natchez, where we left Currer in the hands of the Methodist parson. For many years, Natchez has enjoyed a notoriety for the inhumanity and barbarity of its inhabitants, and the cruel deeds perpetrated there, which have not been equalled in any other city in the Southern States. The following advertisements, which we take from a newspaper published in the vicinity, will show how they catch their negroes who believe in the doctrine that "all men are created free."

"NEGRO DOGS.—The undersigned, having bought the entire pack of negro dogs (of the Hay and Allen stock), *he now proposes to catch runaway negroes*. His charges will be three dollars a day for hunting, and fifteen dollars for catching a runaway. He resides three and one half miles north of Livingston, near the lower Jones' Bluff Road.

"WILLIAM GAMBREL."

"Nov. 6, 1845."

"NOTICE.—The subscriber, living on Carroway Lake, on Hoe's Bayou, in Carroll parish, sixteen miles on the road leading from Bayou Mason to Lake Providence, is ready with a pack of dogs to hunt runaway negroes at any time. These dogs are well trained, and are known throughout the parish. Letters addressed to me at Providence will secure immediate attention. My terms are five dollars per day for hunting the trails, whether the negro is caught or not. Where a twelve hours' trail is shown, and the negro not taken, no charge is made. For taking a negro, twenty-five dollars, and no charge made for hunting.

"JAMES W. HALL."

"Nov. 26, 1847."

These dogs will attack a negro at their master's
bidding and cling to him as the bull-dog will cling
to a beast. Many are the speculations, as to whether
the negro will be secured alive or dead, when these
dogs once get on his track. A slave hunt took place
near Natchez, a few days after Currer's arrival,
which was calculated to give her no favourable
opinion of the people. Two slaves had run off owing
to severe punishment. The dogs were put upon
their trail. The slaves went into the swamps, with
the hope that the dogs when put on their scent
would be unable to follow them through the water.
The dogs soon took to the swamp, which lies between
the highlands, which was now covered with water,
waist deep : here these faithful animals, *swimming*
nearly all the time, followed the zigzag course, the
tortuous twistings and windings of these two fugitives, who, it was afterwards discovered, were lost;
sometimes scenting the tree wherein they had found
a temporary refuge from the mud and water ; at
other places where the deep mud had pulled off a
shoe, and they had not taken time to put it on again.
For two hours and a half, for four or five miles, did
men and dogs wade through this bushy, dismal
swamp, surrounded with grim-visaged alligators,
who seemed to look on with jealous eye at this en-
croachment of their hereditary domain ; now losing
the trail—then slowly and dubiously taking it off
again, until they triumphantly threaded it out,
bringing them back to the river, where it was found
that the negroes had crossed their own trail, near
the place of starting. In the meantime a heavy
shower had taken place, putting out the trail. The
negroes were now at least four miles ahead.

It is well known to hunters that it requires the
keenest scent and best blood to overcome such obstacles,
and yet these persevering and sagacious animals

conquered every difficulty. The slaves now made a
straight course for the Baton Rouge and Bayou Sara
road, about four miles distant.

Feeling hungry now, after their morning walk,
and perhaps thirsty, too, they went about half a mile
off the road, and ate a good, hearty, substantial breakfast. Negroes must eat, as well as other people, but
the dogs will tell on them. Here, for a moment,
the dogs are at fault, but soon unravel the mystery,
and bring them back to the road again; and now
what before was wonderful, becomes almost a miracle.
Here, in this common highway—the thoroughfare
for the whole country around—through mud and
through mire, meeting waggons and teams, and different solitary wayfarers, and, what above all is most
astonishing, actually running through a gang of negroes, their favourite game, who were working on
the road, they pursue the track of the two negroes;
they even ran for eight miles to the very edge of the
plain—the slaves near them for the last mile. At
first they would fain believe it some hunter chasing
deer. Nearer and nearer the whimpering pack
presses on; the delusion begins to dispel; all at once
the truth flashes upon them like a glare of light;
their hair stands on end; 'tis Tabor with his dogs.
The scent becomes warmer and warmer. What was
an irregular cry, now deepens into one ceaseless
roar, as the relentless pack rolls on after its human
prey. It puts one in mind of Actæon and his dogs.
They grow desperate and leave the road, in the vain
hope of shaking them off. Vain hope, indeed! The
momentary cessation only adds new zest to the chase.
The cry grows louder and louder; the yelp grows
short and quick, sure indication that the game is at
hand. It is a perfect rush upon the part of the hunters, while the negroes call upon their weary and
jaded limbs to do their best, but they falter and stag-

ger beneath them. The breath of the hounds is almost upon their very heels, and yet they have a vain hope of escaping these sagacious animals. They can run no longer; the dogs are upon them; they hastily attempt to climb a tree, and as the last one is nearly out of reach, the catch-dog seizes him by the leg, and brings him to the ground; he sings out lustily and the dogs are called off. After this man was secured, the one in the tree was ordered to come down; this, however, he refused to do, but a gun being pointed at him, soon caused him to change his mind. On reaching the ground, the fugitive made one more bound, and the chase again commenced. But it was of no use to run and he soon yielded. While being tied, he committed an unpardonable offence: he resisted, and for that he must be made an example on their arrival home. A mob was collected together, and a Lynch court was held, to determine what was best to be done with the negro who had had the impudence to raise his hand against a white man. The Lynch court decided that the negro should be burnt at the stake. A Natchez newspaper, the *Free Trader*, giving an account of it says,

"The body was taken and chained to a tree immediately on the banks of the Mississippi, on what is called Union Point. Faggots were then collected and piled around him, to which he appeared quite indifferent. When the work was completed, he was asked what he had to say. He then warned all to take example by him, and asked the prayers of all around; he then called for a drink of water, which was handed to him; he drank it, and said, 'Now set fire—I am ready to go in peace!' The torches were lighted, and placed in the pile, which soon ignited. He watched unmoved the curling flame that grew, until it began to entwine itself around and feed upon his body; then he sent forth cries of agony painful to the ear, begging some one to blow his brains out; at the same time surging with almost superhuman strength, until the staple with which the chain was fastened to the tree (not being well secured) drew out, and he leaped from the burning pile. At that moment the sharp ringing of several rifles was heard: the body of the negro fell a corpse on the ground. He was picked up by some two or three, and again thrown into the fire, and consumed, not a vestige remaining to show that such a being ever existed."

Nearly 4,000 slaves were collected from the plantations in the neighbourhood to witness this scene. Numerous speeches were made by the magistrates and ministers of religion to the large concourse of slaves, warning them, and telling them that the same fate awaited them, if they should prove rebellious to their owners. There are hundreds of negroes who run away and live in the woods. Some take refuge in the swamps, because they are less frequented by human beings. A Natchez newspaper gave the following account of the hiding-place of a slave who had been captured: —

"A runaway's den was discovered on Sunday, near the Washington Spring, in a little patch of woods, where it had been for several months so artfully concealed under ground, that it was detected only by accident, though in sight of two or three houses, and near the road and fields where there has been constant daily passing. The entrance was concealed by a pile of pine straw, representing a hog-bed, which being removed, discovered a trap-door and steps that led to a room about six feet square, comfortably ceiled with plank, containing a small fire-place, the flue of which was ingeniously conducted above ground and concealed by the straw. The inmates took the alarm, and made their escape; *but Mr. Adams and his excellent dogs being put upon the trail, soon run down and secured one of them*, which proved to be a negro-fellow who had been out about a year. He stated that the other occupant was a woman, who had been a runaway

a still longer time.   In the den was found a quantity of meal,
bacon, corn, potatoes, &c. and various cooking utensils and
wearing apparel." — *Vicksburgh Sentinel*, Dec. 6th, 1838.

Currer was one of those who witnessed the
execution of the slave at the stake, and it gave her
no very exalted opinion of the people of the cotton
growing district.

CHAPTER IV.

THE QUADROON'S HOME.

" How sweetly on the hill-side sleeps
    The sunlight with its quickening rays !
The verdant trees that crown the steeps,
    Grow greener in its quivering blaze.

ABOUT three miles from Richmond is a pleasant
plain, with here and there a beautiful cottage surrounded by trees so as scarcely to be seen. Among
them was one far retired from the public roads, and
almost hidden among the trees. It was a perfect
model of rural beauty. The piazzas that surrounded
it were covered with clematis and passion flower.
The pride of China mixed its oriental looking foliage
with the majestic magnolia, and the air was redolent
with the fragrance of flowers, peeping out of every
nook and nodding upon you with a most unexpected
welcome. The tasteful hand of art had not learned
to imitate the lavish beauty and harmonious disorder
of nature, but they lived together in loving amity,
and spoke in accordant tones. The gateway rose in
a gothic arch, with graceful tracery in iron work,
surmounted by a cross, round which fluttered and
played the mountain fringe, that lightest and most
fragile of vines. This cottage was hired by Horatio
Green for Clotel, and the quadroon girl soon found
herself in her new home.

The tenderness of Clotel's conscience, together
with the care her mother had with her and the high
value she placed upon virtue, required an outward
marriage ; though she well knew that a union with

her proscribed race was unrecognised by law, and therefore the ceremony would give her no legal hold on Horatio's constancy. But her high poetic nature regarded reality rather than the semblance of things; and when he playfully asked how she could keep him if he wished to run away, she replied, "If the mutual love we have for each other, and the dictates of your own conscience do not cause you to remain my husband, and your affections fall from me, I would not, if I could, hold you by a single fetter." It was indeed a marriage sanctioned by heaven, although unrecognised on earth. There the young couple lived secluded from the world, and passed their time as happily as circumstances would permit. It was Clotel's wish that Horatio should purchase her mother and sister, but the young man pleaded that he was unable, owing to the fact that he had not come into possession of his share of property, yet he promised that when he did, he would seek them out and purchase them. Their first-born was named Mary, and her complexion was still lighter than her mother. Indeed she was not darker than other white children. As the child grew older, it more and more resembled its mother. The iris of her large dark eye had the melting mezzotinto, which remains the last vestige of African ancestry, and gives that plaintive expression, so often observed, and so appropriate to that docile and injured race. Clotel was still happier after the birth of her dear child; for Horatio, as might have been expected, was often absent day and night with his friends in the city, and the edicts of society had built up a wall of separation between the quadroon and them. Happy as Clotel was in Horatio's love, and surrounded by an outward environment of beauty, so well adapted to her poetic spirit, she felt these incidents with inexpressible pain. For herself she cared but little; for she had found a sheltered home in Horatio's heart, which the world might ridicule, but had no power to profane. But when she looked at her beloved Mary, and reflected upon the unavoidable and dangerous position which the tyranny of society had awarded her, her soul was filled with anguish. The rare loveliness of the child increased daily, and was evidently ripening into most marvellous beauty. The father seemed to rejoice in it with unmingled pride; but in the deep tenderness of the mother's eye, there was an indwelling sadness that spoke of anxious thoughts and fearful foreboding. Clotel now urged Horatio to remove to France or England, where both her and her child would be free, and where colour was not a crime. This request excited but little opposition, and was so attractive to his imagination, that he might have overcome all intervening 'obstacles, had not "a change come over the spirit of his dreams." He still loved Clotel; but he was now becoming engaged in political and other affairs which kept him oftener and longer from the young mother; and ambition to become a statesman was slowly gaining the ascendancy over him.

Among those on whom Horatio's political success most depended was a very popular and wealthy man, who had an only daughter. His visits to the house were at first purely of a political nature; but the young lady was pleasing, and he fancied he discovered in her a sort of timid preference for himself. This excited his vanity, and awakened thoughts of the great worldly advantages connected with a union. Reminiscences of his first love kept these vague ideas in check for several months; for with it was associated the idea of restraint. Moreover, Gertrude, though inferior in beauty, was yet a pretty contrast to her rival. Her light hair fell in silken ringlets

G

down her shoulders, her blue eyes were gentle though inexpressive, and her healthy cheeks were like opening rosebuds.   He had already become accustomed to the dangerous experiment of resisting his own inward convictions; and this new impulse to ambition, combined with the strong temptation of variety in love, met the ardent young man weakened in moral principle, and unfettered by laws of the land.   The change wrought upon him was soon noticed by Clotel.

CHAPTER V.

THE SLAVE MARKET.

"What! mothers from their children riven!
    What! God's own image bought and sold!
Americans to market driven,
    And barter'd as the brute for gold."—*Whittier.*

Not far from Canal-street, in the city of New Orleans, stands a large two story flat building surrounded by a stone wall twelve feet high, the top of which is covered with bits of glass, and so constructed as to prevent even the possibility of any one's passing over it without sustaining great injury. Many of the rooms resemble cells in a prison. In a small room near the "office" are to be seen any number of iron collars, hobbles, handcuffs, thumbscrews, cowhides, whips, chains, gags, and yokes. A back yard inclosed by a high wall looks something like the playground attached to one of our large New England schools, and in which are rows of benches and swings. Attached to the back premises is a goodsized kitchen, where two old negresses are at work, stewing, boiling, and baking, and occasionally wiping the sweat from their furrowed and swarthy brows.

The slave-trader Walker, on his arrival in New Orleans, took up his quarters at this slave pen with his gang of human cattle; and the morning after, at ten o'clock, they were exhibited for sale. There, first of all, was the beautiful Althesa, whose pale countenance and dejected look told how many sad hours she had passed since parting with her mother at Natchez. There was a poor woman who had

G 2

been separated from her husband and five children. Another woman, whose looks and manner were expressive of deep anguish, sat by her side. There, too, was "Uncle Geemes," with his whiskers off, his face shaved clean, and the grey hair plucked out, and ready to be sold for ten years younger than he was. Toby was also there, with his face shaved and greased, ready for inspection. The examination commenced, and was carried on in a manner calculated to shock the feelings of any one not devoid of the milk of human kindness. "What are you wiping your eyes for?" inquired a fat, red-faced man, with a white hat set on one side of his head, and a cigar in his mouth, of a woman who sat on one of the stools. "I s'pose I have been crying." "Why do you cry?" "Because I have left my man behind." "Oh, if I buy you I will furnish you with a better man than you left. I have lots of young bucks on my farm." "I don't want, and will never have, any other man," replied the woman. "What's your name?" asked a man in a straw hat of a tall negro man, who stood with his arms folded across his breast, and leaning against the wall. "My name is Aaron, sir." "How old are you?" "Twenty-five." "Where were you raised?" "In old Virginny, sir." "How many men have owned you?" "Four." "Do you enjoy good health?" "Yes, sir." "How long did you live with your first owner?" "Twenty years." "Did you ever run away?" "No, sir." "Did you ever strike your master." "No, sir." "Were you ever whipped much?" "No, sir, I s'pose I did not deserve it." "How long did you live with your second master?" "Ten years, sir." "Have you a good appetite?" "Yes, sir." "Can you eat your allowance?" "Yes, sir, when I can get it." "What were you employed at in Virginia?" "I worked in de terbacar feel." "In the tobacco

field?" "Yes, sir." "How old did you say you
were?" "I will be twenty-five if I live to see next
sweet potater-digging time." "I am a cotton
planter, and if I buy you, you will have to work in
the cotton field. My men pick one hundred and
fifty pounds a day, and the women one hundred and
forty, and those who fail to pick their task receive
five stripes from the cat for each pound that is want-
ing. Now, do you think you could keep up with
the rest of the hands?" "I don't know, sir, I 'spec
I'd have to." "How long did you live with your
third master?" "Three years, sir." "Why, this
makes you thirty-three, I thought you told me you
was only twenty-five?" Aaron now looked first at
the planter, then at the trader, and seemed perfectly
bewildered. He had forgotten the lesson given him
by Pompey as to his age, and the planter's circuitous
talk (doubtless to find out the slave's real age) had
the negro off his guard. "I must see your back, so
as to know how much you have been whipped, before
I think of buying," said the planter. Pompey, who
had been standing by during the examination, thought
that his services were now required, and stepping
forward with a degree of officiousness, said to Aaron,
"Don't you hear de gentman tell you he want to
zamon your limbs. Come, unharness yeself, old boy,
an don't be standing dar." Aaron was soon examined
and pronounced "sound;" yet the conflicting statement about the age was not satisfactory.

Fortunate for Althesa she was spared the pain of
undergoing such an examination, Mr. Crawford, a
teller in one of the banks, had just been married, and
wanted a maid-servant for his wife; and passing
through the market in the early part of the day, was
pleased with the young slave's appearance and purchased her, and in his dwelling the quadroon found a
much better home than often falls to the lot of a

slave sold in the New Orleans market. The heart-rending and cruel traffic in slaves which has been so often described, is not confined to any particular class of persons. No one forfeits his or her character or standing in society, by buying or selling slaves; or even raising slaves for the market. The precise number of slaves carried from the slave-raising to the slave-consuming states, we have no means of knowing. But it must be very great, as more than forty thousand were sold and taken out of the state of Virginia in one year. Known to God only is the amount of human agony and suffering which sends its cry from the slave markets and negro pens, un-heard and unheeded by man, up to his ear; mothers weeping for their children, breaking the night-silence with the shrieks of their breaking hearts. From some you will hear the burst of bitter lamentation, while from others the loud hysteric laugh, denoting still deeper agony. Most of them leave the market for cotton or rice plantations,

> " Where the slave-whip ceaseless swings,
>   Where the noisome insect stings,
>   Where the fever demon strews
>   Poison with the falling dews,
>   Where the sickly sunbeams glare
>   Through the hot and misty air."

CHAPTER VI.

THE RELIGIOUS TEACHER.

" What! preach and enslave men?
　Give thanks — and rob thy own afflicted poor?
　Talk of thy glorious liberty, and then
　Bolt hard the captive's door?"— *Whittier.*

The Rev. John Peck was a native of the state of
Connecticut, where he was educated for the ministry,
in the Methodist persuasion.　His father was a strict
follower of John Wesley, and spared no pains in his
son's education, with the hope that he would one
day be as renowned as the great leader of his sect.
John had scarcely finished his education at New
Haven, when he was invited by an uncle, then on a
visit to his father, to spend a few months at Natchez
in the state of Mississippi.　Young Peck accepted
his uncle's invitation, and accompanied him to the
South.　Few young men, and especially clergymen,
going fresh from a college to the South, but are
looked upon as geniuses in a small way, and who
are not invited to all the parties in the neighbourhood.　Mr. Peck was not an exception to this rule.
The society into which he was thrown on his arrival
at Natchez was too brilliant for him not to be cap-
tivated by it; and, as might have been expected, he
succeeded in captivating a plantation with seventy
slaves, if not the heart of the lady to whom it belonged.
Added to this, he became a popular preacher, had a
large congregation with a snug salary.　Like other
planters, Mr. Peck confided the care of his farm to
Ned Huckelby, an overseer of high reputation in his

way. The Poplar Farm, as it was called, was situated in a beautiful valley nine miles from Natchez, and near the river Mississippi. The once unshorn face of nature had given way, and now the farm blossomed with a splendid harvest, the neat cottage stood in a grove where Lombardy poplars lift their tutted tops almost to prop the skies; the willow, locust, and horse-chesnut spread their branches, and flowers never cease to blossom. This was the parson's country house, where the family spent only two months during the year.

The town residence was a fine villa, seated upon the brow of a hill at the edge of the city. It was in the kitchen of this house that Currer found her new home. Mr. Peck was, every inch of him, a democrat, and early resolved that his "people," as he called his slaves, should be well fed and not over-worked, and therefore laid down the law and gospel to the overseer as well as the slaves.

"It is my wish," said he to Mr. Carlton, an old school-fellow, who was spending a few days with him, "it is my wish that a new system be adopted on the plantations in this estate. I believe that the sons of Ham should have the gospel, and I intend that my negroes shall. The gospel is calculated to make mankind better, and none should be without it." "What say you," replied Carlton, "about the right of man to his liberty?" "Now, Carlton, you have begun again to harp about man's rights; I really wish you could see this matter as I do. I have searched in vain for any authority for man's natural rights; if he had any, they existed before the fall. That is, Adam and Eve may have had some rights which God gave them, and which modern philosophy, in its pretended reverence for the name of God, prefers to call natural rights. I can imagine they had the right to eat of the fruit of the trees of the garden;

they were restricted even in this by the prohibition of one. As far as I know without positive assertion, their liberty of action was confined to the garden. These were not 'inalienable rights,' however, for they forfeited both them and life with the first act of disobedience. Had they, after this, any rights? We cannot imagine them; they were condemned beings; they could have no rights, but by Christ's gift as king. These are the only rights man can have as an independent isolated being, if we choose to consider him in this impossible position, in which so many theorists have placed him. If he had no rights, he could suffer no wrongs. Rights and wrongs are therefore necessarily the creatures of society, such as man would establish himself in his gregarious state. They are, in this state, both artificial and voluntary. Though man has no rights, as thus considered, undoubtedly he has the power, by such arbitrary rules of right and wrong as his necessity enforces." "I regret I cannot see eye to eye with you," said Carlton. "I am a disciple of Rousseau, and have for years made the rights of man my study; and I must confess to you that I can see no difference between white men and black men as it regards liberty." "Now, my dear Carlton, would you really have the negroes enjoy the same rights with ourselves?" "I would, most certainly. Look at our great Declaration of Independence; look even at the constitution of our own Connecticut, and see what is said in these about liberty." "I regard all this talk about rights as mere humbug. The Bible is older than the Declaration of Independence, and there I take my stand. The Bible furnishes to us the armour of proof, weapons of heavenly temper and mould, whereby we can maintain our ground against all attacks. But this is true only when we obey its directions, as well as employ its sanctions.

Our rights are there established, but it is always in connection with our duties. If we neglect the one we cannot make good the other. Our domestic institutions can be maintained against the world, if we but allow Christianity to throw its broad shield over them. But if we so act as to array the Bible against our social economy, they must fall. Nothing ever yet stood long against Christianity. Those who say that religious instruction is inconsistent with our peculiar civil polity, are the worst enemies of that polity. They would drive religious men from its defence. Sooner or later, if these views prevail, they will separate the religious portion of our community from the rest, and thus divided we shall become an easy prey. Why, is it not better that Christian men should hold slaves than unbelievers? We know how to value the bread of life, and will not keep it from our slaves."

" Well, every one to his own way of thinking," said Carlton, as he changed his position. " I confess," added he, " that I am no great admirer of either the Bible or slavery. My heart is my guide : my conscience is my Bible. I wish for nothing further to satisfy me of my duty to man. If I act rightly to mankind, I shall fear nothing." Carlton had drunk too deeply of the bitter waters of infidelity, and had spent too many hours over the writings of Rousseau, Voltaire, and Thomas Paine, to place that appreciation upon the Bible and its teachings that it demands. During this conversation there was another person in the room, seated by the window, who, although at work upon a fine piece of lace, paid every attention to what was said. This was Georgiana, the only daughter of the parson. She had just returned from Connecticut, where she had finished her education. She had had the opportunity of contrasting the spirit of Christianity and liberty in New England with

that of slavery in her native state, and had learned
to feel deeply for the injured negro. Georgiana was
in her nineteenth year, and had been much benefited
by a residence of five years at the North. Her form
was tall and graceful; her features regular and well
defined; and her complexion was illuminated by the
freshness of youth, beauty, and health. The daughter differed from both the father and his visitor upon
the subject which they had been discussing, and as
soon as an opportunity offered, she gave it as her
opinion, that the Bible was both the bulwark of
Christianity and of liberty. With a smile she said,
" Of course, papa will overlook my differing from him,
for although I am a native of the South, I am by education and sympathy a Northerner." Mr. Peck laughed
and appeared pleased, rather than otherwise, at the
manner in which his daughter had expressed herself.

From this Georgiana took courage and said,
"We must try the character of slavery, and our duty
in regard to it, as we should try any other question of
character and duty. To judge justly of the character
of anything, we must know what it does. That
which is good does good, and that which is evil
does evil. And as to duty, God's designs indicate
his claims. That which accomplishes the manifest
design of God is right; that which counteracts it,
wrong. Whatever, in its proper tendency and
general effect, produces, secures, or extends human
welfare, is according to the will of God, and is good;
and our duty is to favour and promote, according to
our power, that which God favours and promotes by
the general law of his providence. On the other hand,
whatever in its proper tendency and general effect destroys, abridges, or renders insecure, human welfare, is opposed to God's will, and is evil. And
as whatever accords with the will of God, in any
manifestation of it should be done and persisted in,

so whatever opposes that will should not be done, and if done, should be abandoned. Can that then be right, be well doing—can that obey God's behest, which makes a man a slave? which dooms him and all his posterity, in limitless generations, to bondage, to unrequited toil through life? 'Thou shalt love thy neighbour as thyself.' This single passage of Scripture should cause us to have respect to the rights of the slave. True Christian love is of an enlarged, disinterested nature. It loves all who love the Lord Jesus Christ in sincerity, without regard to colour or condition." "Georgiana, my dear, you are an abolitionist; your talk is fanaticism," said Mr. Peck in rather a sharp tone; but the subdued look of the girl, and the presence of Carlton, caused the father to soften his language. Mr. Peck having lost his wife by consumption, and Georgiana being his only child, he loved her too dearly to say more, even if he felt displeased. A silence followed this exhortation from the young Christian. But her remarks had done a noble work. The father's heart was touched; and the sceptic, for the first time, was viewing Christianity in its true light.

'I think I must go out to your farm," said Carlton, as if to break the silence. "I shall be pleased to have you go," returned Mr. Peck. "I am sorry I can't go myself, but Huckelby will show you every attention; and I feel confident that when you return to Connecticut, you will do me the justice to say, that I am one who looks after my people, in a moral, social, and religious point of view." "Well, what do you say to my spending next Sunday there?" "Why, I think that a good move; you will then meet with Snyder, our missionary." "Oh, you have missionaries in these parts, have you?" "Yes," replied Mr. Peck; "Snyder is from New York, and is our missionary to the poor, and preaches to our 'people' on Sunday;

you will no doubt like him; he is a capital fellow."
"Then I shall go," said Carlton, "but only wish I
had company." This last remark was intended for
Miss Peck, for whom he had the highest admiration.

It was on a warm Sunday morning, in the month
of May, that Miles Carlton found himself seated beneath a fine old apple tree, whose thick leaves entirely shaded the ground for some distance round.
Under similar trees and near by, were gathered together all the "people" belonging to the plantation.
Hontz Snyder was a man of about forty years of age,
exceedingly low in stature, but of a large frame. He
had been brought up in the Mohawk Valley, in the
state of New York, and claimed relationship with
the oldest Dutch families in that vicinity. He had
once been a sailor, and had all the roughness of
character that a sea-faring man might expect to
possess; together with the half-Yankee, half-German
peculiarities of the people of the Mohawk Valley.
It was nearly eleven o'clock when a one-horse
waggon drove up in haste, and the low squatty preacher got out and took his place at the foot of one
of the trees, where a sort of rough board table was
placed, and took his books from his pocket and commenced.

"As it is rather late," said he, "we will leave
the singing and praying for the last, and take our
text, and commence immediately. I shall base my
remarks on the following passage of Scripture, and
hope to have that attention which is due to the cause
of God: — 'All things whatsoever ye would that
men should do unto you, do ye even so unto them;'
that is, do by all mankind just as you would desire
they should do by you, if you were in their place
and they in yours.

"Now, to suit this rule to your particular circumstances, suppose you were masters and mis-

tresses, and had servants under you, would you not desire that your servants should do their business faithfully and honestly, as well when your back was turned as while you were looking over them? Would you not expect that they should take notice of what you said to them? that they should behave themselves with respect towards you and yours, and be as careful of every thing belonging to you as you would be yourselves? You are servants: do, therefore, as you would wish to be done by, and you will be both good servants to your masters and good servants to God, who requires this of you, and will reward you well for it, if you do it for the sake of conscience, in obedience to his commands.

" You are not to be eye-servants. Now, eye-servants are such as will work hard, and seem mighty diligent, while they think anybody is taking notice of them; but, when their masters' and mistresses' backs are turned they are idle, and neglect their business. I am afraid there are a great many such eye-servants among you, and that you do not consider how great a sin it is to be so, and how severely God will punish you for it. You may easily deceive your owners, and make them have an opinion of you that you do not deserve, and get the praise of men by it; but remember that you cannot deceive Almighty God, who sees your wickedness and deceit, and will punish you accordingly. For the rule is, that you must obey your masters in all things, and do the work they set you about with fear and trembling, in singleness of heart as unto Christ; not with eye-service, as men-pleasers, but as the servants of Christ, doing the will of God from the heart; with good-will doing service as to the Lord, and not as to men.

" *Take care that you do not fret or murmur, grumble or repine at your condition; for this will not only make*

your life uneasy, but will greatly offend Almighty God.
Consider that it is not yourselves, it is not the people
that you belong to, it is not the men who have
brought you to it, but *it is the will of God who hath
by his providence made you servants, because, no doubt,
he knew that condition would be best for you in this
world, and help you the better towards heaven, if you
would but do your duty in it.* So that any discontent
at your not being free, or rich, or great, as you see
some others, is quarrelling with your heavenly Master,
and finding fault with God himself, who hath made
you what you are, and hath promised you as large a
share in the kingdom of heaven as the greatest man
alive, if you will but behave yourself aright, and do
the business he hath set you about in this world
honestly and cheerfully. Riches and power have
proved the ruin of many an unhappy soul, by drawing
away the heart and affections from God, and fixing
them on mean and sinful enjoyments; so that, when
God, who knows our hearts better than we know
them ourselves, sees that they would be hurtful to us,
and therefore keeps them from us, it is the greatest
mercy and kindness he could show us.

" You may perhaps fancy that, if you had riches
and freedom, you could do your duty to God and
man with greater pleasure than you can now. But
pray consider that, if you can but save your souls
through the mercy of God, you will have spent your
time to the best of purposes in this world; and he that
at last can get to heaven has performed a noble
journey, let the road be ever so rugged and difficult.
Besides, you really have a great advantage over most
white people, who have not only the care of their
daily labour upon their hands, but the care of looking
forward and providing necessaries for to-morrow and
next day, and of clothing and bringing up their
children, and of getting food and raiment for as

many of you as belong to their families, which often puts them to great difficulties, and distracts their minds so as to break their rest, and take off their thoughts from the affairs of another world.   Whereas you are quite eased from all these cares, and have nothing but your daily labour to look after, and, when that is done, take your needful rest.   Neither is it necessary for you to think of laying up anything against old age, as white people are obliged to do; for the laws of the country have provided that you shall not be turned off when you are past labour, but shall be maintained, while you live, by those you belong to, whether you are able to work or not.

" There is only one circumstance which may appear grievous, that I shall now take notice of, and that is correction.

" Now, when correction is given you, you either deserve it, or you do not deserve it.   But whether you really deserve it or not, it is your duty, and Almighty God requires that you bear it patiently. You may perhaps think that this is hard doctrine; but, if you consider it right, you must needs think otherwise of it.   Suppose, then, that you deserve correction, you cannot but say that it is just and right you should meet with it.   Suppose you do not, or at least you do not deserve so much, or so severe a correction, for the fault you have committed, you perhaps have escaped a great many more, and are at last paid for all.   Or suppose you are quite innocent of what is laid to your charge, and suffer wrongfully in that particular thing, is it not possible you may have done some other bad thing which was never discovered, and that Almighty God who saw you doing it would not let you escape without punishment one time or another?   And ought you not, in such a case, to give glory to him, and be thankful that he would rather punish you in this life for your wicked-

ness than destroy your souls for it in the next life?
But suppose even this was not the case (a case
hardly to be imagined), and that you have by no
means, known or unknown, deserved the correction
you suffered, there is this great comfort in it, that,
if you bear it patiently, and leave your cause in the
hands of God, he will reward you for it in heaven,
and the punishment you suffer unjustly here shall
turn to your exceeding great glory hereafter.

"Lastly, you should serve your masters faithfully,
because of their goodness to you. See to what trouble
they have been on your account. Your fathers were
poor ignorant and barbarous creatures in Africa, and
the whites fitted out ships at great trouble and expense and brought you from that benighted land to
Christian America, where you can sit under your own
vine and fig tree and no one molest or make you
afraid. Oh, my dear black brothers and sisters, you
are indeed a fortunate and a blessed people. Your
masters have many troubles that you know nothing
about If the banks break, your masters are sure to
lose something. If the crops turn out poor, they lose
by it. If one of you die, your master loses what he
paid for you, while you lose nothing. Now let me
exhort you once more to be faithful."

Often during the delivery of the sermon did
Snyder cast an anxious look in the direction where
Carlton was seated; no doubt to see if he had found
favour with the stranger. Huckelby, the overseer,
was also there, seated near Carlton. With all
Snyder's gesticulations, sonorous voice, and occasionally bringing his fist down upon the table with the
force of a sledge hammer, he could not succeed in
keeping the negroes all interested: four or five were
fast asleep, leaning against the trees; as many more
were nodding, while not a few were stealthily crack-
ing and eating hazlenuts. "Uncle Simon, you may

strike up a hymn," said the preacher as he closed his Bible. A moment more, and the whole company (Carlton excepted) had joined in the well known hymn, commencing with

> " When I can read my title clear
> To mansions in the sky."

After the singing, Sandy closed with prayer, and the following questions and answers read, and the meeting was brought to a close.

" *Q.* What command has God given to servants concerning obedience to their masters?—*A.* ' Servants, obey in all things your masters according to the flesh, not with eye-service as men-pleasers, but in singleness of heart, fearing God.'

" *Q.* What does God mean by masters according to the flesh?—*A.* ' Masters in this world.'

" *Q.* What are servants to count their masters worthy of?—*A.* ' All honour.'

" *Q.* How are they to do the service of their masters?—*A.* ' *With good will*, doing service as unto the Lord, and not unto men.'

" *Q.* 'How are they to try to please their masters?—*A.* ' Please him well in all things, not answering again.'

" *Q.* Is a servant who is an eye-servant to his earthly master an eye-servant to his heavenly master?—*A.* ' Yes.'

" *Q.* Is it right in a servant, when commanded to do any thing, to be sullen and slow, and answer his master again?—*A.* ' No.'

" *Q.* If the servant professes to be a Christian, ought he not to be *as a Christian servant*, an example to all other servants of love and obedience to his master?—*A.* ' Yes.'

" *Q.* And, should his master be a Christian also, ought he not on that account specially to love and obey him?—*A.* ' Yes.'

" *Q.* But suppose the master is hard to please, and threatens and punishes more than he ought, what is the servant to do?—*A.* ' Do his best to please him.'

" *Q.* When the servant suffers *wrongfully* at the hands of his master, and, to please God, takes it patiently, will God reward him for it?—*A.* ' Yes.'

" *Q.* Is it right for the servant to *run away*, or is it right to *harbour* a runaway? — *A.* 'No.'

" *Q.* If a servant runs away, what should be done with him? — *A.* 'He should be caught and brought back.'

" *Q.* When he is brought back, what should be done with him? — *A.* 'Whip him well.'

" *Q.* Why may not the whites be slaves as well as the blacks? — *A.* 'Because the Lord intended the negroes for slaves.'

" *Q.* Are they better calculated for servants than the whites? — *A.* 'Yes, their hands are large, the skin thick and tough, and they can stand the sun better than the whites.'

" *Q.* Why should servants not complain when they are whipped? — *A.* 'Because the Lord has commanded that they should be whipped.'

" *Q.* Where has He commanded it? — *A.* 'He says, He that knoweth his master's will, and doeth it not, shall be beaten with many stripes.'

" *Q.* Then is the master to blame for whipping his servant? — *A.* 'Oh, no! he is only doing his duty as a Christian."

Snyder left the ground in company with Carlton and Huckelby, and the three dined together in the overseer's dwelling.

"Well," said Joe, after the three white men were out of hearing, "Marser Snyder bin try hesef to-day." "Yes," replied Ned; "he want to show de strange gentman how good he can preach." "Dat's a new sermon he gib us to-day," said Sandy. "Dees white fokes is de very dibble," said Dick; "and all dey whole study is to try to fool de black people." "Didn't you like de sermon?" asked Uncle Simon. "No," answered four 'or five voices. "He rared and pitched enough," continued Uncle Simon.

Now Uncle Simon was himself a preacher, or at least he thought so, and was rather pleased than otherwise, when he heard others spoken of in a disparaging manner. "Uncle Simon can beat dat sermon all to pieces," said Ned, as he was filling his mouth with hazelnuts. "I got no notion of dees white fokes, no how," returned Aunt Dafney. "Dey all de time tellin' dat de Lord made us for to work for dem, and I don't believe a word of it." "Marser Peck give dat sermon to Snyder, I know," said Uncle Simon. "He jest de one for dat," replied Sandy. "I think de people dat made de Bible was great fools," said Ned. "Why?" Uncle Simon. "'Cause dey made such a great big book and put nuttin' in it, but servants obey yer masters." "Oh," replied Uncle Simon, "thars more in de Bible den dat, only Snyder never reads any other part to us; I use to hear it read in Maryland, and thar was more den what Synder lets us hear." In the overseer's house there was another scene going on, and far different from what we have here described.

CHAPTER VII.

"No seeming of logic can ever convince the American people, that thousands of our slave-holding brethren are not excellent, humane, and even Christian men, fearing God, and keeping His commandments."—*Rev. Dr. Joel Parker.*

"You like these parts better than New York," said Carlton to Snyder, as they were sitting down to dinner in the overseer's dwelling. "I can't say that I do," was the reply; "I came here ten years ago as missionary, and Mr. Peck wanted me to stay, and I have remained. I travel among the poor whites during the week, and preach for the niggers on Sunday." "Are there many poor whites in this district?" "Not here, but about thirty miles from here, in the Sand Hill district; they are as ignorant as horses. Why it was no longer than last week I was up there, and really you would not believe it, that people were so poor off. In New England, and, I may say, in all the free states, they have free schools, and everybody gets educated. Not so here. In Connecticut there is only one out of every five hundred above twenty-one years that can neither read nor write. Here there is one out of every eight that can neither read nor write. There is not a single newspaper taken in five of the counties in this state. Last week I was at Sand Hill for the first time, and I called at a farmhouse. The man was out. It was a low log-hut, and yet it was the best house in that locality. The woman and nine children were there, and the geese, ducks, chickens, pigs, and children

were all running about the floor. The woman seemed
scared at me when I entered the house. I inquired
if I could get a little dinner, and my horse fed. She
said, yes, if I would only be good enough to feed
him myself, as her 'gal,' as she called her daughter,
would be afraid of the horse. When I returned into
the house again from the stable, she kept her eyes
upon me all the time. At last she said, 'I s'pose you
aint never bin in these parts afore?' 'No,' said I.
'Is you gwine to stay here long?' 'Not very long,'
I replied. 'On business, I s'pose.' 'Yes,' said I,
'I am hunting up the lost sheep of the house of
Israel.' 'Oh,' exclaimed she, 'hunting for lost sheep
is you? Well, you have a hard time to find 'em here.
My husband lost an old ram last week, and he aint found
him yet, and he's hunted every day.' 'I am not
looking for four-legged sheep,' said I, 'I am hunting for sinners.' 'Ah;' she said, 'then you are a
preacher.' 'Yes,' said I. 'You are the first of
that sort that's bin in these diggins for many a day.'
Turning to her eldest daughter, she said in an excited tone, 'Clar out the pigs and ducks, and sweep
up the floor; this is a preacher.' And it was some
time before any of the children would come near me;
one remained under the bed (which, by the by, was in
the same room), all the while I was there. 'Well,'
continued the woman, 'I was a tellin' my man only
yesterday that I would like once more to go to meetin'
before I died, and he said as he should like to do
the same. But as you have come, it will save us
the trouble of going out of the district.'" "Then you
found some of the lost sheep," said Carlton. "Yes,"
replied Snyder, "I did not find anything else up
there. The state makes no provision for educating
the poor: they are unable to do it themselves, and
they grow up in a state of ignorance and degradation.
The men hunt and the women have to go in the

fields and labour." "What is the cause of it?" in-
inquired Carlton; "Slavery," answered Snyder,
"slavery,—and nothing else. Look at the city of
Boston; it pays more taxes for the support of the
government than this entire state. The people of
Boston do more business than the whole population
of Mississippi put together. I was told some very
amusing things while at Sand Hill. A farmer there
told me a story about an old woman, who was very
pious herself. She had a husband and three sons,
who were sad characters, and she had often prayed
for their conversion but to no effect. At last, one
day while working in the corn-field, one of her sons
was bitten by a rattlesnake. He had scarce reached
home before he felt the poison, and in his agony
called loudly on his Maker.

"The pious old woman, when she heard this, for-
getful of her son's misery, and everything else but the
glorious hope of his repentance, fell on her knees,
and prayed as follows,—'Oh! Lord, I thank thee,
that thou hast at last opened Jimmy's eyes to the
error of his ways; and I pray that, in thy Divine
mercy, thou wilt send a rattlesnake to bite the old
man, and another to bite Tom, and another to bite
Harry, for I am certain that nothing but a rattlesnake, or something of the kind, will ever turn them
from their sinful ways, they are so hard-headed.'
When returning home, and before I got out of the
Sand Hill district, I saw a funeral, and thought I
would fasten my horse to a post and attend. The
coffin was carried in a common horse cart, and followed by fifteen or twenty persons very shabbily
dressed, and attended by a man whom I took to be
the religious man of the place. After the coffin had
been placed near the grave, he spoke as follows,—

'Friends and neighbours! you have congregated to see
this lump of mortality put into a hole in the ground. You

all know the deceased — a worthless, drunken, good-for-no
thing vagabond. He lived in disgrace and infamy, and
died in wretchedness. You all despised him — you all know
his brother Joe, who lives on the hill? He's not a bit better
though he has scrap'd together a little property by cheating
his neighbours. His end will be like that of this loathsome
creature, whom you will please put into the hole as soon as
possible. I wont ask you to drop a tear, but brother Bohow
will please raise a hymn while we fill up the grave.'"

"I am rather surprised to hear that any portion
of the whites in this state are in so low a condition."
"Yet it is true," returned Snyder.

"These are very onpleasant facts to be related to
ye, Mr. Carlton," said Huckelby; "but I can bear
witness to what Mr. Snyder has told ye." Huckelby was from Maryland, where many of the poor
whites are in as sad a condition as the Sand Hillers
of Mississippi. He was a tall man, of iron constitution, and could neither read nor write, but was considered one of the best overseers in the country.
When about to break a slave in, to do a heavy task,
he would make him work by his side all day; and
if the new hand kept up with him, he was set down
as an able bodied man. Huckelby had neither moral,
religious, or political principles, and often boasted
that conscience was a matter that never "cost"
him a thought. "Mr. Snyder aint told ye half
about the folks in these parts;" continued he; "we
who comes from more enlightened parts don't know
how to put up with 'em down here. I find the people here knows mighty little indeed; in fact, I may
say they are univarsaly onedicated. I goes out
among none on 'em, 'cause they aint such as I have
been used to 'sociate with. When I gits a little
richer, so that I can stop work, I tend to go back
to Maryland, and spend the rest of my days." "I
wonder the negroes don't attempt to get their freedom by physical force." "It aint no use for 'em

to try that, for if they do, we puts 'em through by daylight," replied Huckelby. "There are some desperate fellows among the slaves," said Snyder. "Indeed," remarked Carlton. "Oh, yes," replied the preacher. "A case has just taken place near here, where a neighbour of ours, Mr. J. Higgerson, attempted to correct a negro man in his employ, who resisted, drew a knife, and stabbed him (Mr. H.) in several places. Mr J. C. Hobbs (a Tennessean) ran to his assistance. Mr. Hobbs stooped to pick up a stick to strike the negro, and, while in that position, the negro rushed upon him, and caused his immediate death. The negro then fled to the woods, but was pursued with dogs, and soon overtaken. He had stopped in a swamp to fight the dogs, when the party who were pursuing him came upon him, and commanded him to give up, which he refused to do. He then made several efforts to stab them. Mr. Roberson, one of the party, gave him several blows on the head with a rifle gun; but this, instead of subduing, only increased his desperate revenge. Mr. R. then discharged his gun at the negro, and missing him, the ball struck Mr. Boon in the face, and felled him to the ground. The negro, seeing Mr. Boon prostrated, attempted to rush up and stab him, but was prevented by the timely interference of some one of the party. He was then shot three times with a revolving pistol, and once with a rifle, and after having his throat cut, he still kept the knife firmly grasped in his hand, and tried to cut their legs when they approached to put an end to his life. This chastisement was given because the negro grumbled, and found fault with his master for flogging his wife." "Well, this is a bad state of affairs indeed, and especially the condition of the poor whites," said Carlton. "You see," replied Snyder, "no white man is respectable in these slave states who works for a living. No community can be prosperous, where honest labour is not honoured. No society can be rightly constituted, where the intellect is not fed. Whatever institution reflects discredit on industry, whatever institution forbids the general culture of the understanding, is palpably hostile to individual rights, and to social well-being. Slavery is the incubus that hangs over the Southern States." "Yes," interrupted Huckelby; "them's just my sentiments now, and no mistake. I think that, for the honour of our country, this slavery business should stop. I don't own any, no how, and I would not be an overseer if I wern't paid for it."

CHAPTER VIII.

THE SEPARATION.

" In many ways does the full heart reveal
  The presence of the love it would conceal;
  But in far more the estranged heart lets know
  The absence of the love, which yet it fain would show."

AT length the news of the approaching marriage of Horatio met the ear of Clotel. Her head grew dizzy, and her heart fainted within her; but, with a strong effort at composure, she inquired all the particulars, and her pure mind at once took its resolution. Horatio came that evening, and though she would fain have met him as usual, her heart was too full not to throw a deep sadness over her looks and tones. She had never complained of his decreasing tenderness, or of her own lonely hours; but he felt that the mute appeal of her heart-broken looks was more terrible than words. He kissed the hand she offered, and with a countenance almost as sad as her own, led her to a window in the recess shadowed by a luxuriant passion flower. It was the same seat where they had spent the first evening in this beautiful cottage, consecrated to their first loves. The same calm, clear moonlight looked in through the trellis. The vine then planted had now a luxuriant growth; and many a time had Horatio fondly twined its sacred blossoms with the glossy ringlets of her raven hair. The rush of memory almost overpowered poor Clotel; and Horatio felt too much oppressed and ashamed to break the long deep silence. At length, in words scarcely audible, Clotel said : "Tell me, dear Horatio, are you to be married next week?" He dropped her hand as if a rifle ball had struck him; and it was not until after long hesitation, that he began to make some reply about the necessity of circumstances. Mildly but earnestly the poor girl begged him to spare apologies. It was enough that he no longer loved her, and that they must bid farewell. Trusting to the yielding tenderness of her character, he ventured, in the most soothing accents, to suggest that as he still loved her better than all the world, she would ever be his real wife, and they might see each other frequently. He was not prepared for the storm of indignant emotion his words excited. True, she was his slave; her bones, and sinews had been purchased by his gold, yet she had the heart of a true woman, and hers was a passion too deep and absorbing to admit of partnership, and her spirit was too pure to form a selfish league with crime.

At length this painful interview came to an end. They stood together by the Gothic gate, where they had so often met and parted in the moonlight. Old remembrances melted their souls. "Farewell, dearest Horatio," said Clotel. "Give me a parting kiss." Her voice was choked for utterance, and the tears flowed freely, as she bent her lips toward him. He folded her convulsively in his arms, and imprinted a long impassioned kiss on that mouth, which had never spoken to him but in love and blessing. With efforts like a death-pang she at length raised her head from his heaving bosom, and turning from him with bitter sobs, "It is our last. To meet thus is henceforth crime. God bless you. I would not have you so miserable as I am. Farewell. A last farewell." "The last?" exclaimed he, with a wild shriek. "Oh God, Clotel, do not say that;" and covering his face with his hands, he wept like a child. Recovering from his emotion, he found himself alone. The moon looked down upon him mild, but very sorrowfully; as the Madonna seems to gaze upon her worshipping children, bowed down with consciousness of sin. At that moment he would have given worlds to have disengaged himself from Gertrude, but he had gone so far, that blame, disgrace, and duels with angry relatives would now attend any effort to obtain his freedom. Oh, how the moonlight oppressed him with its friendly sadness! It was like the plaintive eye of his forsaken one, like the music of sorrow echoed from an unseen world. Long and earnestly he gazed at that cottage, where he had so long known earth's purest foretaste of heavenly bliss. Slowly he walked away; then turned again to look on that charmed spot, the nestling-place of his early affections. He caught a glimpse of Clotel, weeping beside a magnolia, which commanded a long view of the path leading to the public road. He would have sprung toward her but she darted from him, and entered the cottage. That graceful figure, weeping in the moonlight, haunted him for years. It stood before his closing eyes, and greeted him with the morning dawn. Poor Gertrude, had she known all, what a dreary lot would hers have been; but fortunately she could not miss the impassioned tenderness she never experienced; and Horatio was the more careful in his kindness, because he was deficient in love. After Clotel had been separated from her mother and sister, she turned her attention to the subject of Christianity, and received that consolation from her Bible that is never denied to the children of God. Although it was against the laws of Virginia, for a slave to be taught to read, Currer had employed an old free negro, who lived near her, to teach her two daughters to read and write. She felt that the

step she had taken in resolving never to meet
Horatio again would no doubt expose her to his
wrath, and probably cause her to be sold, yet her
heart was too guileless for her to commit a crime,
and therefore she had ten times rather have been
sold as a slave than do wrong. Some months after
the marriage of Horatio and Gertrude their barouche
rolled along a winding road that skirted the forest near
Clotel's cottage, when the attention of Gertrude was
suddenly attracted by two figures among the trees
by the wayside; and touching Horatio's arm, she
exclaimed, "Do look at that beautiful child." He
turned and saw Clotel and Mary. His lips quivered,
and his face became deadly pale. His young wife
looked at him intently, but said nothing. In returning
home, he took another road; but his wife seeing this,
expressed a wish to go back the way they had come.
He objected, and suspicion was awakened in her heart,
and she soon after learned that the mother of that
lovely child bore the name of Clotel, a name which she
had often heard Horatio murmur in uneasy slumbers.
From gossiping tongues she soon learned more than
she wished to know. She wept, but not as poor Clotel
had done; for she never had loved, and been beloved
like her, and her nature was more proud: henceforth
a change came over her feelings and her manners,
and Horatio had no further occasion to assume a
tenderness in return for hers. Changed as he was
by ambition, he felt the wintry chill of her polite
propriety, and sometimes, in agony of heart, compared
it with the gushing love of her who was indeed his
wife. But these and all his emotions were a sealed
book to Clotel, of which she could only guess the
contents. With remittances for her and her child's
support, there sometimes came earnest pleadings that
she would consent to see him again; but these she
never answered, though her heart yearned to do so.

She pitied his young bride, and would not be tempted
to bring sorrow into her household by any fault of
hers. Her earnest prayer was, that she might not
know of her existence. She had not looked on
Horatio since she watched him under the shadow of
the magnolia, until his barouche passsed her in her
rambles some months after. She saw the deadly
paleness of his countenance, and had he dared to look
back, he would have seen her tottering with faintness.
Mary brought water from a rivulet, and sprinkled
her face. When she revived, she clasped the beloved
child to her heart with a vehemence that made her
scream. Soothingly she kissed away her fears, and
gazed into her beautiful eyes with a deep, deep
sadness of expression, which poor Mary never forgot.
Wild were the thoughts that passed round her aching
heart, and almost maddened her poor brain; thoughts
which had almost driven her to suicide the night of
that last farewell. For her child's sake she had conquered the fierce temptation then; and for her sake,
she struggled with it now. But the gloomy atmo-
sphere of their once happy home overclouded the
morning of Mary's life. Clotel perceived this, and
it gave her unutterable pain.

> " Tis ever thus with woman's love,
>   True till life's storms have passed ;
> And, like the vine around the tree,
>   It braves them to the last."

CHAPTER IX.

THE MAN OF HONOUR.

"My tongue could never learn sweet soothing words,
  But now thy beauty is propos'd, my fee,
  My proud heart sues, and prompts my tongue to speak."
                                                    Shakspeare.

JAMES CRAWFORD, the purchaser of Althesa, was from the green mountains of Vermont, and his feelings were opposed to the holding of slaves. But his young wife persuaded him into the idea that it was no worse to own a slave than to hire one and pay the money to another. Hence it was that he had been induced to purchase Althesa. Henry Morton, a young physician from the same state, and who had just commenced the practice of his profession in New Orleans, was boarding with Crawford when Althesa was brought home. The young physician had been in New Orleans but a few weeks, and had seen very little of slavery. In his own mountain home he had been taught that the slaves of the Southern states were negroes, if not from the coast of Africa, the descendants of those who had been imported. He was unprepared to behold with composure a beautiful young white girl of fifteen in the degraded position of a chattel slave. The blood chilled in his young heart as he heard Crawford tell how, by bantering with the trader, he had bought her for two hundred dollars less than he first asked. His very looks showed that the slave girl had the deepest sympathy of his heart. Althesa had been brought up by her mother to look after the domestic concerns of her cottage in Virginia, and knew well the duties imposed upon her. Mrs. Crawford was much pleased with her new servant, and often made mention of her in presence of Morton. The young man's sympathy ripened into love, which was reciprocated by the friendless and injured child of sorrow. There was but one course left; that was, to purchase the young girl and make her his wife, which he did six months after her arrival in Crawford's family. The young physician and his wife immediately took lodgings in another part of the city; a private teacher was called in, and the young wife taught some of those accomplishments which are necessary for one's taking a position in society. Dr. Morton soon obtained a large practice in his profession, and with it increased in wealth—but with all his wealth he never would own a slave. Mrs. Morton was now in a position to seek out and redeem her mother, whom she had not heard of since they parted at Natchez. An agent was immediately despatched to hunt out the mother and to see if she could be purchased. The agent had no trouble in finding out Mr. Peck: but all overtures were unavailable; he would not sell Currer. His excuse was, that she was such a good housekeeper that he could not spare her. Poor Althesa felt sad when she found that her mother could not be bought. However, she felt a consciousness of having done her duty in the matter, yet waited with the hope that the day might come when she should have her mother by her side.

I

CHAPTER X.

THE YOUNG CHRISTIAN.

" HERE we see *God dealing in slaves;* giving them to his own favourite child [Abraham], a man of superlative worth, and as a reward for his eminent goodness."—*Rev. Theodore Clapp, of New Orleans.*"

ON Carlton's return the next day from the farm, he was overwhelmed with questions from Mr. Peck, as to what he thought of the plantation, the condition of the negroes, Huckelby and Snyder; and especially how he liked the sermon of the latter. Mr. Peck was a kind of a patriarch in his own way. To begin with, he was a man of some talent. He not only had a good education, but was a man of great eloquence, and had a wonderful command of language. He too either had, or thought he had, poetical genius; and was often sending contributions to the *Natchez Free Trader*, and other periodicals. In the way of raising contributions for foreign missions, he took the lead of all others in his neighbourhood. Everything he did, he did for the "glory of God," as he said : he quoted Scripture for almost everything he did. Being in good circumstances, he was able to give to almost all benevolent causes to which he took a fancy. He was a most loving father, and his daughter exercised considerable influence over him, and, owing to her piety and judgment, that influence had a beneficial effect. Carlton, though a schoolfellow of the parson's, was nevertheless nearly ten years his junior; and though not an avowed infidel, was, however, a free-thinker, and

one who took no note of to-morrow. And for this
reason Georgiana took peculiar interest in the young
man, for Carlton was but little above thirty and unmarried. The young Christian felt that she would
not be living up to that faith that she professed and
believed in, if she did not exert herself to the utmost
to save the thoughtless man from his downward
career ; and in this she succeeded to her most sanguine expectations. She not only converted him, but in
placing the Scriptures before him in their true light,
she redeemed those sacred writings from the charge
of supporting the system of slavery, which her father
had cast upon them in the discussion some days
before.

Georgiana's first object, however, was to awaken in
Carlton's breast a love for the Lord Jesus Christ.
The young man had often sat under the sound of the
gospel with perfect indifference. He had heard men
talk who had grown grey bending over the Scriptures, and their conversation had passed by him unheeded ; but when a young girl, much younger than
himself, reasoned with him in that innocent and
persuasive manner that woman is wont to use when
she has entered with her whole soul upon an object,
it was too much for his stout heart, and he yielded.
Her next aim was to vindicate the Bible from sustaining the monstrous institution of slavery. She
said, " God has created of one blood all the nations
of men, to dwell on all the face of the earth.' To
claim, hold, and treat a human being as property is
felony against God and man. The Christian religion
is opposed to slaveholding in its spirit and its principles ; it classes men-stealers among murderers ; and
it is the duty of all who wish to meet God in peace,
to discharge that duty in spreading these principles.
Let us not deceive ourselves into the idea that slavery
is right, because it is profitable to us. Slaveholding

is the highest possible violation of the eighth commandment. To take from a man his earnings, is theft; but to take the earner is a compound, life-long theft; and we who profess to follow in the footsteps of our Redeemer, should do our utmost to extirpate slavery from the land. For my own part, I shall do all I can. When the Redeemer was about to ascend to the bosom of the Father, and resume the glory which he had with him before the world was, he promised his disciples that the power of the Holy Ghost should come upon them, and that they should be witnesses for him to the uttermost parts of the earth. What was the effect upon their minds? 'They all continued with one accord in prayer and supplication with the women.' Stimulated by the confident expectation that Jesus would fulfil his gracious promise, they poured out their hearts in fervent supplications, probably for strength to do the work which he had appointed them unto, for they felt that without him they could do nothing, and they consecrated themselves on the altar of God, to the great and glorious enterprise of preaching the unsearchable riches of Christ to a lost and perishing world. Have we less precious promises in the Scriptures of truth? May we not claim of our God the blessing promised unto those who consider the poor: the Lord will preserve them and keep them alive, and they shall be blessed upon the earth? Does not the language, 'Inasmuch as ye did it unto one of the least of these my brethren, ye did it unto me,' belong to all who are rightly engaged in endeavouring to unloose the bondman's fetters? Shall we not then do as the apostles did? Shall we not, in view of the two millions of heathen in our very midst, in view of the souls that are going down in an almost unbroken phalanx to utter perdition, continue in prayer and supplication, that God will grant us the supplies of his Spirit to prepare us for that work which he has given us to do? Shall not the wail of the mother as she surrenders her only child to the grasp of the ruthless kidnapper, or the trader in human blood, animate our devotions? Shall not the manifold crimes and horrors of slavery excite more ardent outpourings at the throne of grace to grant repentance to our guilty country, and permit us to aid in preparing the way for the glorious second advent of the Messiah, by preaching deliverance to the captives, and the opening of the prison doors to those who are bound."

Georgiana had succeeded in rivetting the attention of Carlton during her conversation, and as she was finishing her last sentence, she observed the silent tear stealing down the cheek of the newly born child of God. At this juncture her father entered, and Carlton left the room. "Dear papa," said Georgiana, "will you grant me one favour; or, rather, make me a promise?" "I can't tell, my dear, till I know what it is," replied Mr. Peck. "If it is a reasonable request, I will comply with your wish," continued he. "I hope, my dear," answered she, "that papa would not think me capable of making an unreasonable request." "Well, well," returned he; "tell me what it is." "I hope," said she, "that in your future conversation with Mr. Carlton, on the subject of slavery, you will not speak of the Bible as sustaining it." "Why, Georgiana, my dear, you are mad, aint you?" exclaimed he, in an excited tone. The poor girl remained silent; the father saw in a moment that he had spoken too sharply; and taking her hand in his he said, "Now, my child, why do you make that request?" "Because," returned she, "I think he is on the stool of repentance, if he has not already been received among the elect. He, you know, was bordering upon infidelity, and if the Bible sanctions slavery, then he will naturally enough say that it is not from God; for the argument from internal evidence is not only refuted, but actually turned against the Bible. If the Bible sanctions slavery, then it misrepresents the character of God. Nothing would be more dangerous to the soul of a young convert than to satisfy him that the Scriptures favoured such a system of sin." "Don't you suppose that I understand the Scriptures better than you? I have been in the world longer." "Yes," said she, "you have been in the world longer, and amongst slaveholders so long that you do not regard it in the same light that those do who have not become so familiar with its every-day scenes as you. I once heard you say, that you were opposed to the institution, when you first came to the South." "Yes," answered he, "I did not know so much about it then." "With great deference to you, papa," replied Georgiana, "I don't think that the Bible sanctions slavery. The Old Testament contains this explicit condemnation of it, 'He that stealeth a man, and selleth him, or if he be found in his hand, he shall surely be put to death;' and 'Woe unto him that buildeth his house by unrighteousness, and his chambers by wrong; that useth his neighbour's service without wages, and giveth him not for his work;' when also the New Testament exhibits such words of rebuke as these, 'Behold the hire of the labourers who have reaped down your fields, which is of you kept back by fraud, crieth; and the cries of them who have reaped are entered into the ears of the Lord of Sabaoth.' 'The law is not made for a righteous man, but for the lawless and disobedient, for the ungodly and for sinners, for unholy and profane, for murderers of fathers and murderers of mothers, for manslayers, for whoremongers, for them that defile themselves with mankind, for *menstealers*, for liars,

for perjured persons.' A more scathing denurci-
ation of the sin in question is surely to be found on
record in no other book.   I am afraid," continued the
daughter, " that the acts of the professed friends of
Christianity in the South do more to spread infidelity than the writings of all the atheists which
have ever been published. The infidel watches the
religious world. He surveys the church, and, lo!
thousands and tens of thousands of her accredited
members actually hold slaves. Members 'in good
and regular standing,' fellowshipped throughout
Christendom except by a few anti-slavery churches
generally despised as ultra and radical, reduce their
fellow men to the condition of chattels, and by force
keep them in that state of degradation. Bishops,
ministers, elders, and deacons are engaged in this
awful business, and do not consider their conduct as
at all inconsistent with the precepts of either the Old
or New Testaments. Moreover, those ministers and
churches who do not themselves hold slaves, very
generally defend the conduct of those who do, and
accord to them a fair Christian character, and in the
way of business frequently take mortgages and levy
executions on the bodies of their fellow men, and in
some cases of their fellow Christians.

" Now is it a wonder that infidels, beholding the
practice and listening to the theory of professing
Christians, should conclude that the Bible inculcates
a morality not inconsistent with chattelising human
beings? And must not this conclusion be strength-
ened, when they hear ministers of talent and learning
declare that the Bible does sanction slaveholding, and
that it ought not to be made a disciplinable offence
in churches? And must not all doubt be dissipated,
when one of the most learned professors in our theo-
logical seminaries asserts that the Bible ' recognises
that the relation may still exist, *salva fide et salva*

ecclesia' (without injury to the Christian faith or
church) and that only 'the *abuse* of it is the essential
and fundamental wrong?' Are not infidels bound to
believe that these professors, ministers, and churches
understand their own Bible, and that, consequently,
notwithstanding solitary passages which appear to
condemn slaveholding, the Bible sanctions it?
When nothing can be further from the truth.
And as for Christ, his whole life was a living testimony against slavery and all that it inculcates.
When he designed to do us good, he took upon himself the form of a servant. He took his station at
the bottom of society. He voluntarily identified
himself with the poor and the despised. The warning
voices of Jeremiah and Ezekiel were raised in olden
time, against sin. Let us not forget what followed.
'Therefore, thus saith the Lord — ye have not
hearkened unto me in proclaiming liberty every one
to his brother, and every one to his neighbour — behold I proclaim a liberty for you saith the Lord, to
the sword, to the pestilence, and to the famine.' Are
we not virtually as a nation adopting the same impious language, and are we not exposed to the same
tremendous judgments? Shall we not, in view of
those things, use every laudable means to awaken our
beloved country from the slumbers of death, and
baptize all our efforts with tears and with prayers,
that God may bless them. Then, should our labour
fail to accomplish the end for which we pray, we
shall stand acquitted at the bar of Jehovah, and
although we may share in the national calamities
which await unrepented sins, yet that blessed ap-
proval will be ours.—' Well done good and faithful
servants, enter ye into the joy of your Lord.'"

"My dear Georgiana," said Mr. Peck, "I must
be permitted to entertain my own views on this
subject, and to exercise my own judgment."

"Believe me, dear papa," she replied, "I would not be understood as wishing to teach you, or to dictate to you in the least; but only grant my request, not to allude to the Bible as sanctioning slavery, when speaking with Mr. Carlton."

"Well," returned he, "I will comply with your wish."

The young Christian had indeed accomplished a noble work; and whether it was admitted by the father, or not, she was his superior and his teacher. Georgiana had viewed the right to enjoy perfect liberty as one of those inherent and inalienable rights which pertain to the whole human race, and of which they can never be divested, except by an act of gross injustice. And no one was more able than herself to impress those views upon the hearts of all with whom she came in contact. Modest and self-possessed, with a voice of great sweetness, and a most winning manner, she could, with the greatest ease to herself, engage their attention.

CHAPTER XI.

THE PARSON POET.

"UNBIND, unbind my galling chain,
   And set, oh! set me free:
No longer say that I'll disdain
   The gift of liberty."

THROUGH the persuasion of Mr. Peck, and fascinated with the charms of Georgiana, Carlton had prolonged his stay two months with his old school-fellow. During the latter part of the time he had been almost as one of the family. If Miss Peck was invited out, Mr. Carlton was, as a matter of course. She seldom rode out, unless with him. If Mr. Peck was absent, he took the head of the table; and, to the delight of the young lady, he had on several occasions taken part in the family worship. "I am glad," said Mr. Peck, one evening while at the tea table, "I am glad, Mr. Carlton, that my neighbour Jones has invited you to visit him at his farm. He is a good neighbour, but a very ungodly man; I want that you should see his people, and then, when you return to the North, you can tell how much better a Christian's slaves are situated than one who does nothing for the cause of Christ." "I hope, Mr. Carlton," said Georgiana, "that you will spend the Sabbath with him, and have a religious interview with the negroes." "Yes," replied the parson, "that's well thought of, Georgy." "Well, I think I will go up on Thursday next, and stay till Monday," said Carlton; "and I shall act upon your suggestion, Miss Peck," continued he; "and try to get a religious interview with the blacks.   By-the-by," remarked Carlton, " I saw an advertisement in the *Free Trader* to-day that rather puzzled me. Ah, here it is now ; and,'' drawing the paper from his pocket, " I will read it, and then you can tell me what it means :

'To PLANTERS AND OTHERS. — *Wanted fifty negroes.* Any person having *sick negroes*, considered *incurable* by their respective physicians, (their owners of course,) and wishing to dispose of them, Dr. Stillman will pay cash for negroes affected with scrofula or king's evil, confirmed hypo-chondriacism, apoplexy, or diseases of the brain, kidneys, spleen, stomach and intestines, bladder and its appendages, diarrhœa, dysentery, &c.   *The highest cash price will be paid as above.*'

When I read this to-day I thought that the adver-tiser must be a man of eminent skill as a physician, and that he intended to cure the sick negroes ; but on second thought I find that some of the diseases enumerated are certainly incurable.   What can he do with these sick negroes ? ''   " You see," replied Mr. Peck, laughing, " that he is a doctor, and has use for them in his lectures.   The doctor is con-nected with a small college.   Look at his prospectus, where he invites students to attend, and that will explain the matter to you.''   Carlton turned to another column, and read the following :

" Some advantages of a peculiar character are connected with this institution, which it may be proper to point out. No place in the United States offers as great opportunities for the acquisition of anatomical knowledge.   Subjects being obtained from among the coloured population in suffi-cient numbers *for every purpose*, and proper dissections car-ried on *without offending any individuals in the community!*"

" These are for dissection, then ? " inquired Carlton with a trembling voice.   " Yes," answered the par-son.   " Of course they wait till they die before they

can use them." "They keep them on hand, and
when they need one they bleed him to death,"
returned Mr. Peck. "Yes, but that's murder."
"Oh, the doctors are licensed to commit murder,
you know; and what's the difference, whether one
dies owing to the loss of blood, or taking too many
pills? For my own part, if I had to choose, I
would rather submit to the former." "I have often
heard what I considered hard stories in abolition
meetings in New York about slavery; but now I
shall begin to think that many of them are true."
"The longer you remain here the more you will be
convinced of the iniquity of the institution," remarked Georgiana. "Now, Georgy, my dear, don't
give us another abolition lecture, if you please,"
said Mr. Peck. "Here, Carlton," continued the
parson, "I have written a short poem for your sister's album, as you requested me; it is a domestic
piece, as you will see." "She will prize it the
more for that," remarked Carlton; and taking the
sheet of paper, he laughed as his eyes glanced over
it. "Read it out, Mr. Carlton," said Georgiana,
"and let me hear what it is; I know papa gets off
some very droll things at times." Carlton complied
with the young lady's request, and read aloud the
following rare specimen of poetical genius:

"MY LITTLE NIG.

" I have a little nigger, the blackest thing alive,
 He'll be just four years old if he lives till forty-five;
 His smooth cheek hath a glossy hue, like a new polished
  boot,
 And his hair curls o'er his little head as black as any soot.
 His lips bulge from his countenance — his little ivories
  shine —
 His nose is what we call a little pug, but fashioned very
  fine:
 Although not quite a fairy, he is comely to behold,
 And I wouldn't sell him, 'pon my word, for a hundred all
  in gold.

" He gets up early in the morn, like all the other nigs,
    And runs off to the hog-lot, where he squabbles with the
        pigs—
    And when the sun gets out of bed, and mounts up in the
        sky,
    The warmest corner of the yard is where my nig doth lie.
    And there extended lazily, he contemplates and dreams,
    (I cannot qualify to this, but plain enough it seems;)
    Until 'tis time to take in grub, when you can't find him
        there,
    For, like a politician, he has gone to hunt his share.

" I haven't said a single word concerning my plantation,
    Though a prettier, I guess, cannot be found within the
        nation;
    When he gets a little bigger, I'll take and to him show it,
    And then I'll say, ' My little nig, now just prepare to go it !'
    I'll put a hoe into his hand—he'll soon know what it
        means,
    And every day for dinner, he shall have bacon and greens."

CHAPTER XII.

A NIGHT IN THE PARSON'S KITCHEN.

" AND see the servants met,
    Their daily labour's o'er ;
And with the jest and song they set
    The kitchen in a roar."

MR. PECK kept around him four servants besides
Currer, of whom we have made mention : of these,
Sam was considered the first. If a dinner-party was
in contemplation, or any company to be invited to
the parson's, after all the arrangements had been
talked over by the minister and his daughter, Sam
was sure to be consulted upon the subject by " Miss
Georgy," as Miss Peck was called by the servants.
If furniture, crockery, or anything else was to be
purchased, Sam felt that he had been slighted if his
opinion had not been asked. As to the marketing,
he did it all. At the servants' table in the kitchen,
he sat at the head, and was master of ceremonies.
A single look from him was enough to silence any
conversation or noise in the kitchen, or any other part
of the premises. There is, in the Southern States,
a great amount of prejudice against colour amongst
the negroes themselves. The nearer the negro or
mulatto approaches to the white, the more he seems
to feel his superiority over those of a darker hue.
This is, no doubt, the result of the prejudice that
exists on the part of the whites towards both mulattoes and blacks. Sam was originally from
Kentucky, and through the instrumentality of one
of his young masters whom he had to take to school'

he had learned to read so as to be well understood ; and, owing to that fact, was considered a prodigy among the slaves, not only of his own master's, but those of the town who knew him. Sam had a great wish to follow in the footsteps of his master, and be a poet; and was, therefore, often heard singing doggrels of his own composition. But there was one great drawback to Sam, and that was his colour. He was one of the blackest of his race. This he evidently regarded as a great misfortune. However, he made up for this in his dress. Mr. Peck kept his house servants well dressed ; and as for Sam, he was seldom seen except in a ruffled shirt. Indeed, the washerwoman feared him more than all others about the house.

Currer, as we have already stated, was chief of the kitchen department, and had a general supervision of the household affairs. Alfred the coachman, Peter, and Hetty made up the remainder of the house servants. Besides these, Mr. Peck owned eight slaves who were masons. These worked in the city. Being mechanics, they were let out to greater advantage than to keep them on the farm. However, every Sunday night, Peck's servants, including the bricklayers, usually assembled in the kitchen, when the events of the week were freely discussed and commented on. It was on a Sunday evening, in the month of June, that there was a party at Mr. Peck's, and, according to custom in the Southern States, the ladies had their maid-servants with them. Tea had been served in "the house," and the servants, including the strangers, had taken their seats at the tea table in the kitchen. Sam, being a "single gentleman," was unusually attentive to the "ladies" on this occasion. He seldom or ever let the day pass without spending at least an hour in combing and brushing up his "hair." Sam had an idea that fresh butter was better for his hair than any other kind of grease; and therefore, on churning days, half a pound of butter had always to be taken out before it was salted. When he wished to appear to great advantage, he would grease his face, to make it "shiny." On the evening of the party therefore, when all the servants were at the table, Sam cut a big figure. There he sat with his wool well combed and buttered, face nicely greased, and his ruffles extending five or six inches from his breast. The parson in his own drawing-room did not make a more imposing appearance than did his servant on this occasion. "I jist bin had my fortune told last Sunday night," said Sam, as he helped one of the girls to some sweet hash. "Indeed," cried half-a-dozen voices. "Yes," continued he; "Aunt Winny teld me I is to hab de prettiest yaller gal in town, and dat I is to be free." All eyes were immediately turned toward Sally Johnson, who was seated near Sam. "I speck I see somebody blush at dat remark," said Alfred. "Pass dem pancakes and molasses up dis way, Mr. Alf, and none of your insinawaysion here," rejoined Sam. "Dat reminds me," said Currer, "dat Dorcas Simpson is gwine to git married." "Who to, I want to know?" inquired Peter. "To one of Mr. Darby's field-hands," answered Currer. "I should tink dat dat gal would not trow hersef away in dat manner," said Sally. "She good enough looking to get a house servant, and not to put up wid a fiel' nigger," continued she. "Yes," said Sam, "dat's a wery insensible remark of yours, Miss Sally. I admire your judgment wery much, I assure you. Dah's plenty of suspectible and well-dressed house servants dat a gal of her looks can get, wid out taken up wid dem common darkies." "Is de man black or a mulatto?" inquired one of the company. "He's nearly white," replied Currer. "Well den, dat's some exchuse for her," remarked Sam; "for I don't like to see dis malgemation of blacks and mulattoes, no how," continued Sam. "If I had my rights I would be a mulatto too, for my mother was almost as light-coloured as Miss Sally," said he. Although Sam was one of the blackest men living, he nevertheless contended that his mother was a mulatto, and no one was more prejudiced against the blacks than he. A good deal of work, and the free use of fresh butter, had no doubt done wonders for his "hare" in causing it to grow long, and to this he would always appeal when he wished to convince others that he was part of an Anglo-Saxon. "I always thought you was not clear black, Mr. Sam," said Agnes. "You are right dahr, Miss Agnes. My hare tells what company I belong to," answered Sam. Here the whole company joined in the conversation about colour, which lasted for some time, giving unmistakeable evidence that caste is owing to ignorance. The evening's entertainment concluded by Sam's relating a little of his own experience while with his first master in old Kentucky.

Sam's former master was a doctor, and had a large practice among his neighbours, doctoring both masters and slaves. When Sam was about fifteen years of age, his old master set him to grinding up the ointment, then to making pills. As the young student grew older and became more practised in his profession, his services were of more importance to the doctor. The physician having a good business, and a large number of his patients being slaves, the most of whom had to call on the doctor when ill, he put Sam to bleeding, pulling teeth, and administering medicine to the slaves. Sam soon acquired the name amongst the slaves of the "Black Doctor." With this appellation he was delighted, and no regu-

K

lar physician could possibly have put on more airs than did the black doctor when his services were required. In bleeding, he must have more bandages, and rub and smack the arm more than the doctor would have thought of. We once saw Sam taking out a tooth for one of his patients, and nothing appeared more amusing. He got the poor fellow down on his back, and he got a straddle of the man's chest, and getting the turnkeys on the wrong tooth, he shut both eyes and pulled for his life. The poor man screamed as loud as he could, but to no purpose. Sam had him fast. After a great effort, out came the sound grinder, and the young doctor saw his mistake; but consoled himself with the idea that as the wrong tooth was out of the way, there was more room to get at the right one. Bleeding and a dose of calomel was always considered indispensable by the "Old Boss;" and, as a matter of course, Sam followed in his footsteps.

On one occasion the old doctor was ill himself, so as to be unable to attend to his patients. A slave, with pass in hand, called to receive medical advice, and the master told Sam to examine him and see what he wanted. This delighted him beyond measure, for although he had been acting his part in the way of giving out medicine as the master ordered it, he had never been called upon by the latter to examine a patient, and this seemed to convince him that, after all, he was no sham doctor. As might have been expected, he cut a rare figure in his first examination, placing himself directly opposite his patient, and folding his arms across his breast, and looking very knowingly, he began, "What's de matter wid you?" "I is sick." "Where is you sick?" "Here," replied the man, putting his hand upon his stomach. "Put out your tongue," continued the doctor. The man run out his tongue at full length. "Let me feel your pulse," at the same time taking his patient's hand in his, placing his fingers on his pulse, he said, "Ah, your case is a bad one; if I don't do something for you, and dat pretty quick, you i'll be a gone coon, and dat's sartin." At this the man appeared frightened and inquired what was the matter with him: in answer, Sam said, "I done told you dat your case is a bad one, and dat's enough." On Sam's returning to his master's bedside, the latter said, "Well, Sam, what do you think is the matter with him?" "His stomach is out of order, sir," he replied. "What do you think had best be done for him?" "I think I better bleed him and give him a dose of calomel," returned Sam. So to the latter's gratification the master let him have his own way. We need not further say, that the recital of Sam's experience as a physician gave him a high position amongst the servants that evening, and made him a decided favourite with the ladies, one of whom feigned illness, when the black doctor, to the delight of all, and certainly to himself, gave medical advice. Thus ended the evening amongst the servants in the parson's kitchen.

CHAPTER XIII.

" 'Tis too much prov'd — that with devotion's visage,
And pious action, we do sugar o'er the devil himself."
Shakspeare

" You will, no doubt, be well pleased with neighbour Jones," said Mr. Peck, as Carlton stepped into the chaise to pay his promised visit to the " ungodly man." " Don't forget to have a religious interview with the negroes," remarked Georgiana, as she gave the last nod to her young convert. " I will do my best," returned Carlton, as the vehicle left the door. As might have been expected, Carlton met with a cordial reception at the hands of the proprietor of the Grove Farm. The servants in the " Great House " were well dressed, and appeared as if they did not want for food. Jones knew that Carlton was from the North, and a non-slaveholder, and therefore did everything in his power to make a favourable impression on his mind. " My negroes are well clothed, well fed, and not over worked," said the slaveholder to his visitor, after the latter had been with him nearly a week. " As far as I can see, your slaves appear to good advantage," replied Carlton. " But," continued he, " if it is a fair question, do you have preaching among your slaves on Sunday, Mr. Jones?" " No, no," returned he, " I think that's all nonsense; my negroes do their own preaching." " So you do permit them to have meetings." " Yes, when they wish. There's some very intelligent and clever chaps among them."

"As to-morrow is the Sabbath," said Carlton, "if you have no objection, I will attend meeting with them." "Most certainly you shall, if you will do the preaching," returned the planter. Here the young man was about to decline, but he remembered the parting words of Georgiana, and he took courage and said, "Oh, I have no objection to give the negroes a short talk." It was then understood that Carlton was to have a religious interview with the blacks the next day, and the young man waited with a degree of impatience for the time.

In no part of the South are slaves in a more ignorant and degraded state than in the cotton, sugar, and rice districts.

If they are permitted to cease labour on the Sabbath, the time is spent in hunting, fishing, or ying beneath the shade of a tree, resting for the morrow. Religious instruction is unknown in the far South, except among such men as the Rev. C. C. Jones, John Peck, and some others who regard religious instruction, such as they impart to their slaves, as calculated to make them more trustworthy and valuable as property. Jones, aware that his slaves would make rather a bad show of intelligence if questioned by Carlton, resolved to have them ready for him, and therefore gave his driver orders with regard to their preparation. Consequently, after the day's labour was over, Dogget, the driver, assembled the negroes together and said, "Now, boys and gals, your master is coming down to the quarters to-morrow with his visitor, who is going to give you a preach, and I want you should understand what he says to you. Now many of you who came of Old Virginia and Kentuck, know what preaching is, and others who have been raised in these parts do not. Preaching is to tell you that you are mighty wicked and bad at heart. This, I suppose, you all

know. But if the gentleman should ask you who
made you, tell him the Lord; if he ask if you wish
to go to heaven, tell him yes. Remember that, you
are all Christians, all love the Lord, all want to go
to heaven, all love your masters, and all love me.
Now, boys and gals, I want you to show yourselves
smart to-morrow: be on your p's and q's, and,
Monday morning, I will give you all a glass of
whiskey bright and early." Agreeable to arrangement the slaves were assembled together on Sunday
morning under the large trees near the great
house, and after going through another drilling
from the driver, Jones and Carlton made their
appearance. "You see," said Jones to the negroes,
as he approached them, "you see here's a gentleman that's come to talk to you about your souls,
and I hope you 'ill all pay that attention that you
ought." Jones then seated himself in one of the
two chairs placed there for him and the stranger.

Carlton had already selected a chapter in the Bible
to read to them, which he did, after first prefacing
it with some remarks of his own. Not being accustomed to speak in public, he determined, after reading the Bible, to make it more of a conversational
meeting than otherwise. He therefore began asking
them questions. "Do you feel that you are a Christian?" asked he of a full-blooded negro that sat near
him. "Yes, sir," was the response. "You feel,
then, that you shall go to heaven." "Yes, sir."
"Of course you know who made you?" The man
put his hand to his head and began to scratch his
wool; and, after a little hesitation, answered, "De
overseer told us last night who made us, but indeed
I forgot the gentmun's name." This reply was
almost too much for Carlton, and his gravity was
not a little moved. However, he bit his tongue, and
turned to another man, who appeared, from his

looks, to be more intelligent. "Do you serve the
Lord?" asked he. "No, sir, I don't serve anybody
but Mr. Jones; I neber belong to anybody else."
To hide his feelings at this juncture, Carlton turned
and walked to another part of the grounds, to where
the women were seated, and said to a mulatto woman
who had rather an anxious countenance, "Did you
ever hear of John the Baptist?" "Oh yes, marser,
John de Baptist; I know dat nigger bery well indeed; he libs in Old Kentuck, where I come from."
Carlton's gravity here gave way, and he looked at
the planter and laughed right out. The old woman
knew a slave near her old master's farm in Kentucky, and was ignorant enough to suppose that he
was the John the Baptist inquired about. Carlton
occupied the remainder of the time in reading
Scripture and talking to them. "My niggers aint
shown off very well to-day," said Jones, as he and
his visitor left the grounds. "No," replied Carlton.
"You did not get hold of the bright ones," continued
the planter. "So it seems," remarked Carlton.
The planter evidently felt that his neighbour, Parson
Peck, would have a nut to crack over the account
that Carlton would give of the ignorance of the
slaves, and said and did all in his power to remove
the bad impression already made; but to no purpose.
The report made by Carlton, on his return, amused
the parson very much. It appeared to him the best
reason why professed Christians like himself should
be slave-holders. Not so with Georgiana. She did
not even smile when Carlton was telling his story,
but seemed sore at heart that such ignorance should
prevail in their midst. The question turned upon
the heathen of other lands, and the parson began to
expatiate upon his own efforts in foreign missions,
when his daughter, with a child-like simplicity,
said,

" Send Bibles to the heathen;
    On every distant shore,
From light that's beaming o'er us,
    Let streams increasing pour
But keep it from the millions
    Down-trodden at our door.

"Send Bibles to the heathen,
    Their famished spirits feed;
Oh! haste, and join your efforts,
    The priceless gift to speed;
Then flog the trembling negro
    If he should learn to read."

"I saw a curiosity while at Mr. Jones's that I
shall not forget soon," said Carlton.   "What was
it?" inquired the parson.   "A kennel of bloodhounds; and such dogs I never saw before.   They
were of a species between the bloodhound and the
foxhound, and were ferocious, gaunt, and savage-
looking animals.   They were part of a stock imported
from Cuba, he informed me.   They were kept in an
iron cage, and fed on Indian corn bread.   This kind
of food, he said, made them eager for their business.
Sometimes they would give the dogs meat, but it
was always after they had been chasing a negro."
"Were those the dogs you had, papa, to hunt
Harry?" asked Georgiana.   "No, my dear," was
the short reply : and the parson seemed anxious to
change the conversation to something else.   When
Mr. Peck had left the room, Carlton spoke more
freely of what he had seen, and spoke more pointedly
against slavery; for he well knew that Miss Peck
sympathised with him in all he felt and said.
    "You mentioned about your father hunting a
slave," said Carlton, in an under tone.   "Yes,"
replied she ; "papa went with some slave-catchers
and a parcel of those nasty negro-dogs, to hunt poor
Harry.   He belonged to papa and lived on the farm.
His wife lives in town, and Harry had been to see

A NEGRO HUNT IN THE SOUTHERN STATES. *Page* 137

her, and did not return quite as early as he should; and Huckelby was flogging him, and he got away and came here. I wanted papa to keep him in town, so that he could see his wife more frequently; but he said they could not spare him from the farm, and flogged him again, and sent him back. The poor fellow knew that the overseer would punish him over again, and instead of going back he went into the woods." "Did they catch him?" asked Carlton. "Yes," replied she. "In chasing him through the woods, he attempted to escape by swimming across a river, and the dogs were sent in after him, and soon caught him. But Harry had great courage and fought the dogs with a big club; and papa seeing the negro would escape from the dogs, shot at him, as he says, only to wound him, that he might be caught; but the poor fellow was killed." Overcome by relating this incident, Georgiana burst into tears.

Although Mr. Peck fed and clothed his house servants well, and treated them with a degree of kindness, he was, nevertheless, a most cruel master. He encouraged his driver to work the field-hands from early dawn till late at night; and the good appearance of the house-servants, and the preaching of Snyder to the field negroes, was to cause himself to be regarded as a Christian master. Being on a visit one day at the farm, and having with him several persons from the Free States, and wishing to make them believe that his slaves were happy, satisfied, and contented, the parson got out the whiskey and gave each one a dram, who in return had to drink the master's health, or give a toast of some kind. The company were not a little amused at some of the sentiments given, and Peck was delighted at every indication of contentment on the part of the blacks. At last it came to Jack's turn to drink, and the master expected something good from him, because he was considered the cleverest and most witty slave on the farm.

"Now," said the master, as he handed Jack the cup of whiskey; "now, Jack, give us something rich. You know," continued he, "we have raised the finest crop of cotton that's been seen in these parts for many a day. Now give us a toast on cotton; come, Jack, give us something to laugh at." The negro felt not a little elated at being made the hero of the occasion, and taking the whiskey in his right hand, put his left to his head and began to scratch his wool, and said,

> "The big bee flies high,
> The little bee make the honey;
> The black folks makes the cotton,
> And the white folks gets the money."

CHAPTER XIV.

A FREE WOMAN REDUCED TO SLAVERY.

ALTHESA found in Henry Morton a kind and affectionate husband; and his efforts to purchase her mother, although unsuccessful, had doubly endeared him to her. Having from the commencement resolved not to hold slaves, or rather not to own any, they were compelled to hire servants for their own use. Five years had passed away, and their happiness was increased by two lovely daughters. Mrs. Morton was seated, one bright afternoon, busily engaged with her needle, and near her sat Salome, a servant that she had just taken into her employ. The woman was perfectly white; so much so, that Mrs. Morton had expressed her apprehensions to her husband, when the woman first came, that she was not born a slave. The mistress watched the servant, as the latter sat sewing upon some coarse work, and saw the large silent tear in her eye. This caused an uneasiness to the mistress, and she said, "Salome, don't you like your situation here?" "Oh yes, madam," answered the woman in a quick tone, and then tried to force a smile. "Why is it that you often look sad, and with tears in your eyes?" The mistress saw that she had touched a tender chord, and continued, "I am your friend; tell me your sorrow, and, if I can, I will help you" As the last sentence was escaping the lips of the mistress, the slave woman put her check apron to her face and wept. Mrs. Morton saw plainly that there was cause for this expression of grief, and pressed the woman more closely. "Hear me, then," said the woman calming herself: "I will tell you why I sometimes weep. I was born in Germany, on the banks of the Rhine. Ten years ago my father came to this country, bringing with him my mother and myself. He was poor, and I, wishing to assist all I could, obtained a situation as nurse to a lady in this city. My father got employment as a labourer on the wharf, among the steamboats; but he was soon taken ill with the yellow fever, and died. My mother then got a situation for herself, while I remained with my first employer. When the hot season came on, my master, with his wife, left New Orleans until the hot season was over, and took me with them. They stopped at a town on the banks of the Mississippi river, and said they should remain there some weeks. One day they went out for a ride, and they had not been gone more than half an hour, when two men came into the room and told me that they had bought me, and that I was their slave. I was bound and taken to prison, and that night put on a steamboat and taken up the Yazoo river, and set to work on a farm. I was forced to take up with a negro, and by him had three children. A year since my master's daughter was married, and I was given to her. She came with her husband to this city, and I have ever since been hired out."

"Unhappy woman," whispered Althesa, "why did you not tell me this before?" "I was afraid," replied Salome, "for I was once severely flogged for telling a stranger that I was not born a slave." On Mr. Morton's return home, his wife communicated to him the story which the slave woman had told her an hour before, and begged that something might be done to rescue her from the situation she was then in. In Louisiana as well as many others of the slave states, great obstacles are thrown in the way of persons who have been wrongfully reduced to slavery regaining their freedom. A person claiming to be free must prove his right to his liberty. This, it will be seen, throws the burden of proof upon the slave, who, in all probability, finds it out of his power to procure such evidence. And if any free person shall attempt to aid a freeman in regaining his freedom, he is compelled to enter into security in the sum of one thousand dollars, and if the person claiming to be free shall fail to establish such fact, the thousand dollars are forfeited to the state. This cruel and oppressive law has kept many a freeman from espousing the cause of persons unjustly held as slaves. Mr. Morton inquired and found that the woman's story was true, as regarded the time she had lived with her present owner; but the latter not only denied that she was free, but immediately removed her from Morton's. Three months after Salome had been removed from Morton's and let out to another family, she was one morning cleaning the door steps, when a lady passing by, looked at the slave and thought she recognised some one that she had seen before. The lady stopped and asked the woman if she was a slave, "I am," said she." "Were you born a slave?" "No, I was born in Germany." "What's the name of the ship in which you came to this country?" inquired the lady. "I don't know," was the answer. "Was it the *Amazon*?" At the sound of this name, the slave woman was silent for a moment, and then the tears began to flow freely down her care-worn cheeks. "Would you know Mrs. Marshall, who was a passenger in the *Amazon*, if you should see her?" inquired the lady. At this the woman gazed at the lady with a degree of intensity that can be imagined better than described, and then fell at the lady's feet. The lady was Mrs. Marshall. She had crossed the Atlantic in the same ship with this poor woman. Salome, like many of her countrymen, was a beautiful singer, and had often entertained Mrs. Marshall and the other lady passengers on board the *Amazon*. The poor woman was raised from the ground by Mrs. Marshall, and placed upon the door step that she had a moment before been cleaning. " I will do my utmost to rescue you from the horrid life of a slave," exclaimed the lady, as she took from her pocket her pencil, and wrote down the number of the house, and the street in which the German woman was working as a slave.

After a long and tedious trial of many days, it was decided that Salome Miller was by birth a free woman, and she was set at liberty. The good and generous Althesa had contributed some of the money toward bringing about the trial, and had done much to cheer on Mrs. Marshall in her benevolent object. Salome Miller is free, but where are her three children ? They are still slaves, and in all human probability will die as such.

This, reader, is no fiction; if you think so, look over the files of the New Orleans newspapers of the years 1845-6, and you will there see reports of the trial.

CHAPTER XV.

" I PROMISED thee a sister tale
   Of man's perfidious cruelty ;
   Come, then, and hear what cruel wrong
   Befel the dark ladie."—*Coleridge.*

LET us return for a moment to the home of Clotel.
While she was passing lonely and dreary hours with
none but her darling child, Horatio Green was trying
to find relief in that insidious enemy of man, the
intoxicating cup. Defeated in politics, forsaken in
love by his wife, he seemed to have lost all principle
of honour, and was ready to nerve himself up to any
deed, no matter how unprincipled. Clotel's existence was now well known to Horatio's wife, and
both her and her father demanded that the beautiful
quadroon and her child should be sold and sent out
of the state. To this proposition he at first turned
a deaf ear ; but when he saw that his wife was about
to return to her father's roof, he consented to leave
the matter in the hands of his father-in-law. The
result was, that Clotel was immediately sold to the
slave-trader, Walker, who, a few years previous, had
taken her mother and sister to the far South. But,
as if to make her husband drink of the cup of humiliation to its very dregs, Mrs. Green resolved to take
his child under her own roof for a servant. Mary
was, therefore, put to the meanest work that could
be found, and although only ten years of age, she
was often compelled to perform labour, which, under
ordinary circumstances, would have been thought too

hard for one much older. One condition of the sale of Clotel to Walker was, that she should be taken out of the state, which was accordingly done. Most quadroon women who are taken to the lower countries to be sold are either purchased by gentlemen for their own use, or sold for waiting-maids; and Clotel, like her sister, was fortunate enough to be bought for the latter purpose. The town of Vicksburgh stands on the left bank of the Mississippi, and is noted for the severity with which slaves are treated. It was here that Clotel was sold to Mr. James French, a merchant.

Mrs. French was severe in the extreme to her servants. Well dressed, but scantily fed, and overworked were all who found a home with her. The quadroon had been in her new home but a short time ere she found that her situation was far different from what it was in Virginia. What social virtues are possible in a society of which injustice is the primary characteristic? in a society which is divided into two classes, masters and slaves? Every married woman in the far South looks upon her husband as unfaithful, and regards every quadroon servant as a rival. Clotel had been with her new mistress but a few days, when she was ordered to cut off her long hair. The negro, constitutionally, is fond of dress and outward appearance. He that has short, woolly hair, combs it and oils it to death. He that has long hair, would sooner have his teeth drawn than lose it. However painful it was to the quadroon, she was soon seen with her hair cut as short as any of the full-blooded negroes in the dwelling.

Even with her short hair, Clotel was handsome. Her life had been a secluded one, and though now nearly thirty years of age, she was still beautiful. At her short hair, the other servants laughed, "Miss Clo needn't strut round so big, she got short nappy har well as I," said Nell, with a broad grin that showed her teeth. "She tinks she white, when she come here wid dat long har of hers," replied Mill. "Yes," continued Nell; "missus make her take down her wool so she no put it up to-day."

The fairness of Clotel's complexion was regarded with envy as well by the other servants as by the mistress herself. This is one of the hard features of slavery. To-day the woman is mistress of her own cottage; to-morrow she is sold to one who aims to make her life as intolerable as possible. And be it remembered, that the house servant has the best situation which a slave can occupy. Some American writers have tried to make the world believe that the condition of the labouring classes of England is as bad as the slaves of the United States.

The English labourer may be oppressed, he may be cheated, defrauded, swindled, and even starved; but it is not slavery under which he groans. H- cannot be sold; in point of law he is equal to the prime minister. "It is easy to captivate the unthinke ing and the prejudiced, by eloquent declamation about the oppression of English operatives being worse than that of American slaves, and by exaggerating the wrongs on one side and hiding them on the other. But all informed and reflecting minds, knowing that bad as are the social evils of England, those of Slavery are immeasurably worse." But the degradation and harsh treatment that Clotel experienced in her new home was nothing compared with the grief she underwent at being separated from her dear child. Taken from her without scarcely a moment's warning, she knew not what had become of her. The deep and heartfelt grief of Clotel was soon perceived by her owners, and fearing that her refusal to take food would cause her death, they resolved to sell her. Mr. French found no difficulty

L

in getting a purchaser for the quadroon woman, for such are usually the most marketable kind of property. Clotel was sold at private sale to a young man for a housekeeper; but even he had missed his aim.

CHAPTER XVI.

DEATH OF THE PARSON.

CARLTON was above thirty years of age, standing on the last legs of a young man, and entering on the first of a bachelor. He had never dabbled in matters of love, and looked upon all women alike. Although he respected woman for her virtues, and often spoke of the goodness of heart of the sex, he had never dreamed of marriage. At first he looked upon Miss Peck as a pretty young woman, but after she became his religious teacher, he regarded her in that light, that every one will those whom they know to be their superiors. It was soon seen, however, that the young man not only respected and reverenced Georgiana for the incalculable service she had done him, in awakening him to a sense of duty to his soul, but he had learned to bow to the shrine of Cupid. He found, weeks after he had been in her company, that when he met her at table, or alone in the drawingroom, or on the piazza, he felt a shortness of breath, a palpitating of the heart, a kind of dizziness of the head; but he knew not its cause.

This was love in its first stage. Mr. Peck saw, or thought he saw, what would be the result of Carlton's visit, and held out every inducement in his power to prolong his stay. The hot season was just commencing, and the young Northerner was talking of his return home, when the parson was very suddenly taken ill. The disease was the cholera, and the physicians pronounced the case incurable. In less than five hours John Peck was a corpse. His love for Georgiana, and respect for her father, had induced Carlton to remain by the bedside of the dying man, although against the express orders of the physician. This act of kindness caused the young orphan henceforth to regard Carlton as her best friend. He now felt it his duty to remain with the young woman until some of her relations should be summoned from Connecticut. After the funeral, the family physician advised that Miss Peck should go to the farm, and spend the time at the country seat; and also advised Carlton to remain with her, which he did.

At the parson's death his negroes showed little or no signs of grief. This was noticed by both Carlton and Miss Peck, and caused no little pain to the latter. "They are ungrateful," said Carlton, as he and Georgiana were seated on the piazza. "What," asked she, "have they to be grateful for?" "Your father was kind, was he not?" "Yes, as kind as most men who own slaves; but the kindness meted out to blacks would be unkindness if given to whites. We would think so, should we not?" "Yes," replied he. "If we would not consider the best treatment which a slave receives good enough for us, we should not think he ought to be grateful for it. Everybody knows that slavery in its best and mildest form is wrong. Whoever denies this, his lips libel his heart. Try him! Clank the chains in his ears, and tell him they are for him; give him an hour to prepare his wife and children for a life of slavery; bid him make haste, and get ready their necks for the yoke, and their wrists for the coffle chains, then look at his pale lips and trembling knees, and you have nature's testimony against slavery."

"Let's take a walk," said Carlton, as if to turn the conversation. The moon was just appearing through the tops of the trees, and the animals and insects in an adjoining wood kept up a continued din of music. The croaking of bull-frogs, buzzing of insects, cooing of turtle-doves, and the sound from a thousand musical instruments, pitched on as many different keys, made the welkin ring. But even all this noise did not drown the singing of a party of the slaves, who were seated near a spring that was sending up its cooling waters. "How prettily the negroes sing," remarked Carlton, as they were wending their way towards the place from whence the sound of the voices came. "Yes," replied Georgiana; "master Sam is there, I'll warrant you: he's always on hand when there's any singing or dancing. We must not let them see us, or they will stop singing." "Who makes their songs for them?" inquired the young man. "Oh, they make them up as they sing them; they are all impromptu songs." By this time they were near enough to hear distinctly every word; and, true enough, Sam's voice was heard above all others. At the conclusion of each song they all joined in a hearty laugh, with an expression of "Dats de song for me;" "Dems dems."

"Stop," said Carlton, as Georgiana was rising from the log upon which she was seated; "stop, and let's hear this one." The piece was sung by Sam, the others joining in the chorus, and was as follows:

Sam.

"Come, all my brethren, let us take a rest,
 While the moon shines so brightly and clear;
Old master is dead, and left us at last,
 And has gone at the Bar to appear.
Old master has died, and lying in his grave,
 And our blood will awhile cease to flow;
He will no more trample on the neck of the slave;
 For he's gone where the slaveholders go.

Chorus.

" Hang up the shovel and the hoe —
    Take down the fiddle and the bow —
    Old master has gone to the slaveholder's rest ;
He has gone where they all ought to go.

Sam.

" I heard the old doctor say the other night,
    As he passed by the dining-room door —
' Perhaps the old man may live through the night,
    But I think he will die about four.'
Young mistress sent me, at the peril of my life,
    For the parson to come down and pray,
For says she, ' Your old master is now about to die,'
    And says I, ' God speed him on his way.'

" Hang up the shovel, &c.

" At four o'clock at morn the family was called
    Around the old man's dying bed ;
And oh ! but I laughed to myself when I heard
    That the old man's spirit had fled.
Mr. Carlton cried, and so did I pretend ;
    Young mistress very nearly went mad ;
And the old parson's groans did the heavens fairly rend ;
    But I tell you I felt mighty glad.

" Hang up the shovel, &c.

" We'll no more be roused by the blowing of his horn,
    Our backs no longer he will score ;
He no more will feed us on cotton-seeds and corn ;
    For his reign of oppression now is o'er.
He no more will hang our children on the tree,
    To be ate by the carrion crow ;
He no more will send our wives to Tennessee ;
    For he's gone where the slaveholders go.

" Hang up the shovel and the hoe,
    Take down the fiddle and the bow,
    We'll dance and sing,
    And make the forest ring,
With the fiddle and the old banjo."

The song was not half finished before Carlton regretted that he had caused the young lady to remain and hear what to her must be anything but pleasant reflections upon her deceased parent. "I think we will walk," said he, at the same time extending his arm to Georgiana. "No," said she: "let's hear them out. It is from these unguarded expressions of the feelings of the negroes, that we should learn a lesson." At its conclusion they walked towards the house in silence: as they were ascending the steps, the young man said, "They are happy, after all. The negro, situated as yours are, is not aware that he is deprived of any just rights." "Yes, yes," answered Georgiana: "you may place the slave where you please; you may dry up to your utmost the fountains of his feelings, the springs of his thought; you may yoke him to your labour, as an ox which liveth only to work, and worketh only to live; you may put him under any process which, without destroying his value as a slave, will debase and crush him as a rational being; you may do this, and *the idea that he was born to be free will survive it all.* It is allied to his hope of immortality; it is the ethereal part of his nature, which oppression cannot reach; it is a torch lit up in his soul by the hand of Deity, and never meant to be extinguished by the hand of man."

On reaching the drawing-room, they found Sam snuffing the candles, and looking as solemn and as dignified as if he had never sung a song or laughed in his life. "Will Miss Georgy have de supper got up now?" asked the negro. "Yes," she replied. "Well," remarked Carlton, "that beats anything I ever met with. Do you think that was Sam we heard singing?" "I am sure of it," was the answer. "I could not have believed that that fellow was capable of so much deception," continued he. " Our system of slavery is one of deception ; and Sam, you see, has only been a good scholar. However, he is as honest a fellow as you will find among the slave population here. If we would have them more honest, we should give them their liberty, and then the inducement to be dishonest would be gone. I have resolved that these creatures shall all be free." " Indeed !" exclaimed Carlton. " Yes, I shall let them all go free, and set an example to those about me." " I honour your judgment," said he. " But will the state permit them to remain ? " " If not, they can go where they can live in freedom. I will not be unjust because the state is."

CHAPTER XVII.

RETALIATION.

" I HAD a dream, a happy dream ;
    I thought that I was free :
  That in my own bright land again
    A home there was for me."

WITH the deepest humiliation Horatio Green saw the daughter of Clotel, his own child, brought into his dwelling as a servant. His wife felt that she had been deceived, and determined to punish her deceiver. At first Mary was put to work in the kitchen, where she met with little or no sympathy from the other slaves, owing to the fairness of her complexion. The child was white, what should be done to make her look like other negroes, was the question Mrs. Green asked herself. At last she hit upon a plan : there was a garden at the back of the house over which Mrs. Green could look from her parlour window. Here the white slave-girl was put to work, without either bonnet or handkerchief upon her head. A hot sun poured its broiling rays on the naked face and neck of the girl, until she sank down in the corner of the garden, and was actually broiled to sleep. "Dat little nigger ain't working a bit, missus," said Dinah to Mrs. Green, as she entered the kitchen.

"She's lying in the sun, seasoning ; she will work better by and by," replied the mistress. " Dees white niggers always tink dey sef good as white folks," continued the cook. " Yes, but we will teach them better ; won't we, Dinah ?" " Yes, missus, I don't like dees mularter niggers, no how; dey always want to set dey sef up for something big." The cook was black, and was not without that prejudice which is to be found among the negroes, as well as among the whites of the Southern States. The sun had the desired effect, for in less than a fortnight Mary's fair complexion had disappeared, and she was but little whiter than any other mulatto children running about the yard. But the close resemblance between the father and child annoyed the mistress more than the mere whiteness of the child's complexion. Horatio made proposition after proposition to have the girl sent away, for every time he beheld her countenance it reminded him of the happy days he had spent with Clotel. But his wife had commenced, and determined to carry out her unfeeling and fiendish designs. This child was not only white, but she was the granddaughter of Thomas Jefferson, the man who, when speaking against slavery in the legislature of Virginia, said,

" The whole commerce between master and slave is a perpetual exercise of the most boisterous passions ; *the most unremitting despotism on the one part, and degrading submission on the other*. With what execration should the statesman be loaded who, permitting one half the citizens thus to trample on the rights of the other, transforms those into despots and these into enemies, destroys the morals of the one part, and the *amor patriæ* of the other ! For if the slave can have a country in this world, it must be any other in preference to that in which he is born to live and labour for another; in which he must lock up the faculties of his nature, contribute as far as depends on his individual endeavours to the evanishment of the human race, or entail his own miserable condition on the endless generations proceeding from him. And can the liberties of a nation be thought secure when we have removed their only firm basis, a conviction in the minds of the people that these liberties are the gift of God ? that they are not to be violated

but with his wrath? Indeed, I tremble for my country when
I reflect that God is just; that his justice cannot sleep for
ever; that, considering numbers, nature, and natural means
only, a revolution of the wheel of fortune, an exchange of
situation, is among possible events; that it may become
probable by supernatural interference! The Almighty has
no attribute which can take side with us in such a contest.

. . . .

"What an incomprehensible machine is man! Who can
endure toil, famine, stripes, imprisonment, and death itself,
in vindication of his own liberty, and the next moment be
deaf to all those motives, whose power supported him
through his trial, and inflict on his fellow-men a bondage,
*one hour of which is fraught with more misery than ages of
that which he rose in rebellion to oppose!* But we must wait
with patience the workings of an overruling Providence, and
hope that that is preparing the deliverance of these our suffering brethren. When the measure of their tears shall be
full—when their tears shall have involved heaven itself in
darkness—doubtless a God of justice will awaken to their
distress, and by diffusing light and liberality among their
oppressors, or at length by his exterminating thunder, manifest his attention to things of this world, and that they are
not left to the guidance of blind fatality."

The same man, speaking of the probability that
the slaves might some day attempt to gain their
liberties by a revolution, said,

"I tremble for my country, when I recollect that God is
just, and that His justice cannot sleep for ever. The Almighty has no attribute that can take sides with us in such
a struggle."

But, sad to say, Jefferson is not the only American statesman who has spoken high-sounding
words in favour of freedom, and then left his own
children to die slaves.

CHAPTER XVIII.

THE LIBERATOR.

"WE hold these truths to be self-evident, that all men are created free and equal; that they are endowed by their Creator with certain inalienable rights; among these are life, *liberty*, and the pursuit of happiness."—*Declaration of American Independence.*

THE death of the parson was the commencement of a new era in the history of his slaves. Only a little more than eighteen years of age, Georgiana could not expect to carry out her own wishes in regard to the slaves, although she was sole heir to her father's estate. There were distant relations whose opinions she had at least to respect. And both law and public opinion in the state were against any measure of emancipation that she might think of adopting; unless, perhaps, she might be permitted to send them to Liberia. Her uncle in Connecticut had already been written to, to come down and aid in settling up the estate. He was a Northern man, but she knew him to be a tight-fisted yankee, whose whole counsel would go against liberating the negroes. Yet there was one way in which the thing could be done. She loved Carlton, and she well knew that he loved her; she read it in his countenance every time they met, yet the young man did not mention his wishes to her. There were many reasons why he should not. In the first place, her father was just deceased, and it seemed only right that he should wait a reasonable time. Again, Carlton was poor, and Georgiana was possessed of a large fortune; and his high spirit would not, for a moment, allow him to place himself in a position to be regarded as a fortune-hunter. The young girl hinted, as best she could, at the probable future; but all to no purpose. He took nothing to himself. True, she had read much of "woman's rights;" and had even attended a meeting, while at the North, which had been called to discuss the wrongs of woman; but she could not nerve herself up to the point of putting the question to Carlton, although she felt sure that she should not be rejected. She waited, but in vain. At last, one evening, she came out of her room rather late, and was walking on the piazza for fresh air. She passed near Carlton's room, and heard the voice of Sam. The negro had just come in to get the young man's boots, and had stopped, as he usually did, to have some talk. "I wish," said Sam, "dat Marser Carlton an Miss Georgy would get married; den, I 'spec, we'd have good times." "I don't think your mistress would have me," replied the young man. "What make tink dat, Marser Carlton?" "Your mistress would marry no one, Sam, unless she loved them." "Den I wish she would lub you, cause I tink we have good times den. All our folks is de same 'pinion like me," returned the negro, and then left the room with the boots in his hands. During the conversation between the Anglo-Saxon and the African, one word had been dropped by the former that haunted the young lady the remainder of the night—"Your mistress would marry no one unless she loved them." That word awoke her in the morning, and caused her to decide upon this important subject. Love and duty triumphed over the woman's timid nature, and that day Georgiana informed Carlton that she was ready to become his wife. The young man, with grateful

tears, accepted and kissed the hand that was offered
to him. The marriage of Carlton and Miss Peck
was hailed with delight by both the servants in the
house and the negroes on the farm. New rules were
immediately announced for the working and general
treatment of the slaves on the plantation. With
this, Huckelby, the overseer, saw his reign coming
to an end; and Snyder, the Dutch preacher, felt
that his services would soon be dispensed with, for
nothing was more repugnant to the feelings of Mrs.
Carlton than the sermons preached by Snyder to the
slaves. She regarded them as something intended
to make them better satisfied with their condition,
and more valuable as pieces of property, without
preparing them for the world to come. Mrs. Carlton
found in her husband a congenial spirit, who entered
into all her wishes and plans for bettering the condition of their slaves. Mrs. Carlton's views and
sympathies were all in favour of immediate emancipation; but then she saw, or thought she saw, a
difficulty in that. If the slaves were liberated, they
must be sent out of the state. This, of course,
would incur additional expense; and if they left
the state, where had they better go? "Let's send
them to Liberia," said Carlton. "Why should they
go to Africa, any more than to the Free States or to
Canada?" asked the wife. "They would be in their
native land," he answered. "Is not this their native
land? What right have we, more than the
negro, to the soil here, or to style ourselves native
Americans? Indeed it is as much their homes as
ours, and I have sometimes thought it was more
theirs. The negro has cleared up the lands, built
towns, and enriched the soil with his blood and
tears; and in return, he is to be sent to a country of
which he knows nothing. Who fought more bravely
for American independence than the blacks? A

negro, by the name of Attucks, was the first that fell in Boston at the commencement of the revolutionary war; and, throughout the whole of the struggles for liberty in this country, the negroes have contributed their share. In the last war with Great Britain, the country was mainly indebted to the blacks in New Orleans for the achievement of the victory at that place; and even General Jackson, the commander in chief, called the negroes together at the close of the war, and addressed them in the following terms :—

"Soldiers! — When on the banks of the Mobile I called you to take up arms, inviting you to partake the perils and glory of your *white fellow citizens, I expected much from you;* for I was not ignorant that you possessed qualities most formidable to an invading enemy. I knew with what fortitude you could endure hunger and thirst, and all the fatigues of a campaign. *I knew well how you loved your native country,* and that you, as well as ourselves, had to defend what *man* holds most dear — his parents, wife, children, and property. *You have done more than I expected.* In addition to the previous qualities I before knew you to possess, I found among you a noble enthusiasm, which leads to the performance of great things.

"'Soldiers! The President of the United States shall hear how praiseworthy was your conduct in the hour of danger, and the representatives of the American people will give you the praise your exploits entitle you to. Your general anticipates them in applauding your noble ardour.'

"And what did these noble men receive in return for their courage, their heroism? Chains and slavery. Their good deeds have been consecrated only in their own memories. Who rallied with more alacrity in response to the summons of danger? If in that hazardous hour, when our homes were menaced with the horrors of war, we did not disdain to call upon the negro to assist in repelling invasion, why should we, now that the danger is past, deny him a home in his native land?" "I see," said

Carlton, "you are right, but I fear you will have difficulty in persuading others to adopt your views." "We will set the example," replied she, "and then hope for the best; for I feel that the people of the Southern States will one day see their error. Liberty has always been our watchword, as far as profession is concerned. Nothing has been held so cheap as our common humanity, on a national average. If every man had his aliquot proportion of the injustice done in this land, by law and violence, the present freemen of the northern section would many of them commit suicide in self-defence, and would court the liberties awarded by Ali Pasha of Egypt to his subjects. Long ere this we should have tested, in behalf of our bleeding and crushed American brothers of every hue and complexion, every new constitution, custom, or practice, by which inhumanity was supposed to be upheld, the injustice and cruelty they contained, emblazoned before the great tribunal of mankind for condemnation; and the good and available power they possessed, for the relief, deliverance and elevation of oppressed men, permitted to shine forth from under the cloud, for the refreshment of the human race."

Although Mr. and Mrs. Carlton felt that immediate emancipation was the right of the slave and the duty of the master, they resolved on a system of gradual emancipation, so as to give them time to accomplish their wish, and to prepare the negro for freedom. Huckelby was one morning told that his services would no longer be required. The negroes, ninety-eight in number, were called together and told that the whip would no longer be used, and that they would be allowed a certain sum for every bale of cotton produced. Sam, whose long experience in the cotton-field before he had been taken into the house, and whose general intelligence justly gave him the first place amongst the negroes on the Poplar Farm, was placed at their head. They were also given to understand that the money earned by them would be placed to their credit; and when it amounted to a certain sum, they should all be free

The joy with which this news was received by the slaves, showed their grateful appreciation of the boon their benefactors were bestowing upon them. The house servants were called and told that wages would be allowed them, and what they earned set to their credit, and they too should be free. The next were the bricklayers. There were eight of these, who had paid their master two dollars per day, and boarded and clothed themselves. An arrangement was entered into with them, by which the money they earned should be placed to their credit; and they too should be free, when a certain amount should be accumulated; and great was the change amongst all these people. The bricklayers had been to work but a short time, before their increased industry was noticed by many. They were no longer apparently the same people. A sedateness, a care, an economy, an industry, took possession of them, to which there seemed to be no bounds but in their physical strength. They were never tired of labouring, and seemed as though they could never effect enough. They became temperate, moral, religious, setting an example of innocent, unoffending lives to the world around them, which was seen and admired by all. Mr. Parker, a man who worked nearly forty slaves at the same business, was attracted by the manner in which these negroes laboured. He called on Mr. Carlton, some weeks after they had been acting on the new system, and offered 2,000 dollars for the head workman, Jim. The offer was, of course, refused. A few days after the same gentleman called again, and made an offer of double the sum that he had on the former occa-

M

sion.   Mr. Parker, finding that no money would purchase either of the negroes, said, " Now, Mr. Carlton,
pray tell me what it is that makes your negroes work
so ? What kind of people are they ?"   " I suppose,"
observed Carlton, " that they are like other people,
flesh and blood."   " Why, sir," continued Parker,
" I have never seen such people; building as they
are next door to my residence, I see and have my eye
on them from morning till night.   You are never
there, for I have never met you, or seen you once at
the building.   Why, sir, I am an early riser, getting
up before day; and do you think that I am not
awoke every morning in my life by the noise of their
trowels at work, and their singing and noise before
day; and do you suppose, sir, that they stop or leave
off work at sundown ? No, sir, but they work as
long as they can see to lay a brick, and then they carry
up brick and mortar for an hour or two afterward,
to be ahead of their work the next morning.   And
again, sir, do you think that they walk at their work?
No, sir, they run all day.   You see, sir, those im-
mensely long ladders, five stories in height; do you
suppose they walk up them ? No, sir, they run up
and down them like so many monkeys all day long.
I never saw such people as these in my life.   I don't
know what to make of them.   Were a white man
with them and over them with a whip, then I should
see and understand the cause of the running and in-
cessant labour; but I cannot comprehend it; there is
something in it, sir.   Great man, sir, that Jim; great
man; I should like to own him."   Carlton here informed Parker that their liberties depended upon
their work; when the latter replied, " If niggers can
work so for the promise of freedom, they ought to be
made to work without it."   This last remark was in
the true spirit of the slaveholder, and reminds us of
the fact that, some years since, the overseer of General

Wade Hampton offered the niggers under him a suit
of clothes to the one that picked the most cotton in
one day; and after that time that day's work was
given as a task to the slaves on that plantation; and,
after a while, was adopted by other planters.

The negroes on the farm, under "Marser Sam,"
were also working in a manner that attracted the
attention of the planters round about. They no
longer feared Huckelby's whip, and no longer slept
under the preaching of Snyder. On the Sabbath,
Mr. and Mrs. Carlton read and explained the Scriptures to them; and the very great attention paid by
the slaves showed plainly that they appreciated the
gospel when given to them in its purity. The death
of Currer, from yellow fever, was a great trial to Mrs.
Carlton; for she had not only become much attached
to her, but had heard with painful interest the story
of her wrongs, and would, in all probability, have
restored her to her daughter in New Orleans.

CHAPTER XIX

ESCAPE OF CLOTEL.

" THE fetters galled my weary soul—
 A soul that seemed but thrown away;
I spurned the tyrant's base control,
 Resolved at least the man to play.

No country has produced so much heroism in so short a time, connected with escapes from peril and oppression, as has occurred in the United States among fugitive slaves, many of whom show great shrewdness in their endeavours to escape from this land of bondage. A slave was one day seen passing on the high road from a border town in the interior of the state of Virginia to the Ohio river. The man had neither hat upon his head or coat upon his back. He was driving before him a very nice fat pig, and appeared to all who saw him to be a labourer employed on an adjoining farm. " No negro is permitted to go at large in the Slave States without a written pass from his or her master, except on business in the neighbourhood." " Where do you live, my boy?" asked a white man of the slave, as he passed a white house with green blinds. "Jist up de road, sir," was the answer. "That's a fine pig." " Yes, sir, marser like dis choat berry much." And the negro drove on as if he was in great haste. In this way he and the pig travelled more than fifty miles before they reached the Ohio river. Once at the river they crossed over; the pig was sold; and nine days after the runaway slave passed over the Niagara river, and, for the first time in his life, breathed the air of freedom.   A few weeks later, and, on the same road, two slaves were seen passing; one was on horseback, the other was walking before him with his arms tightly bound, and a long rope leading from the man on foot to the one on horseback.   "Oh, ho, that's a runaway rascal, I suppose," said a farmer, who met them on the road.   " Yes, sir, he bin runaway, and I got him fast.   Marser will tan his jacket for him nicely when he gets him."   "You are a trustworthy fellow, I imagine," continued the farmer.   " Oh yes, sir; marser puts a heap of confidence in dis nigger."   And the slaves travelled on. When the one on foot was fatigued they would change positions, the other being tied and driven on foot.   This they called "ride and tie."   After a journey of more than two hundred miles they reached the Ohio river, turned the horse loose, told him to go home, and proceeded on their way to Canada.   However they were not to have it all their own way.   There are men in the Free States, and especially in the states adjacent to the Slave States, who make their living by catching the runaway slave, and returning him for the reward that may be offered.   As the two slaves above mentioned were travelling on towards the land of freedom, led by the North Star, they were set upon by four of these slave-catchers, and one of them unfortunately captured.   The other escaped.   The captured fugitive was put under the torture, and compelled to reveal the name of his owner and his place of residence. Filled with delight, the kidnappers started back with their victim.   Overjoyed with the prospect of receiving a large reward, they gave themselves up on the third night to pleasure.   They put up at an inn.   The negro was chained to the bed-post, in the same room with his captors.   At dead of night, when all was still, the slave arose from the floor upon which he had been lying, looked around, and saw that the white men were fast asleep. The brandy punch had done its work. With palpitating heart and trembling limbs he viewed his position. The door was fast, but the warm weather had compelled them to leave the window open. If he could but get his chains off, he might escape through the window to the piazza, and reach the ground by one of the posts that supported the piazza. The sleeper's clothes hung upon chairs by the bedside; the slave thought of the padlock key, examined the pockets and found it. The chains were soon off, and the negro stealthily making his way to the window: he stopped and said to himself, "These men are villains, they are enemies to all who like me are trying to be free. Then why not I teach them a lesson?" He then undressed himself, took the clothes of one of the men, dressed himself in them, and escaped through the window, and, a moment more, he was on the high road to Canada. Fifteen days later, and the writer of this gave him a passage across Lake Erie, and saw him safe in her Britannic Majesty's dominions.

We have seen Clotel sold to Mr. French in Vicksburgh, her hair cut short, and everything done to make her realise her position as a servant. Then we have seen her re-sold, because her owners feared she would die through grief. As yet her new purchaser treated her with respectful gentleness, and sought to win her favour by flattery and presents, knowing that whatever he gave her he could take back again. But she dreaded every moment lest the scene should change, and trembled at the sound of every footfall. At every interview with her new master Clotel stoutly maintained that she had left a husband in Virginia, and would never think of taking another. The gold watch and chain, and other glittering presents which he purchased for her, were all laid aside by the quadroon, as if they were of no value to her. In the same house with her was another servant, a man, who had from time to time hired himself from his master. William was his name. He could feel for Clotel, for he, like her, had been separated from near and dear relatives, and often tried to console the poor woman. One day the quadroon observed to him that her hair was growing out again. "Yes," replied William, "you look a good deal like a man with your short hair." "Oh," rejoined she, "I have often been told that I would make a better looking man than a woman. If I had the money," continued she, "I would bid farewell to this place." In a moment more she feared that she had said too much, and smilingly remarked, "I am always talking nonsense." William was a tall, full-bodied negro, whose very countenance beamed with intelligence. Being a mechanic, he had, by his own industry, made more than what he paid his owner; this he laid aside, with the hope that some day he might get enough to purchase his freedom. He had in his chest one hundred and fifty dollars. His was a heart that felt for others, and he had again and again wiped the tears from his eyes as he heard the story of Clotel as related by herself. "If she can get free with a little money, why not give her what I have?" thought he, and then he resolved to do it. An hour after, he came into the quadroon's room, and laid the money in her lap, and said, "There, Miss Clotel, you said if you had the means you would leave this place; there is money enough to take you to England, where you will be free. You are much fairer than many of the white women of the South, and can easily pass for a free white lady." At first Clotel feared that it was a plan by which the negro wished to try her fidelity to her owner; but she was soon convinced by his earnest manner, and the deep feeling with which he spoke, that he was honest. "I will take the money only on one condition," said she; "and that is, that I effect your escape as well as my own." "How can that be done?" he inquired. "I will assume the disguise of a gentleman and you that of a servant, and we will take passage on a steamboat and go to Cincinnati, and thence to Canada." Here William put in several objections to the plan. He feared detection, and he well knew that, when a slave is once caught when attempting to escape, if returned is sure to be worse treated than before. However, Clotel satisfied him that the plan could be carried out if he would only play his part.

The resolution was taken, the clothes for her disguise procured, and before night everything was in readiness for their departure. That night Mr. Cooper, their master, was to attend a party, and this was their opportunity. William went to the wharf to look out for a boat, and had scarcely reached the landing ere he heard the puffing of a steamer. He returned and reported the fact. Clotel had already packed her trunk, and had only to dress and all was ready. In less than an hour they were on board the boat. Under the assumed name of "Mr. Johnson," Clotel went to the clerk's office and took a private state room for herself, and paid her own and servant's fare. Besides being attired in a neat suit of black, she had a white silk handkerchief tied round her chin, as if she was an invalid. A pair of green glasses covered her eyes; and fearing that she would be talked to too much and thus render her liable to be detected, she assumed to be very ill. On the other hand, William was playing his part well in the servants' hall; he was talking loudly of his master's wealth. Nothing appeared as good on the boat as in his master's fine mansion. "I don't like dees steamboats no how," said William; "I hope when marser goes on a journey agin he will take de carriage and de hosses." Mr. Johnson (for such was the name by which Clotel now went) remained in his room, to avoid, as far as possible, conversation with others. After a passage of seven days they arrived at Louisville, and put up at Gough's Hotel. Here they had to await the departure of another boat for the North. They were now in their most critical position. They were still in a slave state, and John C. Calhoun, a distinguished slave-owner, was a guest at this hotel. They feared, also, that trouble would attend their attempt to leave this place for the North, as all persons taking negroes with them have to give bail that such negroes are not runaway slaves. The law upon this point is very stringent: all steamboats and other public conveyances are liable to a fine for every slave that escapes by them, besides paying the full value for the slave. After a delay of four hours, Mr. Johnson and servant took passage on the steamer Rodolph, for Pittsburgh. It is usual, before the departure of the boats, for an officer to examine every part of the vessel to see that no slave secretes himself on board, "Where are you going?" asked the officer of William, as he was doing his duty on this occasion. "I am going with marser," was the quick reply. "Who is your master?" "Mr. Johnson, sir, a gentleman in the cabin." "You must take him to the office and satisfy that captain that all is right, or you can't go on this boat." William informed his master what the officer had said. The boat was on the eve of going, and no time could be lost, yet they knew not what to do. At last they went to the office, and Mr. Johnson, addressing the captain, said, "I am informed that my boy can't go with me unless I give security that he belongs to me." "Yes," replied the captain,

" that is the law." "A very strange law indeed,"
rejoined Mr. Johnson, "that one can't take his property with him." After a conversation of some
minutes, and a plea on the part of Johnson that he
did not wish to be delayed owing to his illness, they
were permitted to take their passage without farther
trouble, and the boat was soon on its way up the
river. The fugitives had now passed the Rubicon,
and the next place at which they would land would
be in a Free State. Clotel called William to her
room, and said to him, " We are now free, you can
go on your way to Canada, and I shall go to Virginia
in search of my daughter." The announcement that
she was going to risk her liberty in a Slave State
was unwelcome news to William. With all the
eloquence he could command, he tried to persuade
Clotel that she could not escape detection, and was
only throwing her freedom away. But she had
counted the cost, and made up her mind for the
worst. In return for the money he had furnished,
she had secured for him his liberty, and their engage-
ment was at an end.

After a quick passage the fugitives arrived at Cincinnati, and there separated. William proceeded
on his way to Canada, and Clotel again resumed her
own apparel, and prepared to start in search of her
child. As might have been expected, the escape of
those two valuable slaves created no little sensation
in Vicksburgh. Advertisements and messages were
sent in every direction in which the fugitives were
thought to have gone. It was soon, however, known
that they had 'left the town as master and servant;
and many were the communications which appeared
in the newspapers, in which the writers thought, or
pretended, that they had seen the slaves in their
disguise. One was to the effect that they had gone
off in a chaise; one as master, and the other as ser-

vant. But the most probable was an account given by a correspondent of one of the Southern newspapers, who happened to be a passenger in the same steamer in which the slaves escaped, and which we here give :—

"One bright starlight night, in the month of December last, I found myself in the cabin of the steamer Rodolph, then lying in the port of Vicksburgh, and bound to Louisville. I had gone early on board, in order to select a good berth, and having got tired of reading the papers, amused myself with watching the appearance of the passengers as they dropped in, one after another, and I being a believer in physiognomy, formed my own opinion of their characters.

"The second bell rang, and as I yawningly returned my watch to my pocket, my attention was attracted by the appearance of a young man who entered the cabin supported by his servant, a strapping negro.

"The man was bundled up in a capacious overcoat; his face was bandaged with a white handkerchief, and its expression entirely hid by a pair of enormous spectacles.

' There was something so mysterious and unusual about the young man as he sat restless in the corner, that curiosity led me to observe him more closely.

"He appeared anxious to avoid notice, and before the steamer had fairly left the wharf, requested, in a low, womanly voice, to be shown his berth, as he was an invalid, and must retire early: his name he gave as Mr. Johnson. His servant was called, and he was put quietly to bed. I paced the deck until Tybee light grew dim in the distance, and then went to my berth.

"I awoke in the morning with the sun shining in my face; we were then just passing St. Helena. It was a mild beautiful morning, and most of the passengers were on deck, enjoying the freshness of the air, and stimulating their appetites for breakfast. Mr. Johnson soon made his appearance, arrayed as on the night before, and took his seat quietly upon the guard of the boat.

"From the better opportunity afforded by daylight, I found that he was a slight built, apparently handsome young man, with black hair and eyes, and of a darkness of complexion that betokened Spanish extraction. Any notice from others seemed painful to him ; so to satisfy my curiosity, I questioned his servant, who was standing near, and gained the following information.

" His master was an invalid — he had suffered for a long time under a complication of diseases, that had baffled the skill of the best physicians in Mississippi he was now suffering principally with the 'rheumatism,' and he was scarcely able to walk or help himself in any way. He came from Vicksburgh, and was now on his way to Philadelphia, at which place resided his uncle, a celebrated physician, and through whose means he hoped to be restored to perfect health.

" This information, communicated in a bold, off-hand manner, enlisted my sympathies for the sufferer, although it occurred to me that he walked rather too gingerly for a person afflicted with so many ailments."

After thanking Clotel for the great service she had done him in bringing him out of slavery, William bade her farewell. The prejudice that exists in the Free States against coloured persons, on account of their colour, is attributable solely to the influence of slavery, and is but another form of slavery itself. And even the slave who escapes from the Southern plantations, is surprised when he reaches the North, at the amount and withering influence of this prejudice. William applied at the railway station for a ticket for the train going to Sandusky, and was told that if he went by that train he would have to ride in the luggage-van. " Why ?" asked the astonished negro. " We don't send a Jim Crow carriage but once a day, and that went this morning." The "Jim Crow" carriage is the one in which the blacks have to ride. Slavery is a school in which its victims learn much shrewdness, and William had been an apt scholar. Without asking any more questions, the negro took his seat in one of the first-class carriages. He was soon seen and ordered out. Afraid to remain in the town longer, he resolved to go by that train ; and consequently seated himself on a goods' box in the luggage-van. The train started at its proper time,

and all went on well. Just before arriving at the
end of the journey, the conductor called on William
for his ticket. "I have none," was the reply.
"Well, then, you can pay your fare to me," said the
officer. "How much is it?" asked the black man.
"Two dollars." "What do you charge those in the
passenger-carriage?" "Two dollars." "And do
you charge me the same as you do those who ride in
the best carriages?" asked the negro. "Yes," was
the answer. "I shan't pay it," returned the man.
"You black scamp, do you think you can ride on this
road without paying your fare?" "No, I don't want
to ride for nothing; I only want to pay what's
right." "Well, launch out two dollars, and that's
right." "No, I shan't; I will pay what I ought,
and won't pay any more." "Come, come, nigger,
your fare and be done with it," said the conductor, in
a manner that is never used except by Americans to
blacks. "I won't pay you two dollars, and that
enough," said William. "Well, as you have come
all the way in the luggage-van, pay me a dollar and
a half and you may go." "I shan't do any such
thing." "Don't you mean to pay for riding?"
"Yes, but I won't pay a dollar and a half for riding
up here in the freight-van. If you had let me come
in the carriage where others ride, I would have paid
you two dollars." "Where were you raised? You
seem to think yourself as good as white folks." "I
want nothing more than my rights." "Well, give
me a dollar, and I will let you off." "No, sir, I
shan't do it." "What do you mean to do then—don't
you wish to pay anything?" "Yes, sir, I want to
pay you the full price." "What do you mean by full
price?" "What do you charge per hundred-weight
for goods?" inquired the negro with a degree of gravity that would have astonished Diogenes himself.
"A quarter of a dollar per hundred," answered the

conductor. "I weigh just one hundred and fifty pounds," returned William, "and will pay you three-eighths of a dollar." "Do you expect that you will pay only thirty-seven cents for your ride?" "This, sir, is your own price. I came in a luggage-van, and I'll pay for luggage." After a vain effort to get the negro to pay more, the conductor took the thirty-seven cents, and noted in his cash-book, "Received for one hundred and fifty pounds of luggage, thirty-seven cents." This, reader, is no fiction; it actually occurred in the railway above described.

Thomas Corwin, a member of the American Congress, is one of the blackest white men in the United States. He was once on his way to Congress, and took passage in one of the Ohio river steamers. As he came just at the dinner hour, he immediately went into the dining saloon, and took his seat at the table. A gentleman with his whole party of five ladies at once left the table. "Where is the captain," cried the man in an angry tone. The captain soon appeared, and it was sometime before he could satisfy the old gent. that Governor Corwin was not a nigger. The newspapers often have notices of mistakes made by innkeepers and others who undertake to accommodate the public, one of which we give below.

On the 6th inst., the Hon. Daniel Webster and family entered Edgartown, on a visit for health and recreation. Arriving at the hotel, without alighting from the coach, the landlord was sent for to see if suitable accommodation could be had. That dignitary appearing, and surveying Mr. Webster, while the hon. senator addressed him, seemed woefully to mistake the dark features of the traveller as he sat back in the corner of the carriage, and to suppose him a *coloured man*, particularly as there were two coloured servants of Mr. W. outside. So he promptly declared that there was no room for him and his family, and he could not be accommodated there — at the same time suggesting that he might perhaps find accommodation at some of the huts "up back," to which he pointed. So deeply did the prejudice of looks possess him, that he appeared not to notice that the stranger introduced himself to him as Daniel Webster, or to be so ignorant as not to have heard of such a personage; and turning away, he expressed to the driver his astonishment that he should bring *black* people there for *him* to take in. It was not till he had been repeatedly assured and made to understand that the said Daniel Webster was a real live senator of the United States, that he perceived his awkward mistake and the distinguished honour which he and his house were so near missing.

In most of the Free States, the coloured people are disfranchised on account of their colour. The following scene, which we take from a newspaper in the state of Ohio, will give some idea of the extent to which this prejudice is carried.

"The whole of Thursday last was occupied by the Court of Common Pleas for this county in trying to find out whether one Thomas West was of the VOTING COLOUR, as some had very *constitutional doubts* as to whether his colour was orthodox, and whether his hair was of the official crisp! Was it not a dignified business? Four profound judges, four acute lawyers, twelve grave jurors, and I don't know how many venerable witnesses, making in all about thirty men, perhaps, all engaged in the profound, laborious, and illustrious business, of finding out whether a man who pays tax, works on the road, and is an industrious farmer, has been born according to the republican, Christian constitution of Ohio — so that he can vote! And they wisely, gravely, and 'JUDGMATICALLY' decided that he should not vote! What wisdom — what research it must have required to evolve this truth! It was left for the Court of Common Pleas for Columbian county, Ohio, in the United States of

North America, to find out what Solomon never dreamed of—the courts of all civilised, heathen, or Jewish countries, never contemplated. Lest the wisdom of our courts should be circumvented by some such men as might be named, who are so near being born constitutionally that they might be taken for white by sight, I would suggest that our court be invested with SMELLING powers, and that if a man don't exhale the constitutional smell, he shall not vote! This would be an additional security to our liberties."

William found, after all, that liberty in the so-called Free States was more a name than a reality; that prejudice followed the coloured man into every place that he might enter. The temples erected for the worship of the living God are no exception. The finest Baptist church in the city of Boston has the following paragraph in the deed that conveys its seats to pewholders:

" And it is a further condition of these presents, that if the owner or owners of said pew shall determine hereafter to sell the same, it shall first be offered, in writing, to the standing committee of said society for the time being. at such price as might otherwise be obtained for it; and the said committee shall have the right, for ten days after such offer, to purchase said pew for said society, at that price, first deducting therefrom all taxes and assessments on said pew then remaining unpaid. And if the said committee shall not so complete such purchase within said ten days, then the pew may be sold by the owner or owners thereof (after payment of all such arrears) to any one respectable *white person*, but upon the same conditions as are contained in this instrument; and immediate notice of such sale shall be given in writing, by the vendor, to the treasurer of said society."

Such are the conditions upon which the Rowe Street Baptist Church, Boston, disposes of its seats. The writer of this is able to put that whole congregation, minister and all, to flight, by merely putting his coloured face in that church. We once visited a church in New York that had a place set apart for the sons of Ham. It was a dark, dismal looking place in one corner of the gallery, grated in front like a hen-coop, with a black border around it. It had two doors; over one was B. M.—black men; over the other B. W.—black women.

N

CHAPTER XX.

A TRUE DEMOCRAT.

" Who can, with patience, for a moment see
　The medley mass of pride and misery,
　Of whips and charters, manacles and rights,
　Of slaving blacks and democratic whites,
　And all the piebald policy that reigns
　In free confusion o'er Columbia's plains?
　To think that man, thou just and gentle God!
　Should stand before thee with a tyrant's rod,
　O'er creatures like himself, with souls from thee,
　Yet dare to boast of perfect liberty! — *Thomas Moore.*

EDUCATED in a free state, and marrying a wife who had been a victim to the institution of slavery, Henry Morton became strongly opposed to the system. His two daughters, at the age of twelve years, were sent to the North to finish their education, and to receive that refinement that young ladies cannot obtain in the Slave States. Although he did not publicly advocate the abolition of slavery, he often made himself obnoxious to private circles, owing to the denunciatory manner in which he condemned the "peculiar institution." Being one evening at a party, and hearing one of the company talking loudly of the glory and freedom of American institutions, he gave it as his opinion that, unless slavery was speedily abolished, it would be the ruin of the Union. "It is not our boast of freedom," said he, "that will cause us to be respected abroad. It is not our loud talk in favour of liberty that will cause us to be regarded as friends of human freedom; but our acts will be scrutinised by the people of other countries. We say much against European despotism; let us look to ourselves. That government is despotic where the rulers govern subjects by their own mere will — by decrees and laws emanating from their uncontrolled will, in the enactment and execution of which the ruled have no voice, and under which they have no right except at the will of the rulers. Despotism does not depend upon the number of the rulers, or the number of the subjects. It may have one ruler or many. Rome was a despotism under Nero; so she was under the triumvirate. Athens was a despotism under Thirty Tyrants; under her Four Hundred Tyrants; under her Three Thousand Tyrants. It has been generally observed that despotism increases in severity with the number of despots; the responsibility is more divided, and the claims more numerous. The triumvirs each demanded his victims. The smaller the number of subjects in proportion to the tyrants, the more cruel the oppression, because the less danger from rebellion. In this government, the free white citizens are the rulers — the sovereigns, as we delight to be called. All others are subjects. There are, perhaps, some sixteen or seventeen millions of sovereigns, and four millions of subjects.

" The rulers and the ruled are of all colours, from the clear white of the Caucasian tribes to the swarthy Ethiopian. The former, by courtesy, are all called white, the latter black. In this government the subject has no rights, social, political, or personal. He has no voice in the laws which govern him. He can hold no property. His very wife and children are not his. His labour is another's. He, and all that appertain to him, are the absolute property of his rulers. He is governed, bought, sold, punished, executed, by laws to which he never gave his assent, and by rulers whom he never chose. He is not a serf merely, with half the rights of men like the subjects of despotic Russia; but a native slave, stripped of every right which God and nature gave him, and which the high spirit of our revolution declared inalienable — which he himself could not surrender, and which man could not take from him. Is he not then the subject of despotic sway?

"The slaves of Athens and Rome were free in comparison. They had some rights — could acquire some property; could choose their own masters, and purchase their own freedom; and, when free, could rise in social and political life. The slaves of America, then, lie under the most absolute and grinding despotism that the world ever saw. But who are the despots? The rulers of the country — tho sovereign people! Not merely the slaveholder who cracks the lash. He is but the instrument in tho hands of despotism. That despotism is the government of the Slave States, and the United States, consisting of all its rulers — all the free citizens. Do not look upon this as a paradox, because you and I and the sixteen millions of rulers are free. The rulers of every despotism are free. Nicholas of Russia is free. The grand Sultan of Turkey is free. The butcher of Austria is free. Augustus, Anthony, and Lepidus were free, while they drenched Rome in blood. The Thirty Tyrants — the Four Hundred — the Three Thousand, were free while they bound their countrymen in chains. You, and I, and the sixteen millions are free, while we fasten iron chains, and rivet manacles on four millions of our fellowmen — tear their wives and children from them — separate them — sell them, and doom them to perpetual, eternal bondage. Are we not then despots — despots such as history will brand and God abhor?"

" We, as individuals, are fast losing our reputation for honest dealing. Our nation is losing its character. The loss of a firm national character, or the degradation of a nation's honour, is the inevitable prelude to her destruction. Behold the once proud fabric of a Roman empire — an empire carrying its arts and arms into every part of the Eastern continent; the monarchs of mighty kingdoms dragged at the wheels of her triumphal chariots; her eagle waving over the ruins of desolated countries;—where is her splendour, her wealth, her power, her glory? Extinguished for ever. Her mouldering temples, the mournful vestiges of her former grandeur, afford a shelter to her muttering monks. Where are her statesmen, her sages, her philosophers, her orators, generals? Go to their solitary tombs and inquire? She lost her national character, and her destruction followed. The ramparts of her national pride were broken down, and Vandalism desolated her classic fields. Then let the people of our country take warning ere it is too late. But most of us say to ourselves,

"'Who questions the right of mankind to be free?
Yet, what are the rights of the *negro* to me?
I'm well fed and clothed, I have plenty of pelf —
I'll care for the blacks when I turn black myself.'

" New Orleans is doubtless the most immoral place in the United States. The theatres are open on the Sabbath. Bull-fights, horse-racing, and other cruel amusements are carried on in this city to an extent unknown in any other part of the Union. The most stringent laws have been passed in that city against negroes, yet a few years since the State Legislature passed a special act to enable a white man to marry a coloured woman, on account of her being possessed of a large fortune. And, very recently, the following paragraph appeared in the city papers:—

" 'There has been quite a stir recently in this city, in consequence of a marriage of a white man, named Buddington, a teller in the Canal Bank, to the negro daughter of one of the wealthiest merchants. Buddington, before he could be married, was obliged to swear that he had negro blood in his veins, and to do this he made an incision in his arm, and put some of her blood in the cut. The ceremony was performed by a Catholic clergyman, and the bridegroom has received with his wife a fortune of fifty or sixty thousand dollars.'

"It seems that the fifty or sixty thousand dollars entirely covered the negro woman's black skin, and the law prohibiting marriage between blacks and whites was laid aside for the occasion."

Althesa felt proud, as well she might, at her husband's taking such high ground in a slaveholding city like New Orleans.

CHAPTER XXI.

"O WEEP, ye friends of freedom weep !
Your harps to mournful measures sweep."

ON the last day of November, 1620, on the con-
fines of the Grand Bank of Newfoundland, lo! we
behold one little solitary tempest-tost and weather-
beaten ship; it is all that can be seen on the length
and breadth of the vast intervening solitudes, from
the melancholy wilds of Labrador and New England's
iron-bound shores, to the western coasts of Ireland
and the rock-defended Hebrides, but one lonely ship
greets the eye of angels or of men, on this great thoroughfare of nations in our age. Next in moral
grandeur, was this ship, to the great discoverer's :
Columbus found a continent; the May-flower brought
the seed-wheat of states and empire. That is the
May-flower, with its servants of the living God, their
wives and little ones, hastening to lay the foundations
of nations in the occidental lands of the setting-sun.
Hear the voice of prayer to God for his protection,
and the glorious music of praise, as it breaks into the
wild tempest of the mighty deep, upon the ear of
God. Here in this ship are great and good men.
Justice, mercy, humanity, respect for the rights of
all ; each man honoured, as he was useful to himself
and others; labour respected, law-abiding men, con-
stitution-making and respecting men ; men, whom no
tyrant could conquer, or hardship overcome, with the
high commission sealed by a Spirit divine, to esta-

blish religious and political liberty for all. This ship had the embryo elements of all that is useful, great, and grand in Northern institutions; it was the great type of goodness and wisdom, illustrated in two and a quarter centuries gone by; it was the good genius of America.

But look far in the South-east, and you behold on the same day, in 1620, a low rakish ship hastening from the tropics, solitary and alone, to the New World. What is she? She is freighted with the elements of unmixed evil. Hark! hear those rattling chains, hear that cry of despair and wail of anguish, as they die away in the unpitying distance. Listen to those shocking oaths, the crack of that flesh-cutting whip. Ah! it is the first cargo of slaves on their way to Jamestown, Virginia. Behold the Mayflower anchored at Plymouth Rock, the slave-ship in James River. Each a parent, one of the prosperous, labour-honouring, law-sustaining institutions of the North; the other the mother of slavery, idleness, lynch-law, ignorance, unpaid labour, poverty, and duelling, despotism, the ceaseless swing of the whip, and the peculiar institutions of the South. These ships are the representation of good and evil in the New World, even to our day. When shall one of those parallel lines come to an end?

The origin of American slavery is not lost in the obscurity of by-gone ages. It is a plain historical fact, that it owes its birth to the African slave trade, now pronounced by every civilised community the greatest crime ever perpetrated against humanity. Of all causes intended to benefit mankind, the abolition of chattel slavery must necessarily be placed amongst the first, and the negro hails with joy every new advocate that appears in his cause. Commiseration for human suffering and human sacrifices awakened the capacious mind, and brought into action the enlarged benevolence, of Georgiana Carlton. With respect to her philosophy — it was of a noble cast. It was, that all men are by nature equal; that they are wisely and justly endowed by the Creator with certain rights, which are irrefragable; and that, however human pride and human avarice may depress and debase, still God is the author of good to man — and of evil, man is the artificer to himself and to his species. Unlike Plato and Socrates, her mind was free from the gloom that surrounded theirs; her philosophy was founded in the school of Christianity; though a devoted member of her father's church, she was not a sectarian.

We learn from Scripture, and it is a little remarkable that it is the only exact definition of religion found in the sacred volume, that "pure religion and undefiled before God, even the Father, is this, to visit the fatherless and widows in their affliction, and to keep oneself unspotted from the world." "Look not every man on his own things, but every man also on the things of others." "Remember them that are in bonds as bound with them." "Whatsoever ye would that others should do to you, do ye even so to them."

This was her view of Christianity, and to this end she laboured with all her energies to convince her slaveholding neighbours that the negro could not only take care of himself, but that he also appreciated liberty, and was willing to work and redeem himself. Her most sanguine wishes were being realized when she suddenly fell into a decline. Her mother had died of consumption, and her physician pronounced this to be her disease. She was prepared for this sad intelligence, and received it with the utmost composure. Although she had confidence in her husband that he would carry out her wishes in freeing the negroes after her death, Mrs. Carlton resolved upon their immediate liberation. Consequently the slaves were all summoned before the noble woman, and informed that they were no longer bondsmen. "From this hour," said she, "you are free, and all eyes will be fixed upon you. I dare not predict how far your example may affect the welfare of your brethren yet in bondage. If you are temperate, industrious, peaceable, and pious, you will show to the world that slaves can be emancipated without danger. Remember what a singular relation you sustain to society. The necessities of the case require not only that you should behave as well as the whites, but better than the whites; and for this reason: if you behave no better than they, your example will lose a great portion of its influence. Make the Lord Jesus Christ your refuge and exemplar. His is the only standard around which you can successfully rally. If ever there was a people who needed the consolations of religion to sustain them in their grievous afflictions, you are that people. You had better trust in the Lord than to put confidence in man. Happy is that people whose God is the Lord. Get as much education as possible for yourselves and your children. An ignorant people can never occupy any other than a degraded station in society; they can never be truly free until they are intelligent. In a few days you will start for the state of Ohio, where land will be purchased for some of you who have families, and where I hope you will all prosper. We have been urged to send you to Liberia, but we think it wrong to send you from your native land. We did not wish to encourage the Colonization Society, for it originated in hatred of the free coloured people. Its pretences are false, its doctrines odious, its means contemptible. Now, whatever may be your situation in life, 'Remember those in bonds as bound with them.' You must get ready as soon as you can for your journey to the North."

Seldom was there ever witnessed a more touching scene than this. There sat the liberator,—pale, feeble, emaciated, with death stamped upon her countenance, surrounded by the sons and daughters of Africa; some of whom had in former years been separated from all that they had held near and dear, and the most of whose backs had been torn and gashed by the negro whip. Some were upon their knees at the feet of their benefactress; others were standing round her weeping. Many begged that they might be permitted to remain on the farm and work for wages, for some had wives and some husbands on other plantations in the neighbourhood, and would rather remain with them.

But the laws of the state forbade any emancipated negroes remaining, under penalty of again being sold into slavery. Hence the necessity of sending them out of the state. Mrs. Carlton was urged by her friends to send the emancipated negroes to Africa. Extracts from the speeches of Henry Clay, and other distinguished Colonization Society men, were read to her to induce her to adopt this course. Some thought they should be sent away because the blacks are vicious; others because they would be missionaries to their brethren in Africa. "But," said she, "if we send away the negroes because they are profligate and vicious, what sort of missionaries will they make? Why not send away the vicious among the whites for the same reason, and the same purpose?"

Death is a leveller, and neither age, sex, wealth, nor usefulness can avert when he is permitted to strike. The most beautiful flowers soon fade, and droop, and die; this is also the case with man; his days are uncertain as the passing breeze. This hour he glows in the blush of health and vigour, but the next he may be counted with the number no more known on earth.

Although in a low state of health, Mrs. Carlton had the pleasure of seeing all her slaves, except Sam and three others, start for a land of freedom. The morning they were to go on board the steamer, bound for Louisville, they all assembled on the large grass plot, in front of the drawing-room window, and wept while they bid their mistress farewell. When they were on the boat, about leaving the wharf, they were heard giving the charge to those on shore — "Sam, take care of Misus, take care of Marser, as you love us, and hope to meet us in de Hio (Ohio), and in heben; be sure and take good care of Misus and Marser."

In less than a week after her emancipated people had started for Ohio, Mrs. Carlton was cold in death. Mr. Carlton felt deeply, as all husbands must who love their wives, the loss of her who had been a lamp to his feet, and a light to his path. She had converted him from infidelity to Christianity; from the mere theory of liberty to practical freedom. He had looked upon the negro as an ill-treated distant link of the human family; he now regarded them as a part of God's children. Oh, what a silence pervaded the house when the Christian had been removed. His indeed was a lonesome position.

> "'Twas midnight, and he sat alone —
>   The husband of the dead,
> That day the dark dust had been thrown
>   Upon the buried head."

In the midst of the buoyancy of youth, this cherished one had drooped and died. Deep were the sounds of grief and mourning heard in that stately dwelling, when the stricken friends, whose office it had been to nurse and soothe the weary sufferer, beheld her pale and motionless in the sleep of death.

Oh what a chill creeps through the breaking heart when we look upon the insensible form, and feel that it no longer contains the spirit we so dearly loved! How difficult to realise that the eye which always glowed with affection and intelligence—that the ear which had so often listened to the sounds of sorrow and gladness — that the voice whose accents had been to us like sweet music, and the heart, the habitation of benevolence and truth, are now powerless and insensate as the bier upon which the form rests. Though faith be strong enough to penetrate the cloud of gloom which hovers near, and to behold the freed spirit safe, *for ever*, safe in its home in heaven, yet the thoughts *will* linger sadly and cheerlessly upon the grave.

Peace to her ashes! she fought the fight, obtained the Christian's victory, and wears the crown. But if it were that departed spirits are permitted to note the occurrences of this world, with what a frown of disapprobation would hers view the effort being made in the United States to retard the work of emancipation for which she laboured and so wished to see brought about.

In what light would she consider that hypocritical priesthood who gave their aid and sanction to the infamous "Fugitive Slave Law." If true greatness consists in doing good to mankind, then was Georgiana Carlton an ornament to human nature. Who can think of the broken hearts made whole, of sad and dejected countenances now beaming with contentment and joy, of the mother offering her free-born babe to heaven, and of the father whose cup of joy seems overflowing in the presence of his family, where none can molest or make him afraid. Oh, that God may give more such persons to take the whip-

scarred negro by the hand, and raise him to a level
with our common humanity! May the professed
lovers of freedom in the new world see that true
liberty is freedom for all! and may every American
continually hear it sounding in his ear : —

> " Shall every flap of England's flag
>   Proclaim that all around are free,
> From ' farthest Ind ' to each blue crag
>   That beetles o'er the Western Sea?
> And shall we scoff at Europe's kings,
>   When Freedom's fire is dim with us,
> And round our country's altar clings
>   The damning shade of Slavery's curse?

CHAPTER XXII.

A RIDE IN A STAGE-COACH.

WE shall now return to Cincinnati, where we left Clotel preparing to go to Richmond in search of her daughter. Tired of the disguise in which she had escaped, she threw it off on her arrival at Cincinnati. But being assured that not a shadow of safety would attend her visit to a city in which she was well known, unless in some disguise, she again resumed men's apparel on leaving Cincinnati. This time she had more the appearance of an Italian or Spanish gentleman. In addition to the fine suit of black cloth, a splendid pair of dark false whiskers covered the sides of her face, while the curling moustache found its place upon the upper lip. From practice she had become accustomed to high-heeled boots, and could walk without creating any suspicion as regarded her sex. It was on a cold evening that Clotel arrived at Wheeling, and took a seat in the coach going to Richmond. She was already in the state of Virginia, yet a long distance from the place of her destination.

A ride in a stage-coach, over an American road, is unpleasant under the most favourable circumstances. But now that it was winter, and the roads unusually bad, the journey was still more dreary. However, there were eight passengers in the coach, and I need scarcely say that such a number of genuine Americans could not be together without whiling away the time somewhat pleasantly. Be-

sides Clotel, there was an elderly gentleman with
his two daughters—one apparently under twenty
years, the other a shade above. The pale, spectacled face of another slim, tall man, with a white
neckerchief, pointed him out as a minister. The
rough featured, dark countenance of a stout looking
man, with a white hat on one side of his head, told
that he was from the sunny South. There was
nothing remarkable about the other two, who might
pass for ordinary American gentlemen. It was on
the eve of a presidential election, when every man
is thought to be a politician. Clay, Van Buren, and
Harrison were the men who expected the indorse-
ment of the Baltimore Convention. "Who does
this town go for?" asked the old gent. with the
ladies, as the coach drove up to an inn, where groups
of persons were waiting for the latest papers. "We
are divided," cried the rough voice of one of the
outsiders. "Well, who do you think will get the
majority here?" continued the old gent. "Can't
tell very well; I go for 'Old Tip,'" was the answer
from without. This brought up the subject fairly
before the passengers, and when the coach again
started a general discussion commenced, in which all
took a part except Clotel and the young ladies. Some
were for Clay, some for Van Buren, and others for
"Old Tip." The coach stopped to take in a real
farmer-looking man, who no sooner entered than he
was saluted with "Do you go for Clay?" "No,"
was the answer. "Do you go for Van Buren?"
"No." "Well, then, of course you will go
for Harrison." "No." "Why, don't you mean
to work for any of them at the election?"
"No." "Well, who will you work for?" asked one
of the company. "I work for Betsy and the children,
and I have a hard job of it at that," replied the
farmer, without a smile. This answer, as a matter

of course, set the new comer down as one upon whom the rest of the passengers could crack their jokes with the utmost impunity. "Are you an Odd Fellow?" asked one. "No, sir, I've been married more than a month." "I mean, do you belong to the order of Odd Fellows?" "No, no; I belong to the order of married men." "Are you a mason?" "No, I am a carpenter by trade." "Are you a Son of Temperance?" "Bother you, no; I am a son of Mr. John Gosling." After a hearty laugh in which all joined, the subject of Temperance became the theme for discussion. In this the spectacled gent. was at home. He soon showed that he was a New Englander, and went the whole length of the "Maine Law." The minister was about having it all his own way, when the Southerner, in the white hat, took the opposite side of the question. "I don't bet a red cent on these teetotlars," said he, and at the same time looking round to see if he had the approbation of the rest of the company. "Why?" asked the minister. "Because they are a set who are afraid to spend a cent. They are a bad lot, the whole on 'em." It was evident that the white hat gent. was an uneducated man. The minister commenced in full earnest, and gave an interesting account of the progress of temperance in Connecticut, the state from which he came, proving, that a great portion of the prosperity of the state was attributable to the disuse of intoxicating drinks. Every one thought the white hat had got the worst of the argument, and that he was settled for the remainder of the night. But not he; he took fresh courage and began again. "Now," said he, "I have just been on a visit to my uncle's in Vermont, and I guess I knows a little about these here teetotlars. You see, I went up there to make a little stay of a fortnight. I got there at night, and they seemed glad

o

to see me, but they didn't give me a bit of anything to drink. Well, thinks I to myself, the jig's up: I sha'n't get any more liquor till I get out of the state." We all sat up till twelve o'clock that night, and I heard nothing but talk about the 'Juvinal Temperance Army,' the 'Band of Hope,' the 'Rising Generation,' the 'Female Dorcas Temperance Society,' 'The None Such,' and I don't know how many other names they didn't have. As I had taken several pretty large 'Cock Tails' before I entered the state, I thought upon the whole that I would not spile for the want of liquor. The next morning, I commenced writing back to my friends, and telling them what's what. Aunt Polly said, 'Well, Johnny, I s'pose you are given 'em a pretty account of us all here.' 'Yes,' said I; I am tellin' 'em if they want anything to drink when they come up here, they had better bring it with 'em.' 'Oh,' said aunty, 'they would search their boxes; can't bring any spirits in the state.' Well, as I was saying, jist as I got my letters finished, and was going to the post office (for uncle's house was two miles from the town), aunty says, 'Johnny, I s'pose you'll try to get a little somthin' to drink in town won't you?' Says I, 'I s'pose it's no use. 'No,' said she, 'you can't; it aint to be had no how, for love nor money.' So jist as I was puttin' on my hat, 'Johnny,' cries out aunty, 'What,' says I. 'Now I'll tell you, I don't want you to say nothin' about it, but I keeps a little rum to rub my head with, for I am troubled with the headache; now I don't want you to mention it for the world, but I'll give you a little taste, the old man is such a teetotaller, that I should never hear the last of it, and I would not like for the boys to know it, they are members of the "Cold Water Army."'

"Aunty now brought out a black bottle and gave

me a cup, and told me to help myself, which I assure you I did. I now felt ready to face the cold. As I was passing the barn I heard uncle thrashing oats, so I went to the door and spoke to him. 'Come in, John,' says he. 'No,' said I; 'I am goin' to post some letters,' for I was afraid that he would smell my breath if I went too near to him. 'Yes, yes, come in.' So I went in, and says he, 'It's now eleven o'clock; that's about the time you take your grog, I s'pose, when you are at home.' 'Yes,' said I. 'I am sorry for you, my lad; you can't get anything up here; you can't even get it at the chemist's, except as medicine, and then you must let them mix it and you take it in their presence.' 'This is indeed hard,' replied I; 'Well, it can't be helped,' continued he: 'and it ought not to be if it could. It's best for society; people's better off without drink. I recollect when your father and I, thirty years ago, used to go out on a spree and spend more than half a dollar in a night. Then here's the rising generation; there's nothing like settin' a good example. Look how healthy your cousins are—there's Benjamin, he never tasted spirits in his life. Oh, John, I would you were a teetotaller.' 'I suppose,' said I, 'I'll have to be one till I leave the state.' 'Now,' said he, 'John, I don't want you to mention it, for your aunt would go into hysterics if she thought there was a drop of intoxicating liquor about the place, and I would not have the boys to know it for anything, but I keep a little brandy to rub my joints for the rheumatics, and being it's you, I'll give you a little dust.' So the old man went to one corner of the barn, took out a brown jug and handed it to me, and I must say it was a little the best cogniac that I had tasted for many a day. Says I, 'Uncle, you are a good judge of brandy.' 'Yes,' said he, 'I learned when I was young.' So off I started for the post office. In returnin' I thought I'd jist go through the woods where the boys were chopping wood, and wait and go to the house with them when they went to dinner. I found them hard at work, but as merry as crickets. 'Well, cousin John, are you done writing?' 'Yes,' answered I. 'Have you posted them?' 'Yes.' 'Hope you didn't go to any place inquiring for grog.' 'No, I knowed it was no good to do that.' 'I suppose a cock-tail would taste good now.' 'Well, I guess it would,' says I. The three boys then joined in a hearty laugh. 'I suppose you have told 'em that we are a dry set up here?' 'Well, I aint told 'em anything else.' 'Now, cousin John,' said Edward, 'if you wont say anything, we will give you a small taste. For mercy's sake don't let father or mother know it; they are such rabid teetotallers, that they would not sleep a wink to-night if they thought there was any spirits about the place.' 'I am mum,' says I. And the boys took a jug out of a hollow stump, and gave me some first-rate peach brandy. And during the fortnight that I was in Vermont, with my teetotal relations, I was kept about as well corned as if I had been among my hot water friends in Tennessee."

This narrative, given by the white hat man, was received with unbounded applause by all except the pale gent. in spectacles, who showed, by the way in which he was running his fingers between his cravat and throat, that he did not intend to "give it up so." The white hat gent. was now the lion of the company.

"Oh, you did not get hold of the right kind of teetotallers," said the minister. "I can give you a tale worth a dozen of yours," continued he. "Look at society in the states where temperance views prevail, and you will there see real happiness. The people are taxed less, the poor houses are shut up for want of occupants, and extreme destitution is unknown. Every one who drinks at all is liable to become an habitual drunkard. Yes, I say boldly, that no man living who uses intoxicating drinks, is free from the danger of at least occasional, and if of occasional, ultimately of habitual excess. There seems to be no character, position, or circumstances that free men from the danger. *I have known* many young men of the finest promise, led by the drinking habit into vice, ruin, and early death. *I have known* many tradesmen whom it has made bankrupt. *I have known* Sunday scholars whom it has led to prison—teachers, and even superintendents, whom it has dragged down to profligacy. *I have known* ministers of high academic honours, of splendid eloquence, nay, of vast usefulness, whom it has fascinated, and hurried over the precipice of public infamy with their eyes open, and gazing with horror on their fate. *I have known* men of the strongest and clearest intellect and of vigorous resolution, whom it has made weaker than children and fools—gentlemen of refinement and taste whom it has debased into brutes—poets of high genius whom it has bound in a bondage worse than the galleys, and ultimately cut short their days. *I have known* statesmen, lawyers, and judges whom it has killed—kind husbands and fathers whom it has turned into monsters. *I have known* honest men whom it has made villains—elegant and Christian *ladies* whom it has *converted into bloated sots*."

"But you talk too fast," replied the white hat man. "You don't give a feller a chance to say nothin'." "I heard you," continued the minister, "and now you hear me out. It is indeed wonderful how people become lovers of strong drink. Some years since, before I became a teetotaller I kept spirits

about the house, and I had a servant who was much
addicted to strong drink. He used to say that he
could not make my boots shine, without mixing the
blacking with whiskey. So to satisfy myself that the
whiskey was put in the blacking, one morning I made
him bring the dish in which he kept the blacking,
and poured in the whiskey myself. And now, sir,
what do you think?" "Why, I s'pose your boots
shined better than before," replied the white hat.
"No," continued the minister. "He took the blacking out, and I watched him, and he drank down the
whiskey, blacking, and all."

This turned the joke upon the advocate of strong
drink, and he began to put his wits to work for arguments. "You are from Connecticut, are you?"
asked the Southerner. "Yes, and we are an orderly,
pious, peaceable people. Our holy religion is respected, and we do more for the cause of Christ than
the whole Southern States put together." "I don't
doubt it," said the white hat gent. "You sell wooden
nutmegs and other spurious articles enough to do some
good. You talk of your 'holy religion;' but your
robes' righteousness are woven at Lowell and Manchester; your paradise is high per centum on factory
stocks; your palms of victory and crowns of rejoic-
ing are triumphs over a rival party in politics, on
the questions of banks and tariffs. If you could,
you would turn heaven into Birmingham, make
every angel a weaver, and with the eternal din of
looms and spindles drown all the anthems of the
morning stars. Ah! I know you Connecticut people
like a book. No, no, all hoss; you can't come it on
me." This last speech of the rough featured man
again put him in the ascendant, and the spectacled
gent. once more ran his fingers between his cravat
and throat. "You live in Tennessee, I think," said
the minister. "Yes," replied the Southerner, "I used

to live in Orleans, but now I claim to be a Tennessean." "Your people of New Orleans are the most ungodly set in the United States," said the minister. Taking a New Orleans newspaper from his pocket he continued, "Just look here, there are not less than three advertisements of bull fights to take place on the Sabbath. You people of the Slave States have no regard for the Sabbath, religion, morality or anything else intended to make mankind better." Here Clotel could have borne ample testimony, hàd she dared to have taken sides with the Connecticut man. Her residence in Vicksburgh had given her an opportunity of knowing something of the character of the inhabitants of the far South. "Here is an account of a grand bull fight that took place in New Orleans a week ago last Sunday. I will read it to you." And the minister read aloud the following:

"Yesterday, pursuant to public notice, came off at Gretna, opposite the Fourth District, the long heralded fight between the famous grizzly bear, General Jackson (victor in fifty battles), and the Attakapas bull, Santa Anna.

"The fame of the coming conflict had gone forth to the four winds, and women and children, old men and boys, from -all parts of the city, and from the breezy banks of Lake Pontchartrain and Borgne, brushed up their Sunday suit, and prepared to see the fun. Long before the published hour, the quiet streets of the rural Gretna were filled with crowds of anxious denizens, flocking to the arena, and before the fight commenced, such a crowd had collected as Gretna had not seen, nor will be likely to see again.

"The arena for the sports was a cage, twenty feet square, built upon the ground, and constructed of heavy timbers and iron bars. Around it were seats, circularly placed, and intended to accommodate many thousands. About four or five thousand persons assembled, covering the seats as with a cloud, and crowding down around the cage, were within reach of the bars.

"The bull selected to sustain the honour and verify the pluck of Attakapas on this trying occasion was a black animal from the Opelousas, lithe and sinewy as a four year old courser, and with eyes like burning coals. His horns bore the appearance of having been filed at the tips, and wanted that keen and slashing appearance so common with others of his kith and kin; otherwise it would have been ' all day ' with Bruin at the first pass, and no mistake.

" The bear was an animal of note, and called General Jackson, from the fact of his licking up everything that came in his way, and taking 'the responsibility' on all occasions. He was a wicked looking beast, very lean and unamiable in aspect, with hair all standing the wrong way. He had fought some fifty bulls (so they said), always coming out victorious, but that either one of the fifty had been an Attakapas bull, the bills of the performances did not say. Had he tackled Attakapas first it is likely his fifty battles would have remained unfought.

" About half past four o'clock the performances commenced.

" The bull was first seen, standing in the cage alone, with head erect, and looking a very monarch in his capacity. At an appointed signal, a cage containing the bear was placed alongside the arena, and an opening being made, bruin stalked into the battle ground — not, however, without sundry stirrings up with a ten foot pole, he being experienced in such matters, and backwards in raising a row.

" Once on the battle-field, both animals stood, like wary champions, eyeing each other, the bear cowering low, with head upturned and fangs exposed, while Attakapas stood wondering, with his eye dilated, lashing his sides with his long and bushy tail, and pawing up the earth in very wrath.

" The bear seemed little inclined to begin the attack, and the bull, standing a moment, made steps first backward and then forward, as if measuring his antagonist, and meditating where to plant a blow. Bruin wouldn't come to the scratch no way, till one of the keepers, with an iron rod, tickled his ribs and made him move. Seeing this, Attakapas took it as a hostile demonstration, and, gathering his strength, dashed savagely at the enemy, catching him on the points of his horns, and doubling him up like a sack of bran against the bars. Bruin ' sung out' at this, and made a dash for his opponent's nose.

" Missing this, the bull turned to the ' about face,' and the bear caught him by the ham, inflicting a ghastly wound. But Attakapas with a kick shook him off, and renewing the attack, went at him again, head on and with a rush. This time he was not so fortunate, for the bear caught him above the eye, burying his fangs in the tough hide, and holding him as in a vice. It was now the bull's turn to 'sing out,' and he did it, bellowing forth with a voice more hideous than that of all the bulls of Bashan. Some minutes stood matters thus, and the cries of the bull, mingled with the hoarse growls of the bear, made hideous music, fit only for a dance of devils. Then came a pause (the bear having relinquished his hold), and for a few minutes it was doubtful whether the fun was not up. But the magic wand of the keeper (the ten foot pole) again stirred up bruin, and at it they went, and with a rush.

" Bruin now tried to fasten on the bull's back, and drove his tusks in him in several places, making the red blood flow like wine from the vats of Luna. But Attakapas was pluck to the back bone, and, catching bruin on the tips of his horns, shuffled him up right merrily, making the fur fly like feathers in a gale of wind. Bruin cried ' Nuff' (in bear language), but the bull followed up his advantage, and, making one furious plunge full at the figure head of the enemy, struck a horn into his eye, burying it there, and dashing the tender organ into darkness and atoms. Blood followed the blow, and poor bruin, blinded, bleeding, and in mortal agony, turned with a howl to leave, but Attakapas caught him in the retreat, and rolled him over like a ball. Over and over again this rolling over was enacted, and finally, after more than an hour, bruin curled himself up on his back, bruised, bloody, and dead beat. The thing was up with California, and Attakapas was declared the victor amidst the applause of the multitude that made the heavens ring."

" There," said he, " can you find anything against Connecticut equal to that?" The Southerner had to admit that he was beat by the Yankee. During all this time, it must not be supposed that the old gent. with the two daughters, and even the young ladies themselves, had been silent. Clotel and they had not only given their opinions as regarded the merits of the discussion, but that sly glance of the eye, which is ever given where the young of both sexes meet, had been freely at work. The American ladies are rather partial to foreigners, and Clotel had the appearance of a fine Italian. The old gentleman

was now near his home, and a whisper from the
eldest daughter, who was unmarried but marriage-
able, induced him to extend to "Mr. Johnson" an
invitation to stop and spend a week with the young
ladies at their family residence. Clotel excused
herself upon various grounds, and at last, to cut
short the matter, promised that she would pay them
a visit on her return. The arrival of the coach at
Lynchburgh separated the young ladies from the
Italian gent., and the coach again resumed its
journey.

CHAPTER XXIII.

TRUTH STRANGER THAN FICTION.

"Is the poor privilege to turn the key
　Upon the captive, freedom ?　He's as far
　From the enjoyment of the earth and air
　Who watches o'er the chains, as they who wear."

Byron.

DURING certain seasons of the year, all tropical climates are subject to epidemics of a most destructive nature.　The inhabitants of New Orleans look with as much certainty for the appearance of the yellow-fever, small-pox, or cholera, in the hot-season, as the Londoner does for fog in the month of November. In the summer of 1831, the people of New Orleans were visited with one of these epidemics.　It appeared in a form unusually repulsive and deadly.　It seized persons who were in health, without any premonition.　Sometimes death was the immediate consequence.　The disorder began in the brain, by an oppressive pain accompanied or followed by fever. The patient was devoured with burning thirst.　The stomach, distracted by pains, in vain sought relief in efforts to disburden itself.　Fiery veins streaked the eye ; the face was inflamed, and dyed of a dark dull red colour ; the ears from time to time rang painfully. Now mucous secretions surcharged the tongue, and took away the power of speech ; now the sick one spoke, but in speaking had a foresight of death. When the violence of the disease approached the heart, the gums were blackened.　The sleep, broken, troubled by convulsions, or by frightful visions, was worse than the waking hours; and when the reason sank under a delirium which had its seat in the brain, repose utterly forsook the patient's couch. The progress of the heat within was marked by yellowish spots, which spread over the surface of the body. If, then, a happy crisis came not, all hope was gone. Soon the breath infected the air with a fetid odour, the lips were glazed, despair painted itself in the eyes, and sobs, with long intervals of silence, formed the only language. From each side of the mouth spread foam, tinged with black and burnt blood. Blue streaks mingled with the yellow all over the frame. All remedies were useless. This was the Yellow Fever. The disorder spread alarm and confusion throughout the city. On an average, more than 400 died daily. In the midst of disorder and confusion, death heaped victims on victims. Friend followed friend in quick succession. The sick were avoided from the fear of contagion, and for the same reason the dead were left unburied. Nearly 2000 dead bodies lay uncovered in the burial-ground, with only here and there a little lime thrown over them, to prevent the air becoming infected.

The negro, whose home is in a hot climate, was not proof against the disease. Many plantations had to suspend their work for want of slaves to take the places of those carried off by the fever. Henry Morton and wife were among the thirteen thousand swept away by the raging disorder that year. Like too many, Morton had been dealing extensively in lands and stocks; and though apparently in good circumstances was, in reality, deeply involved in debt. Althesa, although as white as most white women in a southern clime, was, as we already know, born a slave. By the laws of all the Southern States the children follow the condition of the mother. If the mother is free the children are free; if a slave, they

are slaves.   Morton was unacquainted with the laws
of the land ; and although he had married Althesa,
it was a marriage which the law did not recognise ;
and therefore she whom he thought to be his wife
was, in fact, nothing more than his slave.   What
would have been his feelings had he known this,
and also known that his two daughters, Ellen and
Jane, were his slaves?   Yet such was the fact.
After the disappearance of the disease with which
Henry Morton had so suddenly been removed, his
brother went to New Orleans to give what aid he
could in settling up the affairs.   James Morton, on
his arrival in New Orleans, felt proud of his nieces,
and promised them a home with his own family in
Vermont ; little dreaming that his brother had married a slave woman, and that his nieces were slaves.
The girls themselves had never heard that their
mother had been a slave, and therefore knew nothing
of the danger hanging over their heads.   An inven-
tory of the property was made out by James Morton,
and placed in the hands of the creditors ; and the
young ladies, with their uncle, were about leaving
the city to reside for a few days on the banks of
Lake Ponchetain, where they could enjoy a fresh air
that the city could not afford.   But just as they
were about taking the train, an officer arrested the
whole party ; the young ladies as slaves, and the
uncle upon the charge of attempting to conceal the
property of his deceased brother.   Morton was overwhelmed with horror at the idea of his nieces being
claimed as slaves, and asked for time, that he might
save them from such a fate.   He even offered to
mortgage his little farm in Vermont for the amount
which young slave women of their ages would fetch.
But the creditors pleaded that they were " an extra
article," and would sell for more than common
slaves ; and must, therefore, be sold at auction.

They were given up, but neither ate nor slept, nor separated from each other, till they were taken into the New Orleans slave market, where they were offered to the highest bidder. There they stood, trembling, blushing, and weeping; compelled to listen to the grossest language, and shrinking from the rude hands that examined the graceful proportions of their beautiful frames.

After a fierce contest between the bidders, the young ladies were sold, one for 2,300 dollars, and the other for 3,000 dollars. We need not add that had those young girls been sold for mere house servants or field hands, they would not have brought one half the sums they did. The fact that they were the grand-daughters of Thomas Jefferson, no doubt, increased their value in the market. Here were two of the softer sex, accustomed to the fondest indulgence, surrounded by all the refinements of life, and with all the timidity that such a life could produce, bartered away like cattle in Smithfield market. Ellen, the eldest, was sold to an old gentleman, who purchased her, as he said, for a housekeeper. The girl was taken to his residence, nine miles from the city. She soon, however, knew for what purpose she had been bought; and an educated and cultivated mind and taste, which made her see and understand how great was her degradation, now armed her hand with the ready means of death. The morning after her arrival, she was found in her chamber, a corpse. She had taken poison. Jane was purchased by a dashing young man, who had just come into the possession of a large fortune. The very appearance of the young Southerner pointed him out as an unprincipled profligate; and the young girl needed no one to tell her of her impending doom. The young maid of fifteen was immediately removed to his country seat, near the junction of the Mississippi river with the sea. This was a most singular spot, remote, in a dense forest spreading over the summit of a cliff that rose abruptly to a great height above the sea; but so grand in its situation, in the desolate sublimity which reigned around, in the reverential murmur of the waves that washed its base, that, though picturesque, it was a forest prison. Here the young lady saw no one, except an old negress who acted as her servant. The smiles with which the young man met her were indignantly spurned. But she was the property of another, and could hope for justice and mercy only through him.

Jane, though only in her fifteenth year, had become strongly attached to Volney Lapuc, a young Frenchman, a student in her father's office. The poverty of the young man, and the youthful age of the girl, had caused their feelings to be kept from the young lady's parents. At the death of his master, Volney had returned to his widowed mother at Mobile, and knew nothing of the misfortune that had befallen his mistress, until he received a letter from her. But how could he ever obtain a sight of her, even if he wished, locked up as she was in her master's mansion? After several days of what her master termed "obstinacy" on her part, the young girl was placed in an upper chamber, and told that that would be her home, until she should yield to her master's wishes. There she remained more than a fortnight, and with the exception of a daily visit from her master, she saw no one but the old negress who waited upon her. One bright moonlight evening as she was seated at the window, she perceived the figure of a man beneath her window. At first, she thought it was her master; but the tall figure of the stranger soon convinced her that it was another. Yes, it was Volney! He had no sooner received her letter, than he set out for New Orleans; and finding on his arrival there, that his mistress had been taken away, resolved to follow her. There he was; but how could she communicate with him? She dared not trust the old negress with her secret, for fear that it might reach her master. Jane wrote a hasty note and threw it out of the window, which was eagerly picked up by the young man, and he soon disappeared in the woods. Night passed away in dreariness to her, and the next morning she viewed the spot beneath her window with the hope of seeing the footsteps of him who had stood there the previous night. Evening returned, and with it the hope of again seeing the man she loved. In this she was not disappointed; for daylight had scarcely disappeared, and the moon once more rising through the tops of the tall trees, when the young man was seen in the same place as on the previous night. He had in his hand a rope ladder. As soon as Jane saw this, she took the sheets from her bed, tore them into strings, tied them together, and let one end down the side of the house. A moment more, and one end of the rope-ladder was in her hand, and she fastened it inside the room. Soon the young maiden was seen descending, and the enthusiastic lover, with his arms extended, waiting to receive his mistress. The planter had been out on an hunting excursion, and returning home, saw his victim as her lover was receiving her in his arms. At this moment the sharp sound of a rifle was heard. and the young man fell weltering in his blood, at the feet of his mistress. Jane fell senseless by his side. For many days she had a confused consciousness of some great agony, but knew not where she was, or by whom surrounded. The slow recovery of her reason settled into the most intense melancholy, which gained at length the compassion even of her cruel master. The beautiful bright eyes, always pleading in expression, were now so heart-piercing in their sadness, that he could not endure their gaze. In a few days the poor girl died of a broken heart, and was buried at night at the back of the garden by the negroes; and no one wept at the grave of her who had been so carefully cherished, and so tenderly beloved.

This, reader, is an unvarnished narrative of one doomed by the laws of the Southern States to be a slave. It tells not only its own story of grief, but speaks of a thousand wrongs and woes beside, which never see the light; all the more bitter and dreadful, because no help can relieve, no sympathy can mitigate, and no hope can cheer.

P

CHAPTER XXIV.

THE ARREST.

" THE fearful storm — it threatens lowering,
   Which God in mercy long delays ;
 Slaves yet may see their masters cowering,
    While whole plantations smoke and blaze !
                                        Carter.

IT was late in the evening when the coach arrived at Richmond, and Clotel once more alighted in her native city. She had intended to seek lodgings somewhere in the outskirts of the town, but the lateness of the hour compelled her to stop at one of the principal hotels for the night. She had scercely entered the inn, when she recognised among the numerous black servants one to whom she was well known ; and her only hope was, that her disguise would keep her from being discovered. The imperturbable calm and entire forgetfulness of self which induced Clotel to visit a place from which she could scarcely hope to escape, to attempt the rescue of a beloved child, demonstrate that over-willingness of woman to carry out the promptings of the finer feelings of her heart. True to woman's nature, she had risked her own liberty for another.

She remained in the hotel during the night, and the next morning, under the plea of illness, she took her breakfast alone. That day the fugitive slave paid a visit to the suburbs of the town, and once more beheld the cottage in which she had spent so many happy hours. It was winter, and the clematis and passion flower were not there ; but there were the same walks she had so often pressed with her feet, and the same trees which had so often shaded her as she passed through the garden at the back of the house. Old remembrances rushed upon her memory, and caused her to shed tears freely. Clotel was now in her native town, and near her daughter; but how could she communicate with her? How could she see her? To have made herself known, would have been a suicidal act; betrayal would have followed, and she arrested. Three days had passed away, and Clotel still remained in the hotel at which she had first put up; and yet she had got no tidings of her child. Unfortunately for Clotel, a disturbance had just broken out amongst the slave population in the state of Virginia, and all strangers were eyed with suspicion.

The evils consequent on slavery are not lessened by the incoming of one or two rays of light. If the slave only becomes aware of his condition, and conscious of the injustice under which he suffers, if he obtains but a faint idea of these things, he will seize the first opportunity to possess himself of what he conceives to belong to him. The infusion of Anglo-Saxon with African blood has created an insurrectionary feeling among the slaves of America hitherto unknown. Aware of their blood connection with their owners, these mulattoes labour under the sense of their personal and social injuries; and tolerate, if they do not encourage in themselves, low and vindictive passions. On the other hand, the slave owners are aware of their critical position, and are ever watchful, always fearing an outbreak among the slaves.

True, the Free States are equally bound with the Slave States to suppress any insurrectionary movement that may take place among the slaves. The Northern freemen are bound by their constitutional obligations to aid the slaveholder in keeping his slaves in their chains. Yet there are, at the time we write, four millions of bond slaves in the United States. The insurrection to which we now refer was headed by a full-blooded negro, who had been born and brought up a slave. He had heard the twang of the driver's whip, and saw the warm blood streaming from the negro's body; he had witnessed the separation of parents and children, and was made aware, by too many proofs, that the slave could expect no justice at the hand of the slave owner. He went by the name of "Nat Turner." He was a preacher amongst the negroes, and distinguished for his eloquence, respected by the whites, and loved and venerated by the negroes. On the discovery of the plan for the outbreak, Turner fled to the swamps, followed by those who had joined in the insurrection. Here the revolted negroes numbered some hundreds, and for a time bade defiance to their oppressors. The Dismal Swamps cover many thousands of acres of wild land, and a dense forest, with wild animals and insects, such as are unknown in any other part of Virginia. Here runaway negroes usually seek a hiding-place, and some have been known to reside here for years. The revolters were joined by one of these. He was a large, tall, full-blooded negro, with a stern and savage countenance; the marks on his face showed that he was from one of the barbarous tribes in Africa, and claimed that country as his native land; his only covering was a girdle around his loins, made of skins of wild beasts which he had killed; his only token of authority among those that he led, was a pair of epaulettes made from the tail of a fox, and tied to his shoulder by a cord. Brought from the coast of Africa when only fifteen years of age to the island of Cuba, he was smuggled from thence into Virginia. He had been two years in the swamps, and considered it his future home. He had met a negro woman who was also a runaway; and, after the fashion of his native land, had gone through the process of oiling her as the marriage ceremony. They had built a cave on a rising mound in the swamp; this was their home. His name was Picquilo. His only weapon was a sword, made from the blade of a scythe, which he had stolen from a neighbouring plantation. His dress, his character, his manners, his mode of fighting, were all in keeping with the early training he had received in the land of his birth. He moved about with the activity of a cat, and neither the thickness of the trees, nor the depth of the water could stop him. He was a bold, turbulent spirit; and from revenge imbrued his hands in the blood of all the whites he could meet. Hunger, thirst, fatigue, and loss of sleep he seemed made to endure as if by peculiarity of constitution. His air was fierce, his step oblique, his look sanguinary. Such was the character of one of the leaders in the Southampton insurrection. All negroes were arrested who were found beyond their master's threshhold, and all strange whites watched with a great degree of alacrity.

Such was the position in which Clotel found affairs when she returned to Virginia in search of her Mary. Had not the slave-owners been watchful of strangers, owing to the outbreak, the fugitive could not have escaped the vigilance of the police; for advertisements, announcing her escape and offering a large reward for her arrest, had been received in the city previous to her arrival, and the officers were therefore on the look-out for the runaway slave. It was on the third day, as the quadroon was seated in her room at the inn, still in the disguise of a gentleman, that two of the city officers entered the room, and informed her that they were authorised to examine all strangers, to assure the authorities that they were not in league with the revolted negroes. With trembling heart the fugitive handed the key of her trunk to the officers. To their surprise, they found nothing but woman's apparel in the box, which raised their curiosity, and caused a further investigation that resulted in the arrest of Clotel as a fugitive slave. She was immediately conveyed to prison, there to await the orders of her master. For many days, uncheered by the voice of kindness, alone, hopeless, desolate, she waited for the time to arrive when the chains were to be placed on her limbs, and she returned to her inhuman and unfeeling owner.

The arrest of the fugitive was announced in all the newspapers, but created little or no sensation. The inhabitants were too much engaged in putting down the revolt among the slaves; and although all the odds were against the insurgents, the whites found it no easy matter, with all their caution. Every day brought news of fresh outbreaks. Without scruple and without pity, the whites massacred all blacks found beyond their owners' plantations: the negroes, in return, set fire to houses, and put those to death who attempted to escape from the flames. Thus carnage was added to carnage, and the blood of the whites flowed to avenge the blood of the blacks. These were the ravages of slavery. No graves were dug for the negroes; their dead bodies became food for dogs and vultures, and their bones, partly calcined by the sun, remained scattered about, as if to mark the mournful fury of servitude and lust of power. When the slaves were subdued, except a few in the swamps, bloodhounds were put in this dismal place to hunt out the remaining re-volters. Among the captured negroes was one of whom we shall hereafter make mention.

CHAPTER XXV.

DEATH IS FREEDOM.

"I ASKED but freedom, and ye gave
Chains, and the freedom of the grave." — *Snelling.*

THERE are, in the district of Columbia, several slave prisons, or "negro pens," as they are termed. These prisons are mostly occupied by persons to keep their slaves in, when collecting their gangs together for the New Orleans market. Some of them belong to the government, and one, in particular, is noted for having been the place where a number of free coloured persons have been incarcerated from time to time. In this district is situated the capitol of the United States. Any free coloured persons visiting Washington, if not provided with papers asserting and proving their right to be free, may be arrested and placed in one of these dens. If they succeed in showing that they are free, they are set at liberty, provided they are able to pay the expenses of their arrest and imprisonment; if they cannot pay these expenses, they are sold out. Through this unjust and oppressive law, many persons born in the Free States have been consigned to a life of slavery on the cotton, sugar, or rice plantations of the Southern States. By order of her master, Clotel was removed from Richmond and placed in one of these prisons, to await the sailing of a vessel for New Orleans. The prison in which she was put stands midway between the capitol at Washington and the president's house. Here the fugitive saw nothing but slaves brought in and taken out, to be placed in ships and sent away to the same part of the country to which she herself would soon be compelled to go. She had seen or heard nothing of her daughter while in Richmond, and all hope of seeing her now had fled. If she was carried back to New Orleans, she could expect no mercy from her master.

At the dusk of the evening previous to the day when she was to be sent off, as the old prison was being closed for the night, she suddenly darted past her keeper, and ran for her life. It is not a great distance from the prison to the Long Bridge, which passes from the lower part of the city across the Potomac, to the extensive forests and woodlands of the celebrated Arlington Place, occupied by that distinguished relative and descendant of the immortal Washington, Mr. George W. Curtis. Thither the poor fugitive directed her flight. So unexpected was her escape, that she had quite a number of rods the start before the keeper had secured the other prisoners, and rallied his assistants in pursuit. It was at an hour when, and in a part of the city where, horses could not be readily obtained for the chase; no bloodhounds were at hand to run down the flying woman; and for once it seemed as though there was to be a fair trial of speed and endurance between the slave and the slave-catchers. The keeper and his forces raised the hue and cry on her pathway close behind; but so rapid was the flight along the wide avenue, that the astonished citizens, as they poured forth from their dwellings to learn the cause of alarm, were only able to comprehend the nature of the case in time to fall in with the motley mass in pursuit, (as many a one did that night,) to raise an anxious prayer to heaven, as they refused to join in the pursuit, that the panting fugitive might escape, and the merciless soul dealer for once be disappointed of his prey. And now with the speed of an arrow—having passed the avenue—with the distance between her and her pursuers constantly increasing, this poor hunted female gained the "*Long Bridge*," as it is called, where interruption seemed improbable, and already did her heart begin to beat high with the hope of success. She had only to pass three-fourths of a mile across the bridge, and she could bury herself in a vast forest, just at the time when the curtain of night would close around her, and protect her from the pursuit of her enemies.

But God by his Providence had otherwise determined. He had determined that an appalling tragedy should be enacted that night, within plain sight of the President's house and the capital of the Union, which should be an evidence wherever it should be known, of the unconquerable love of liberty the heart may inherit; as well as a fresh admonition to the slave dealer, of the cruelty and enormity of his crimes. Just as the pursuers crossed the high draw for the passage of sloops, soon after entering upon the bridge, they beheld three men slowly approaching from the Virginia side. They immediately called to them to arrest the fugitive, whom they proclaimed a runaway slave. True to their Virginian instincts as she came near, they formed in line across the narrow bridge, and prepared to seize her. Seeing escape impossible in that quarter, she stopped suddenly, and turned upon her pursuers. On came the profane and ribald crew, faster than ever, already exulting in her capture, and threatening punishment for her flight. For a moment she looked wildly and anxiously around to see if there was no hope of escape. On either hand, far down below, rolled the deep foamy waters of the Potomac, and before and behind the rapidly approaching step and noisy voices of pursuers, showing how vain would be any further effort for freedom. Her resolution was taken. She clasped her *hands* convulsively, and raised *them*, as she at the same time raised her *eyes* towards heaven, and begged for that mercy and compassion *there*, which had been denied her on earth; and then, with a single bound, she vaulted over the railings of the bridge, and sunk for ever beneath the waves of the river!

Thus died Clotel, the daughter of Thomas Jefferson, a president of the United States; a man distinguished as the author of the Declaration of American Independence, and one of the first statesmen of that country.

Had Clotel escaped from oppression in any other land, in the disguise in which she fled from the Mississippi to Richmond, and reached the United States, no honour within the gift of the American people would have been too good to have been heaped upon the heroic woman. But she was a slave, and therefore out of the pale of their sympathy. They have tears to shed over Greece and Poland; they have an abundance of sympathy for "poor Ireland;" they can furnish a ship of war to convey the Hungarian refugees from a Turkish prison to the "land of the free and home of the brave." They boast that America is the "cradle of liberty;" if it is, I fear they have rocked the child to death. The body of Clotel was picked up from the bank of the river, where it had been washed by the strong current, a hole dug in the sand, and there deposited, without either inquest being held over it, or religious service being performed. Such was the life and such the death of a woman whose virtues and goodness of heart would have done honour to one in a higher station of life, and who, if she had been born in any other land but that of slavery, would have been honoured and

THE DEATH OF CLOTEL. *Page* 218.

loved. A few days after the death of Clotel, the following poem appeared in one of the newspapers:

" Now, rest for the wretched! the long day is past,
  And night on yon prison descendeth at last.
  Now lock up and bolt! Ha, jailor, look there!
  Who flies like a wild bird escaped from the snare?
      A woman, a slave — up, out in pursuit,
        While linger some gleams of day!
      Let thy call ring out! — now a rabble rout
        Is at thy heels — speed away!

" A bold race for freedom! — On, fugitive, on!
  Heaven help but the right, and thy freedom is won.
  How eager she drinks the free air of the plains;
  Every limb, every nerve, every fibre she strains;
      From Columbia's glorious capitol,
        Columbia's daughter flees
      To the sanctuary God has given —
        The sheltering forest trees.

" Now she treads the Long Bridge — joy lighteth her eye —
  Beyond her the dense wood and darkening sky —
  Wild hopes thrill her heart as she neareth the shore:
  O, despair! there are *men* fast advancing before!
      Shame, shame on their manhood! they hear, they heed
        The cry, her flight to stay,
      And like demon forms with their outstretched arms,
        They wait to seize their prey!

" She pauses, she turns! Ah, will she flee back?
  Like wolves, her pursuers howl loud on their track;
  She lifteth to Heaven one look of despair —
  Her anguish breaks forth in one hurried prayer —
      Hark! her jailor's yell! like a bloodhound's bay
        On the low night wind it sweeps!
      Now, death or the chain! to the stream she turns,
        And she leaps! O God, she leaps!

" The dark and the cold, yet merciful wave,
  Receives to its bosom the form of the slave:
  She rises — earth's scenes on her dim vision gleam,
  Yet she struggleth not with the strong rushing stream:
      And low are the death-cries her woman's heart gives,
        As she floats adown the river,
      Faint and more faint grows the drowning voice,
        And her cries have ceased for ever!

" Now back, jailor, back to thy dungeons, again,
  To swing the red lash and rivet the chain!
  The form thou would'st fetter—returned to its God;
      The universe holdeth no realm of night
        More drear than her slavery—
      More merciless fiends than here stayed her flight—
        Joy! the hunted slave is free!

" That bond-woman's corse—let Potomac's proud wave
  Go bear it along *by our Washington's grave*,
  And heave it high up on that hallowed strand,
  To tell of the freedom he won for our land.
      A weak woman's corse, by freemen chased down;
        Hurrah for our country! hurrah!
      To freedom she leaped, through drowning and death—
        Hurrah for our country! hurrah!"

CHAPTER XXVI.

THE ESCAPE.

" No refuge is found on our unhallowed ground,
    For the wretched in Slavery's manacles bound;
    While our star-spangled banner in vain boasts to wave
    O'er the land of the free and the home of the brave!"

WE left Mary, the daughter of Clotel, in the capacity
of a servant in her own father's house, where she
had been taken by her mistress for the ostensible
purpose of plunging her husband into the depths of
humiliation. At first the young girl was treated
with great severity; but after finding that Horatio
Green had lost all feeling for his child, Mrs. Green's
own heart became touched for the offspring of her
husband, and she became its friend. Mary had
grown still more beautiful, and, like most of her sex
in that country, was fast coming to maturity.

The arrest of Clotel, while trying to rescue her
daughter, did not reach the ears of the latter till
her mother had been removed from Richmond to
Washington. The mother had passed from time to
eternity before the daughter knew that she had been
in the neighbourhood. Horatio Green was not in
Richmond at the time of Clotel's arrest; had he
been there, it is not probable but he would have
made an effort to save her. She was not his slave,
and therefore was beyond his power, even had he
been there and inclined to aid her. The revolt
amongst the slaves had been brought to an end, and
most of the insurgents either put to death or sent

out of the state. One, however, remained in prison.
He was the slave of Horatio Green, and had been a
servant in his master's dwelling. He, too, could
boast that his father was an American statesman,
His name was George. His mother had been employed as a servant in one of the principal hotels in
Washington, where members of Congress usually
put up. After George's birth his mother was sold
to a slave trader, and he to an agent of Mr. Green,
the father of Horatio. George was as white as most
white persons. No one would suppose that any
African blood coursed through his veins. His hair
was straight, soft, fine, and light; his eyes blue,
nose prominent, lips thin, his head well formed,
forehead high and prominent; and he was often
taken for a free white person by those who did know
him. This made his condition still more intolerable;
for one so white seldom ever receives fair treatment
at the hands of his fellow slaves; and the whites
usually regard such slaves as persons who, if not
often flogged, and otherwise ill treated, to remind
them of their condition, would soon "forget" that
they were slaves, and "think themselves as good
as white folks." George's opportunities were far
greater than most slaves. Being in his master's
house, and waiting on educated white people, he had
become very familiar with the English language.
He had heard his master and visitors speak of the
down-trodden and oppressed Poles; he heard them
talk of going to Greece to fight for Grecian liberty,
and against the oppressors of that ill-fated people.
George, fired with the love of freedom, and zeal for the
cause of his enslaved countrymen, joined the insurgents,
and with them had been defeated and captured. He
was the only one remaining of these unfortunate
people, and he would have been put to death with
them but for a circumstance that occurred some

weeks before the outbreak. The court house had, by accident, taken fire, and was fast consuming. The engines could not be made to work, and all hope of saving the building seemed at an end. In one of the upper chambers there was a small box containing some valuable deeds belonging to the city; a ladder was placed against the house, leading from the street to the window of the room in which the box stood. The wind blew strong, and swept the flames in that direction. Broad sheets of fire were blown again and again over that part of the building, and then the wind would lift the pall of smoke, which showed that the work of destruction was not yet accomplished. While the doomed building was thus exposed, and before the destroying element had made its final visit, as it did soon after, George was standing by, and hearing that much depended on the contents of the box, and seeing no one disposed to venture through the fiery element to save the treasure, mounted the ladder and made his way to the window, entered the room, and was soon seen descending with the much valued box. Three cheers rent the air as the young slave fell from the ladder when near the ground; the white men took him up in their arms, to see if he had sustained any injury. His hair was burnt, eyebrows closely singed, and his clothes smelt strongly of smoke; but the heroic young slave was unhurt. The city authorities, at their next meeting, passed a vote of thanks to George's master for the lasting benefit that the slave had rendered the public, and commended the poor boy to the special favour of his owner. When George was on trial for participating in the revolt, this "meritorious act," as they were pleased to term it, was brought up in his favour. His trial was put off from session to session, till he had been in prison more than a year. At last, however, he was convicted of high treason, and sentenced to be hanged within ten days of that time. The judge asked the slave if he had anything to say why sentence of death should not be passed on him. George stood for a moment in silence, and then said, "As I cannot speak as I should wish, I will say nothing." "You may say what you please," said the judge. "You had a good master," continued he, "and still you were dissatisfied; you left your master and joined the negroes who were burning our houses and killing our wives." "As you have given me permission to speak," remarked George, "I will tell you why I joined the revolted negroes. I have heard my master read in the Declaration of Independence 'that all men are created free and equal,' and this caused me to inquire of myself why I was a slave. I also heard him talking with some of his visitors about the war with England, and he said, all wars and fightings for freedom were just and right. If so, in what am I wrong? The grievances of which your fathers complained, and which caused the Revolutionary War, were trifling in comparison with the wrongs and sufferings of those who were engaged in the late revolt. Your fathers were never slaves, ours are; your fathers were never bought and sold like cattle, never shut out from the light of knowledge and religion, never subjected to the lash of brutal task-masters. For the crime of having a dark skin, my people suffer the pangs of hunger, the infliction of stripes, and the ignominy of brutal servitude. We are kept in heathenish darkness by laws expressly enacted to make our instruction a criminal offence. What right has one man to the bones, sinews, blood, and nerves of another? Did not one God make us all? You say your fathers fought for freedom—so did we. You tell me that I am to be put to death for violating the laws of the land. Did not the American revolutionists violate the laws when they struck for liberty? They were revolters, but their success made them patriots—we were revolters, and our failure makes us rebels. Had we succeeded, we would have been patriots too. Success makes all the difference. You make merry on the 4th of July; the thunder of cannon and ringing of bells announce it as the birthday of American independence. Yet while these cannons are roaring and bells ringing, one-sixth of the people of this land are in chains and slavery. You boast that this is the 'Land of the Free;' but a traditionary freedom will not save you. It will not do to praise your fathers and build their sepulchres. Worse for you that you have such an inheritance, if you spend it foolishly and are unable to appreciate its worth. Sad if the genius of a true humanity, beholding you with tearful eyes from the mount of vision, shall fold his wings in sorrowing pity, and repeat the strain, 'O land of Washington, how often would I have gathered thy children together, as a hen doth gather her brood under her wings, and ye would not; behold your house is left unto you desolate.' This is all I have to say; I have done." Nearly every one present was melted to tears; even the judge seemed taken by surprise at the intelligence of the young slave. But George was a slave, and an example must be made of him, and therefore he was sentenced. Being employed in the same house with Mary, the daughter of Clotel, George had become attached to her, and the young lovers fondly looked forward to the time when they should be husband and wife.

After George had been sentenced to death, Mary was still more attentive to him, and begged and obtained leave of her mistress to visit him in his cell. The poor girl paid a daily visit to him to whom she had pledged her heart and hand. At one of these meetings, and only four days from the time fixed for the execution, while Mary was seated in George's cell, it occurred to her that she might yet save him from a felon's doom. She revealed to him the secret that was then occupying her thoughts, viz. that George should exchange clothes with her, and thus attempt his escape in disguise. But he would not for a single moment listen to the proposition. Not that he feared detection; but he would not consent to place an innocent and affectionate girl in a position where she might have to suffer for him. Mary pleaded, but in vain—George was inflexible. The poor girl left her lover with a heavy heart, regretting that her scheme had proved unsuccessful.

Towards the close of the next day, Mary again appeared at the prison door for admission, and was soon by the side of him whom she so ardently loved. While there the clouds which had overhung the city for some hours broke, and the rain fell in torrents amid the most terrific thunder and lightning. In the most persuasive manner possible, Mary again importuned George to avail himself of her assistance to escape from an ignominious death. After assuring him that she, not being the person condemned, would not receive any injury, he at last consented, and they began to exchange apparel. As George was of small stature, and both were white, there was no difficulty in his passing out without detection; and as she usually left the cell weeping, with handkerchief in hand, and sometimes at her face, he had only to adopt this mode and his escape was safe. They had kissed each other, and Mary had told George where he would find a small parcel of provisions which she had placed in a secluded spot, when the prison-keeper opened the door and said, "Come, girl, it is time for you to go." George again embraced Mary, and passed out of the jail. It was already dark, and the street lamps were lighted, so that our hero in his new dress had no dread of detection. The provisions were sought out and found, and poor George was soon on the road towards Canada. But neither of them had once thought of a change of dress for George when he should have escaped, and he had walked but a short distance before he felt that a change of his apparel would facilitate his progress. But he dared not go amongst even his coloured associates for fear of being betrayed. However, he made the best of his way on towards Canada, hiding in the woods during the day, and travelling by the guidance of the North Star at night.

With the poet he could truly say,

> "Star of the North! while blazing day
> Pours round me its full tide of light,
> And hides thy pale but faithful ray,
> I, too, lie hid, and long for night."

One morning, George arrived on the banks of the Ohio river, and found his journey had terminated, unless he could get some one to take him across the river in a secret manner, for he would not be permitted to cross in any of the ferry boats, it being a penalty for crossing a slave, besides the value of the slave. He concealed himself in the tall grass and weeds near the river, to see if he could embrace an opportunity to cross. He had been in his hiding place but a short time, when he observed a man in a small boat, floating near the shore, evidently fishing. His first impulse was to call out to the man and ask him to take him over to the Ohio side, but the fear that the man was a slaveholder, or one who might possibly arrest him, deterred him from it. The

man after rowing and floating about for some time
fastened the boat to the root of a tree, and started
to a neighbouring farmhouse.

This was George's moment, and he seized it.
Running down the bank, he unfastened the boat,
jumped in, and with all the expertness of one accustomed to a boat, rowed across the river and landed
on the Ohio side.

Being now in a Free State, he thought he might
with perfect safety travel on towards Canada. He
had, however, gone but a very few miles when he
discovered two men on horseback coming behind him.
He felt sure that they could not be in pursuit of him,
yet he did not wish to be seen by them, so he turned
into another road leading to a house near by. The
men followed, and were but a short distance from
George, when he ran up to a farmhouse, before
which was standing a farmer-looking man, in a broad-
brimmed hat and straight-collared coat, whom he
implored to save him from the "slave-catchers."
The farmer told him to go into the barn near by; he
entered by the front door, the farmer following, and
closing the door behind George, but remaining outside, and gave directions to his hired man as to what
should be done with George. The slaveholders by
this time had dismounted, and were in front of the
barn demanding admittance, and charging the farmer
with secreting their slave woman, for George was
still in the dress of a woman. The Friend, for the
farmer proved to be a member of the Society of
Friends, told the slave-owners that if they wished to
search his barn, they must first get an officer and a
search warrant. While the parties were disputing,
the farmer began nailing up the front door, and the
hired man served the back door in the same way.
The slaveholders, finding that they could not prevail
on the Friend to allow them to get the slave, deter-

mined to go in search of an officer. One was left to
see that the slave did not escape from the barn, while
the other went off at full speed to Mount Pleasant,
the nearest town. George was not the slave of
either of these men, nor were they in pursuit of him,
but they had lost a woman who had been seen in
that vicinity, and when they saw poor George in the
disguise of a female, and attempting to elude pursuit,
they felt sure they were close upon their victim.
However, if they had caught him, although he was
not their slave, they would have taken him back and
placed him in jail, and there he would have remained
until his owner arrived.

After an absence of nearly two hours, the slave-
owner returned with an officer and found the Friend
still driving large nails into the door. In a triumphant
tone and with a corresponding gesture, he handed
the search-warrant to the Friend, and said, " There,
sir, now I will see if I can't get my nigger."
" Well," said the Friend, " thou hast gone to work
according to law, and thou canst now go into my
barn." " Lend me your hammer that I may get the
door open," said the slaveholder. " Let me see the
warrant again." And after reading it over once
more, he said, " I see nothing in this paper which
says I must supply thee with tools to open my door;
if thou wishest to go in, thou must get a hammer
elsewhere." The sheriff said, " I will go to a neighbouring farm and borrow something which will in-
troduce us to Miss Dinah;" and he immediately
went in search of tools. In a short time the officer
returned, and they commenced an assault and battery
upon the barn door, which soon yielded; and in
went the slaveholder and officer, and began turning
up the hay and using all other means to find the lost
property; but, to their astonishment, the slave was
not there. After all hope of getting Dinah was gone,

the slave-owner in a rage said to the Friend, "My nigger is not here." "I did not tell thee there was any one here." "Yes, but I saw her go in, and you shut the door behind her, and if she was not in the barn, what did you nail the door for?" "Can't I do what I please with my own barn door? Now I will tell thee; thou need trouble thyself no more, for the person thou art after entered the front door and went out at the back door, and is a long way from here by this time. Thou and thy friend must be somewhat fatigued by this time; wont thou go in and take a little dinner with me?" We need not say that this cool invitation of the good Quaker was not accepted by the slaveholders. George in the meantime had been taken to a friend's dwelling some miles away, where, after laying aside his female attire, and being snugly dressed up in a straight collared coat, and pantaloons to match, was again put on the right road towards Canada.

The fugitive now travelled by day, and laid by during night. After a fatiguing and dreary journey of two weeks, the fugitive arrived in Canada, and took up his abode in the little town of St. Catherine's, and obtained work on the farm of Colonel Street. Here he attended a night-school, and laboured for his employer during the day. The climate was cold, and wages small, yet he was in a land where he was free, and this the young slave prized more than all the gold that could be given to him. Besides doing his best to obtain education for himself, he imparted what he could to those of his fellow-fugitives about him, of whom there were many.

CHAPTER XXVII.

THE MYSTERY.

GEORGE, however, did not forget his promise to use all the means in his power to get Mary out of slavery. He, therefore, laboured with all his might to obtain money with which to employ some one to go back to Virginia for Mary. After nearly six months' labour at St. Catherine's, he employed an English missionary to go and see if the girl could be purchased, and at what price. The missionary went accordingly, but returned with the sad intelligence that, on account of Mary's aiding George to escape, the court had compelled Mr. Green to sell her out of the state, and she had been sold to a negro trader, and taken to the New Orleans market. As all hope of getting the girl was now gone, George resolved to quit the American continent for ever. He immediately took passage in a vessel laden with timber, bound for Liverpool, and in five weeks from that time he was standing on the quay of the great English seaport. With little or no education, he found many difficulties in the way of getting a respectable living. However he obtained a situation as porter in a large house in Manchester, where he worked during the day, and took private lessons at night. In this way he laboured for three years, and was then raised to the situation of clerk. George was so white as easily to pass for a white man, and being somewhat ashamed of his African descent, he never once mentioned the fact of his having been a slave. He soon became a partner in the firm that employed him, and was now on the road to wealth.

In the year 1842, just ten years after George Green (for he adopted his master's name) arrived in England, he visited France, and spent some days at Dunkirk. It was towards sunset, on a warm day in the month of October, that Mr. Green, after strolling some distance from the Hotel de Leon, entered a burial ground, and wandered long alone among the silent dead, gazing upon the many green graves and marble tombstones of those who once moved on the theatre of busy life, and whose sounds of gaiety once fell upon the ear of man. All nature around was hushed in silence, and seemed to partake of the general melancholy which hung over the quiet resting-place of departed mortals. After tracing the varied inscriptions which told the characters or conditions of the departed, and viewing the mounds beneath which the dust of mortality slumbered, he had now reached a secluded spot, near to where an aged weeping willow bowed its thick foliage to the ground, as though anxious to hide from the scrutinising gaze of curiosity the grave beneath it. Mr. Green seated himself upon a marble tomb, and began to read Roscoe's *Leo X.*, a copy of which he had under his arm. It was then about twilight, and he had scarcely gone through half a page, when he observed a lady in black, leading a boy, some five years old, up one of the paths ; and as the lady's black veil was over her face, he felt somewhat at liberty to eye her more closely. While looking at her, the lady gave a scream, and appeared to be in a fainting position, when Mr. Green sprang from his seat in time to save her from falling to the ground. At this moment, an elderly gentleman was seen approaching with a rapid step, who, from his appearance, was evidently the lady's father, or one intimately connected with her. He came up, and, in a confused manner, asked what was the matter. Mr. Green explained as well as he could. After taking up the smelling bottle which had fallen from her hand, and holding it a short time to her face, she soon began to revive. During all this time the lady's veil had so covered her face, that Mr. Green had not seen it. When she had so far recovered as to be able to raise her head, she again screamed, and fell back into the arms of the old man. It now appeared quite certain, that either the countenance of George Green, or some other object, was the cause of these fits of fainting; and the old gentleman, thinking it was the former, in rather a petulant tone said, "I will thank you, sir, if you will leave us alone." The child whom the lady was leading, had now set up a squall; and amid the death-like appearance of the lady, the harsh look of the old man, and the cries of the boy, Mr. Green left the grounds, and returned to his hotel.

Whilst seated by the window, and looking out upon the crowded street, with every now and then the strange scene in the grave-yard vividly before him, Mr. Green thought of the book he had been reading, and, remembering that he had left it on the tomb, where he had suddenly dropped it when called to the assistance of the lady, he immediately determined to return in search of it. After a walk of some twenty minutes, he was again over the spot where he had been an hour before, and from which he had been so unceremoniously expelled by the old man. He looked in vain for the book; it was nowhere to be found: nothing save the bouquet which the lady had dropped, and which lay half-buried in the grass from having been trodden upon, indicated that any one had been there that evening. Mr.

Green took up the bunch of flowers, and again returned to the hotel.

After passing a sleepless night, and hearing the clock strike six, he dropped into a sweet sleep, from which he did not awake until roused by the rap of a servant, who, entering his room, handed him a note which ran as follows :—" Sir,—I owe you an apology for the inconvenience to which you were subjected last evening, and if you will honour us with your presence to dinner to-day at four o'clock, I shall be most happy to give you due satisfaction. My servant will be in waiting for you at half-past three. I am, sir, your obedient servant, J. Devenant. October 23. To George Green, Esq."

The servant who handed this note to Mr. Green, informed him that the bearer was waiting for a reply. He immediately resolved to accept the invitation, and replied accordingly. Who this person was, and how his name and the hotel where he was stopping had been found out, was indeed a mystery. However, he waited impatiently for the hour when he was to see this new acquaintance, and get the mysterious meeting in the grave-yard solved.

CHAPTER XXVIII.

THE HAPPY MEETING.

" Man's love is of man's life, a thing apart;
    'Tis woman's whole existence."—*Byron.*

THE clock on a neighbouring church had scarcely
ceased striking three, when the servant announced
that a carriage had called for Mr. Green. In less
than half an hour he was seated in a most sumptuous
barouche, drawn by two beautiful iron greys, and rolling along over a splendid gravel road completely
shaded by large trees, which appeared to have been
the accumulating growth of many centuries. The
carriage soon stopped in front of a low villa, and this
too was embedded in magnificent trees covered with
moss. Mr. Green alighted and was shown into a
superb drawing room, the walls of which were hung
with fine specimens from the hands of the great
Italian painters, and one by a German artist representing a beautiful monkish legend connected with
" The Holy Catherine," an illustrious lady of Alex-
andria. The furniture had an antique and dignified
appearance. High backed chairs stood around the
room ; a venerable mirror stood on the mantle shelf;
rich curtains of crimson damask hung in folds at
either side of the large windows ; and a rich Turkey
carpet covered the floor. In the centre stood a table
covered with books, in the midst of which was an
old-fashioned vase filled with fresh flowers, whose
fragrance was exceedingly pleasant. A faint light,

together with the quietness of the hour, gave beauty beyond description to the whole scene.

Mr. Green had scarcely seated himself upon the sofa, when the elderly gentleman whom he had met the previous evening made his appearance, followed by the little boy, and introduced himself as Mr. Devenant. A moment more, and a lady — a beautiful brunette — dressed in black, with long curls of a chesnut colour hanging down her cheeks, entered the room. Her eyes were of a dark hazel, and her whole appearance indicated that she was a native of a southern clime. The door at which she entered was opposite to where the two gentlemen were seated. They immediately rose; and Mr. Devenant was in the act of introducing her to Mr. Green, when he observed that the latter had sunk back upon the sofa, and the last word that he remembered to have heard was, "It is her." After this, all was dark and dreamy: how long he remained in this condition it was for another to tell. When he awoke, he found himself stretched upon the sofa, with his boots off, his neckerchief removed, shirt collar unbuttoned, and his head resting upon a pillow. By his side sat the old man, with the smelling bottle in the one hand, and a glass of water in the other, and the little boy standing at the foot of the sofa. As soon as Mr. Green had so far recovered as to be able to speak, he said, "Where am I, and what does this mean?" "Wait a while," replied the old man, "and I will tell you all." After a lapse of some ten minutes he rose from the sofa, adjusted his apparel, and said, "I am now ready to hear anything you have to say." "You were born in America?" said the old man. "Yes," he replied. "And you were acquainted with a girl named Mary?" continued the old man. "Yes, and I loved her as I can love none other." "The lady whom you met so mys-

teriously last evening is Mary," replied Mr. Devenant.
George Green was silent, but the fountains of
mingled grief and joy stole out from beneath his eye-
lashes, and glistened like pearls upon his pale and
marble-like cheeks. At this juncture the lady again
entered the room. Mr. Green sprang from the sofa,
and they fell into each other's arms, to the surprise
of the old man and little George, and to the amuse-
ment of the servants who had crept up one by one,
and were hid behind the doors, or loitering in the
hall. When they had given vent to their feelings,
they resumed their seats, and each in turn related
the adventures through which they had passed.
"How did you find out my name and address,"
asked Mr. Green? "After you had left us in the
grave-yard, our little George said, ' O, mamma, if
there aint a book!' and picked it up and brought it
to us. Papa opened it, and said, ' The gentleman's
name is written in it, and here is a card of the Hotel
de Leon, where I suppose he is stopping.' Papa
wished to leave the book, and said it was all a fancy
of mine that I had ever seen you before, but I was
perfectly convinced that you were my own George
Green. Are you married?" "No, I am not."
"Then, thank God!" exclaimed Mrs. Devenant.
"And are you single now?" inquired Mr. Green.
"Yes," she replied. "This is indeed the Lord's
doings," said Mr. Green, at the same time bursting
into a flood of tears. Mr. Devenant was past the
age when men should think upon matrimonial subjects, yet the scene brought vividly before his eyes
the days when he was a young man, and had a wife
living. After a short interview, the old man called
their attention to the dinner, which was then waiting.
We need scarcely add, that Mr. Green and Mrs.
Devenant did very little towards diminishing the
dinner that day.

After dinner the lovers (for such we have to call them) gave their experience from the time that George left the jail dressed in Mary's clothes. Up to that time Mr. Green's was substantially as we have related it. Mrs. Devenant's was as follows: — "The night after you left the prison," said she, "I did not shut my eyes in sleep. The next morning, about eight o'clock, Peter the gardener came to the jail to see if I had been there the night before, and was informed that I had, and that I had left a little after dark. About an hour after, Mr. Green came himself, and I need not say that he was much surprised on finding me there, dressed in your clothes. This was the first tidings they had of your escape." "What did Mr. Green say when he found that I had fled?" "Oh!" continued Mrs. Devenant, "he said to me when no one was near, I hope George will get off, but I fear you will have to suffer in his stead. I told him that if it must be so I was willing to die if you could live." At this moment George Green burst into tears, threw his arms around her neck, and exclaimed, "I am glad I have waited so long, with the hope of meeting you again."

Mrs. Devenant again resumed her story:—"I was kept in jail three days, during which time I was visited by the magistrates, and two of the judges. On the third day I was taken out, and master told me that I was liberated, upon condition that I should be immediately sent out of the state. There happened to be just at the time in the neighbourhood a negro-trader, and he purchased me, and I was taken to New Orleans. On the steam-boat we were kept in a close room, where slaves are usually confined, so that I saw nothing of the passengers on board, or the towns we passed. We arrived at New Orleans, and were all put into the slave-market for sale. I was examined by many persons, but none seemed willing to purchase me, as all thought me too white, and said I would run away and pass as a free white woman. On the second day, while in the slave-market, and while planters and others were examining slaves and making their purchases, I observed a tall young man, with long black hair, eyeing me very closely, and then talking to the trader. I felt sure that my time had now come, but the day closed without my being sold. I did not regret this, for I had heard that foreigners made the worst of masters, and I felt confident that the man who eyed me so closely was not an American.

" The next day was the Sabbath. The bells called the people to the different places of worship. Methodists sang, and Baptists immersed, and Presbyterians sprinkled, and Episcopalians read their prayers, while the ministers of the various sects preached that Christ died for all; yet there were some twenty-five or thirty of us poor creatures confined in the 'Negro Pen,' awaiting the close of the holy Sabbath, and the dawn of another day, to be again taken into the market, there to be examined like so many beasts of burden. I need not tell you with what anxiety we waited for the advent of another day. On Monday we were again brought out and placed in rows to be inspected; and, fortunately for me, I was sold before we had been on the stand an hour. I was purchased by a gentleman residing in the city, for a waiting-maid for his wife, who was just on the eve of starting for Mobile, to pay a visit to a near relation. I was then dressed to suit the situation of a maid-servant; and upon the whole, I thought that, in my new dress, I looked as much the lady as my mistress.

" On the passage to Mobile, who should I see among the passengers but the tall, long-haired man that had eyed me so closely in the slave-market a few days before. His eyes were again on me, and he appeared anxious to speak to me, and I as reluctant to be spoken to. The first evening after leaving New Orleans, soon after twilight had let her curtain down, and pinned it with a star, and while I was seated on the deck of the boat near the ladies' cabin, looking upon the rippled waves, and the reflection of the moon upon the sea, all at once I saw the tall young man standing by my side. I immediately rose from my seat, and was in the act of returning to the cabin, when he in a broken accent said, 'Stop a moment; I wish to have a word with you. I am your friend.' I stopped and looked him full in the face, and he said, 'I saw you some days since in the slave-market, and I intended to have purchased you to save you from the condition of a slave. I called on Monday, but you had been sold and had left the market. I inquired and learned who the purchaser was, and that you had to go to Mobile, so I resolved to follow you. If you are willing I will try and buy you from your present owner, and you shall be free.' Although this was said in an honest and off-hand manner, I could not believe the man to be sincere in what he said. 'Why should you wish to set *me* free?' I asked. 'I had an only sister,' he replied, 'who died three years ago in France, and you are so much like her that had I not known of her death, I would most certainly have taken you for her.' 'However much I may resemble your sister, you are aware that I am not her, and why take so much interest in one whom you never saw before?' 'The love,' said he, 'which I had for my sister is transferred to you.' I had all along suspected that the man was a knave, and this profession of love confirmed me in my former belief, and I turned away and left him.

"The next day, while standing in the cabin and

looking through the window, the French gentleman
(for such he was) came to the window while walking
on the guards, and again commenced as on the previous evening. He took from his pocket a bit of
paper and put it into my hand, at the same time
saying, 'Take this, it may some day be of service to
you; remember it is from a friend,' and left me in-
stantly. I unfolded the paper, and found it to be a
100 dollars bank note, on the United States Branch
Bank, at Philadelphia. My first impulse was to
give it to my mistress, but, upon a second thought, I
resolved to seek an opportunity, and to return the
hundred dollars to the stranger.

"Therefore I looked for him, but in vain; and
had almost given up the idea of seeing him again,
when he passed me on the guards of the boat and
walked towards the stem of the vessel. It being
now dark, I approached him and offered the money
to him. He declined, saying at the same time, ' I
gave it to you — keep it.' ' I do not want it,' I
said. 'Now,' said he, ' you had better give your
consent for me to purchase you, and you shall go
with me to France.' 'But you cannot buy me now,'
I replied, 'for my master is in New Orleans, and
he purchased me not to sell, but to retain in his own
family.' ' Would you rather remain with your
present mistress than be free?' ' No,' said I. ' Then
fly with me to-night; we shall be in Mobile in two
hours from this, and when the passengers are going
on shore, you can take my arm, and you can escape
unobserved. The trader who brought you to New
Orleans exhibited to me a certificate of your good
character, and one from the minister of the church
to which you were attached in Virginia; and upon
the faith of these assurances, and the love I bear
you, I promise before high heaven that I will marry
you as soon as it can be done.' This solemn promise,

R

coupled with what had already transpired, gave me confidence in the man; and rash as the act may seem, I determined in an instant to go with him. My mistress had been put under the charge of the captain; and as it would be past ten o'clock when the steamer would land, she accepted an invitation of the captain to remain on board with several other ladies till morning. I dressed myself in my best clothes, and put a veil over my face, and was ready on the landing of the boat. Surrounded by a number of passengers, we descended the stage leading to the wharf, and were soon lost in the crowd that thronged the quay. As we went on shore we encountered several persons announcing the names of hotels, the starting of boats for the interior, and vessels bound for Europe. Among these was the ship Utica, Captain Pell, bound for Havre. 'Now,' said Mr. Devenant, 'this is our chance.' The ship was to sail at twelve o'clock that night, at high tide; and following the men who were seeking passengers, we went immediately on board. Devenant told the captain of the ship that I was his sister, and for such we passed during the voyage. At the hour of twelve the Utica set sail, and we were soon out at sea.

"The morning after we left Mobile, Devenant met me as I came from my state-room, and embraced me for the first time. I loved him, but it was only that affection which we have for one who has done us a lasting favour: it was the love of gratitude rather than that of the heart. We were five weeks on the sea, and yet the passage did not seem long, for Devenant was so kind. On our arrival at Havre we were married and came to Dunkirk, and I have resided here ever since."

At the close of this narrative, the clock struck ten, when the old man, who was accustomed to retire at an early hour, rose to take leave, saying at the same time, "I hope you will remain with us to-night." Mr. Green would fain have excused himself, on the ground that they would expect him and wait at the hotel, but a look from the lady told him to accept the invitation. The old man was the father of Mrs. Devenant's deceased husband, as you will no doubt long since have supposed. A fortnight from the day on which they met in the graveyard, Mr. Green and Mrs. Devenant were joined in holy wedlock; so that George and Mary, who had loved each other so ardently in their younger days, were now husband and wife.

A celebrated writer has justly said of woman, "A woman's whole life is a history of the affections. The heart is her world; it is there her ambition strives for empire; it is there her avarice seeks for hidden treasures. She sends forth her sympathies on adventure; she embarks her whole soul in the traffic of affection; and, if shipwrecked, her case is hopeless, for it is a bankruptcy of the heart."

Mary had every reason to believe that she would never see George again; and although she confesses that the love she bore him was never transferred to her first husband, we can scarcely find fault with her for marrying Mr. Devenant. But the adherence of George Green to the resolution never to marry, unless to his Mary, is, indeed, a rare instance of the fidelity of man in the matter of love. We can but blush for our country's shame when we recal to mind the fact, that while George and Mary Green, and numbers of other fugitives from American slavery, can receive protection from any of the governments of Europe, they cannot return to their native land without becoming slaves.

CHAPTER XXIX.

CONCLUSION.

My narrative has now come to a close. I may be asked, and no doubt shall, Are the various incidents and scenes related founded in truth? I answer, Yes. I have personally participated in many of those scenes. Some of the narratives I have derived from other sources; many from the lips of those who, like myself, have run away from the land of bondage. Having been for nearly nine years employed on Lake Erie, I had many opportunities for helping the escape of fugitives, who, in return for the assistance they received, made me the depositary of their sufferings and wrongs. Of their relations I have made free use. To Mrs. Child, of New York, I am indebted for part of a short story. American Abolitionist journals are another source from whence some of the characters appearing in my narrative are taken. All these combined have made up my story. Having thus acknowledged my resources, I invite the attention of my readers to the following statement, from which I leave them to draw their own conclusions: — "It is estimated that in the United States, members of the Methodist church own 219,363 slaves; members of the Baptist church own 226,000 slaves; members of the Episcopalian church own 88,000 slaves; members of the Presbyterian church own 77,000 slaves; members of all other churches own 50,000 slaves; in all, 660,563 slaves owned by members of the Christian church in this pious democratic republic!"

May these facts be pondered over by British Christians, and at the next anniversaries of the various religious denominations in London may their influence be seen and felt! The religious bodies of American Christians will send their delegates to these meetings. Let British feeling be publicly manifested. Let British sympathy express itself in tender sorrow for the condition of my unhappy race. Let it be understood, unequivocally understood, that no fellowship can be held with slaveholders professing the same common Christianity as yourselves. And until this stain from America's otherwise fair escutcheon be wiped away, let no Christian association be maintained with those who traffic in the blood and bones of those whom God has made of one flesh as yourselves. Finally, let the voice of the whole British nation be heard across the Atlantic, and throughout the length and breadth of the land of the Pilgrim Fathers, beseeching their descendants, as they value *the* common salvation, which knows no distinction between the bond and the free, to proclaim the Year of Jubilee. Then shall the "earth indeed yield her increase, and God, even our own God, shall bless us; and all the ends of the earth shall fear Him."